AN UNWELCOME VISITOR

Her open journal lay facedown on the blotter where she'd left it that afternoon. She fervently hoped he hadn't read any of her recent entries.

"I cannot believe you snuck into this house. Are you purposely courting the gallows?"

"Man's got to be courting something." His eyes narrowed as he studied her, lingering somewhere in the vicinity of her bodice. "And on that note, let me express my admiration for your . . . gown."

Sara set her chin. "I won't be cozened, Gren. I thought you'd decided to stop wandering in and out of my life."

"Maybe I can't help it," he said. "Maybe that fatal charm you once spoke of is your own."

When her frosty manner didn't thaw, he frowned. "Ah, I see I've fallen from your favor, Miss Crab. And yet you smuggle notes to my farm and ask me to meet you on the terrace. You can't blame a man for getting his thoughts in a tangle after that."

"Nothing's changed," she assured him. "And even though I was not the one who insisted we keep apart, I'm more than willing to adhere to that arrangement. You'd better go."

"Aren't you going to thank me first?"

"For what?"

"For not reading your journal. I admit I was sorely tempted."

Her chin thrust up. "Trust me, there's nothing in there that could interest you."

"No? Perhaps you're right. Perhaps there was no point in reading it. . . ." His hand stroked over her cheek for an instant as he leaned in close and whispered, "Not when I see all the answers in your eyes."

The
Kindness
of a Rogue

Nancy Butler

A SIGNET BOOK

SIGNET
Published by New American Library, a division of
Penguin Group (USA) Inc., 375 Hudson Street,
New York, New York 10014, USA
Penguin Group (Canada), 10 Alcorn Avenue, Toronto,
Ontario M4V 3B2, Canada (a division of Pearson Penguin Canada Inc.)
Penguin Books Ltd., 80 Strand, London WC2R 0RL, England
Penguin Ireland, 25 St. Stephen's Green, Dublin 2,
Ireland (a division of Penguin Books Ltd.)
Penguin Group (Australia), 250 Camberwell Road, Camberwell, Victoria 3124,
Australia (a division of Pearson Australia Group Pty. Ltd.)
Penguin Books India Pvt. Ltd., 11 Community Centre, Panchsheel Park,
New Delhi - 110 017, India
Penguin Group (NZ), Cnr Airborne and Rosedale Roads, Albany,
Auckland 1310, New Zealand (a division of Pearson New Zealand Ltd.)
Penguin Books (South Africa) (Pty.) Ltd., 24 Sturdee Avenue,
Rosebank, Johannesburg 2196, South Africa

Penguin Books Ltd., Registered Offices:
80 Strand, London WC2R 0RL, England

First published by Signet, an imprint of New American Library,
a division of Penguin Group (USA) Inc.

First Printing, November 2004
10 9 8 7 6 5 4 3 2 1

This is for Helen Flanagan,
practically family

and

Al Weiss,
teacher and faithful reader

Through his honor I conquered him. For these peasants carry their honor in their hands so that they may constantly consult it; this same honor that once felt so much at home in the city but now has taken refuge in a more rural setting.

—Tirso de Molina
The Rogue of Seville

Chapter One

"*You're making a mistake.*"

Sara Cobb looked up sharply. The man across from her had muttered the words without opening his eyes or straightening from his slouch on the seat. He had spoken softly enough not to disturb the other four passengers, who'd fallen into the inevitable listing doze peculiar to coach travel.

Sara could barely make him out in the dimly lit interior, though she'd observed him briefly when he climbed aboard in Plymouth an hour earlier, just as night was falling. After wedging himself opposite her, between a stout tradesman and a long-nosed clerk, he had proceeded to wage war on her toes with his muddied hobnail boots. Her kidskin half boots had finally withdrawn from the field, and she was not feeling any great charity toward him at the moment.

He appeared to be somewhere between twenty-five and thirty, and in addition to the ponderous footgear, he sported worn corduroy breeches and a threadbare woolen coat topped by a moth-eaten muffler. A low-crowned felt hat had been tugged down over a thatch of black hair badly in need of a barber.

During her brief assessment, Sara hadn't missed another salient point—in spite of his ragged apparel, the man was as handsome as the devil. Definitely someone Miss Bonnet, her friend and former employer, would have termed a "rogue."

"What was that you just said?" she hissed under her breath, unsettled to hear her own private misgivings spoken aloud by a stranger.

He didn't respond at first, and she assumed he'd been mum-

bling in his sleep. She was about to lower her gaze when the
man pushed himself upright. His head lolled back against the
seat cushion as he regarded her with one slightly bleary blue
eye.

"It's a mistake," he said again.

Sara's lips pursed into a frown. Miss Bonnet always said
she resembled a grouper when she did that. Forcing her mouth
to relax, she said, "I have no idea to what you are referring."
She purposely avoided looking directly at the stranger, settling
her gaze instead on the tradesman to his left, who slept on un-
aware.

He nodded to the woman dozing beside her. "I heard what
you told yon farm wife outside Plymouth, that you are bound
for Tregallion."

"And so I am. I don't see anything remarkable in that."

He leaned forward a few inches. "Tregallion House . . . it
has a sorry reputation hereabouts. There's a nasty odor rises
from that place."

Sara put her chin up. "Perhaps they have trouble with their
drains."

He gave an abrupt laugh, loud enough to set the tradesman
sputtering.

"You can joke about it, ma'am, but that doesn't change anything. Tregallion's got an ugly character, if a house can be said
to have such. And Sir Kenneth and Lady Brashear are not quite
as they appear."

"It happens I've met the Brashears while instructing their
daughter at a seminary for young ladies. They seemed quite
unexceptionable."

"So you're to be a governess then? I'd taken you for an
upper house servant."

Sara bristled. His comment drove home just how threadbare
and out-of-date her traveling costume was. Not that it mattered
a whit what this unkempt fellow thought of her.

"Odd," he mused, "that they didn't send you fare for a post
chaise. Still, isn't that always the way? Those who have the
most blunt being the biggest nipfarthings. It's not what you're
used to, eh, sitting elbow-to-elbow with the riffraff?" He

paused, his mouth compressing almost into a scowl. "Ah, but a governess going to Tregallion . . . that makes it even worse."

Sara forced herself to meet his gaze. Even in the dim coach she was struck by the vivid hue of his eyes, the rich, opaque blue startling against a smudge of thick, sooty lashes. "I have no wish to continue this conversation. You seem to find some amusement in trying to frighten me, but you are wasting your time. I do not start at hobgoblins."

She leaned back and closed her eyes, effectively ending their tête-à-tête. Instead, she focused on blocking out the numerous offensive odors permeating the closed coach. Garlic, unwashed bodies, the cloying scent of hair oil and cheap perfume—and the unmistakable aroma of gin. She wondered if her provoker had been imbibing in Plymouth. That might explain his flights of fancy.

Her own apprehension had nothing to do with some imaginary danger at Tregallion. She was sure it was a lovely old house, and from her recollection the Brashears were an elegant, intelligent couple. She'd passed all of ten minutes speaking to them and could find nothing to complain of. It was their daughter Ileana who was at the root of her worries. Less than five months from her comeout and blessed with breeding *and* beauty, the girl would likely take the *ton* by storm. But appearances aside, Ileana was headstrong, temperamental, possibly even malicious.

Sara hadn't a clue why the Brashears had chosen her to complete their daughter's education. There were other teachers at Miss Bonnet's school they might have hired, those who had not formed such a negative opinion of the girl. Not that Sara wasn't grateful for the post. Grateful didn't begin to do justice to her feelings. She had been down to her last few shillings when she received the written offer from Lady Brashear. It had been a godsend, and she wasn't about to let some uncouth ruffian talk her out of taking the position.

She was just nodding off when she sensed the stranger shifting on his seat, heard his boots stamp down on the hard wooden floor. When she opened her eyes, he was staring at her.

"Just hear me out," he said. "I take it you're to instruct Miss Ileana. Her older sister Amelie had two different governesses before she went off to London. Now you'll not hear this from anyone inside the house, but it's the truth nonetheless."

"What?" she asked in a tone of long suffering.

"Disappeared they did. Both of them without a trace."

In spite of herself, Sara's heartbeat quickened.

The man looked at her intently for a moment, then settled back against the cushions. He burrowed his chin into his muffler and shot her a swift, devilish smile. "Pleasant dreams."

Sara did sleep, but her dreams were not troubled by nameless perils. Rather they were filled with visions of a warm bedroom, a schoolroom stocked with books and maps and all the accoutrements teachers held dear, and delicious—and unlimited—meals. There was a lot she could overlook, including Ileana's vindictiveness, in the face of such comfort and security.

Sara awoke when the coach slowed upon entering the village of Penwreath—her destination. Her tormentor had lit a pipe, adding the not unpleasant odor of cherry tobacco to the general fog. He seemed to be paying her no mind, thank heaven.

The other four passengers were also stirring, rooting around in their hand luggage or patting their pockets, as though they had been somewhere other than this snug coach where they might have misplaced their coin purse or gloves. She couldn't know that coaches were rife with petty crime and that to nod off meant risking the loss of one's personal articles. When the passengers had assured themselves that all possessions were intact, they began to comment on the unnaturally cold weather that was afflicting the south coast of Cornwall.

It wasn't until she stepped out into the lantern-lit yard of the inn and was buffeted by a stiff, icy wind that Sara realized the truth of their observations. The interior of the coach, warmed by the body heat of six people, had remained fairly comfortable. Now she stood shivering on the cobblestones, waiting for the coachman to retrieve her travel bag from the boot. She had a cloak in there, not very thick but surely sufficient to keep out some of the bone-deep chill.

The stranger climbed out after Sara and went past her without a word, heading toward the front door of the inn. He was tall, with a loose-limbed, swinging gait that reminded Sara of a yearling colt.

The innkeeper greeted him cheerfully in the doorway. "Sold off old Curry's cattle, did you?"

"Every last one," he replied. "And I've coppers burning a hole in my pocket."

"I think we can do something about that," the landlord said, ushering him inside.

Sara took her bag from the coachman, then went along the flagged path, her own gait awkward and shambling after five days of travel. She practically fell through the front door.

The innkeeper now stood in the entrance to his dining parlor at the far end of the low-ceilinged hall. Once she was able to gain his attention, Sara told him she expected to be met by a carriage from Tregallion House.

The landlord, tall and rawboned, rubbed one hand over his close-cropped hair and whistled an indrawn breath. "Tedn't likely, miss. We do not enjoy the custom of the Brashears."

"I sent them a letter detailing my travel arrangements," she explained. "I am only a half hour past the time I wrote. Surely the carriage waited."

"There's no carriage been sent here." He spun from her abruptly as a young woman hurried past with a tureen. "You there, Angie, clean up that muck of soup you spilled. You'll slip in it and be on your arse in a minute an you don't." He turned back to her and grunted softly. "Ah, these farm girls, ham-handed to the last and no more sense than a widgeon."

He motioned her aside, to a quieter corner of the hall. "Now here's the way of it, miss. I misdoubt the Brashears would agree to such a plan. There be bad blood between that family and myself, and I do fear Sir Kenneth still blames me for a certain fire on his property."

Sara goggled a moment, fearing she had been set down in Bedlam. "But this is the Constant Star, is it not? I am sure I told them that this is where the mail coach stops off."

"That it does," he agreed. "But there's been no sign of a carriage." His eyes brightened. "I do have a nice little gig I could rent you, but I'd advise you against driving along the coast at night. Best leave in the morning. I'll have the missus make up one of the rooms for you."

Sara was ashamed to admit she hadn't any money for a gig or a room. She barely whispered, "No, thank you," before he was off, striding into the dining parlor to scold another luck-less farm girl.

Sara sank down onto a rush-seated chair, wondering what on earth she was to do. No one had ever faulted her for lack of fortitude, but she was weary and hungry—and still weighted down by a mindless grief.

She heard a thrum of soft laughter and looked up.

The tall stranger stood canted in the doorway of the tap-room opposite her, holding a mug of hot rum curled against his chest. "It's the hand of Providence," he said with dark humor. "You're not meant to go to Tregallion."

"Oh, bosh," she said irritably. "There's simply been some sort of mix-up. I got the date wrong . . . or they did. If no car-riage arrives within the next hour, I will walk there."

He chuffed softly. "Well, that's fairly daft. It's all of seven miles to Tregallion. You won't get far over rough country in those shoes." He eyed her half boots peeping beneath the hem of her pelisse.

"No," she agreed, "especially after you stomped all over them in the coach."

He reared back in mock dismay. "I do beg your ladyship's pardon."

The innkeeper reappeared, bearing a tray of clean glasses for the taproom. He frowned down at Sara and muttered, "Still here, I see." He made a beeline for the stranger and had a few words with him in an undertone before passing through to the bar.

The stranger was frowning now.

"What is it?" she asked.

"He wants me to take you to Tregallion. Said it doesn't look right to have women sitting in his hallway like misplaced bag-gage."

Sara's jaw clenched. "Where would he prefer I wait, out in the cold?"

"In truth, it's a small inconvenience. I'm headed that way myself."

"I'll be fine," she assured him. "You needn't trouble yourself over me."

"I don't trouble myself over anyone as a general rule," he said matter-of-factly. "Still, I'll tell you outright, you don't present a very inspiring picture of . . . capability. You're bound to wander off the track and get yourself lost. And dead bodies on the moor tend to make the sheep fretful."

Sara couldn't prevent a tiny *humph* from escaping, something halfway between a sputter of affront and a chuckle.

He shrugged. "It's on your head then. I've done my duty by you. Like most women, you won't listen to reason." He gave her a curt nod and faded back into the taproom.

Before long Sara heard a burst of raucous laughter. She had an uncanny feeling the stranger had just made her the butt of a joke—the harebrained woman who was going to walk seven miles at night.

She waited another half hour, trying to ignore the landlord's dark looks. His wife went past several times before stopping to ask Sara if she wouldn't rather wait in the dining parlor with a cup of tea. Sara refused as graciously as she could, her words followed by a loud rumbling from her stomach.

The wall clock was striking nine when she picked up her bag and went outside. It hadn't grown any warmer. The coach from Plymouth had long since departed, but there was a gangling young ostler lounging in the lantern-lit stableyard. Sara asked him if he knew the way to Tregallion.

"Aye," he said. "'Tis along the coast road . . . about six mile before the turnin'." He cocked his head. "Has your driver lost his way?"

"I have no driver," she said, "or carriage. I intend to walk. So if you could just tell me how to find the estate."

The young man leaned forward and peered at her. "Are 'ee daft, ma'am?"

"Not a bit," she said as staunchly as she could. "The Brashears were to send a carriage—"

"Not to this place they weren't."

"—and I expect there was some mix-up. I am due at the house tonight."

"Tell 'ee what," he said. "Hang on a bit, and old Gren Martyn can give 'ee a ride. He lives beyond Tregallion, up onto the moor."

"Please," said Sara, "just tell me where I am to turn off. I promise you I won't come to any harm."

He thought a moment. "Well, then, it's like this. . . . There be a pile of stones where the road to Tregallion veers off."

Sara nearly wept. If there was one thing rife in Cornwall, it was piles of stones.

"Not just any pile," he continued, "but a great heaping pile. They do say it was the cairn of a Cornish chieftain, but I be thinkin' it's just where some farmer cleared his field."

She thanked him, wishing she had a spare groat to offer for his troubles, but he seemed anxious to head back to the stable, no doubt to entertain his cronies with the tale of the madwoman who intended to walk to Tregallion.

The road beyond the inn was rutted with hardened cart tracks, but Sara marched forward briskly, hoping to keep the cold at bay. She'd wrapped herself in her cloak and tied her shawl over her bonnet, but after five minutes she felt colder than she ever had in her life. The wind swept off the open fields on her right and swirled in, wet and sharp, from the sea on her left. Once she left Penwreath behind, the darkness closed about her like a shroud. Fortunately the luminescence from the sea below gave off enough light for her to keep to the road, else she'd have tumbled down the cliffs to her death— and ended up fretting the gulls instead of the sheep.

She'd gone perhaps a mile and was wondering how she would manage to keep walking since she could no longer feel her toes, when she heard the steady tattoo of hoofbeats on the road behind her. She moved to one side and watched as a lone horseman trotted past.

He went thirty feet beyond her, then drew to a halt.

No, she moaned silently. It was her tormenter from the coach. "Changed your mind yet?" he said without turning around.

"No, I have not," she said, all the while wondering where

self-sufficiency ended and pure pig-headed stubbornness began.

"Suit yourself," he said and clucked to his horse.

Sara watched him disappear into the darkness of the road ahead.

That was exactly what her life felt like these days . . . a dark road with only vague and shadowy prospects looming before her. It was true she had the schooling of Ileana Brashear for at least three or four months, but after that she'd be forced to seek another position. A dowdy governess with neither charm nor any great accomplishments to recommend her. What did it matter that Miss Bonnet had told her she was a born teacher? Imparting knowledge was one thing; getting her pupils to like her was quite another. She knew all the names they called her behind her back. And now she was to instruct the worst of the girls who had mocked her.

She tried to thrust away any thoughts of all she had lost in the past five years—her family home . . . her parents, dead within a year of each other . . . her dear, wry Miss Bonnet now also gone from her life. She couldn't shake off the sinking feeling that her stature had again been reduced—as a well-regarded schoolteacher, she hadn't minded toiling for a living, but now desperation had forced her into the tenuous position of governess in this remote Duchy of Cornwall.

Sara shuffled forward, fighting off the urge to sit down and have a good cry. The way the temperature was dropping, her tears would likely freeze on her cheeks.

After another half mile, she decided to leave her bag behind in the bushes—it was starting to weigh her down like an anchor. Surely someone from the house would agree to fetch it in the morning. She was rustling around in a clump of low scrub, looking for the densest part, when she heard hoofbeats again, coming from the road ahead. Without thinking, she crouched down.

He pulled up directly opposite where she was hiding.

"I don't know what it is," he mused. "Something about you that puts me in mind of a defenseless fawn or a stray kitten. Not that I'd go out of my way for you, mind. But my route home happens to pass fairly near the gates of Tregallion."

When she didn't respond, he nudged his horse closer to the bushes. "What the devil are you doing in there—answering the call of nature?"

Sara stood up immediately. "Certainly not. I am hiding my bag."

"Oh," he drawled. "That makes a world of sense." He set one hand on his hip. "But unless you plan to sleep in the altogether, I suggest we bring it with us. I'll hold it in front of me, and you can ride pillion behind."

Sara couldn't move. "I . . . I don't even know your name."

"Martyn," he said. "Grenville Martyn."

She cocked her head. "The boy in the stableyard called you 'old' Gren Martyn."

He laughed. "To a sprat like Georgie Hobblyn I suppose I am old. Now will you bide or will you go?"

Just then, a fierce wind slashed in from the sea, whipping the tail of Sara's cloak and cutting right through her layers of clothing. She decided she was done being a martyr to her pride.

"Very well," she said as she stepped from the bushes and handed up her bag.

He balanced it before him, then freed one stirrup so she could boost herself off the ground. As she stepped up, he caught her easily under her right arm and swung her behind him.

"Sorry there's no pillion," he said, "but I wager Cap's got a nice soft rump."

Sara shifted back a bit to make sure she wouldn't go flying the first time they hit a bump in the road. Cap's broad rump wasn't exactly soft, but it was wonderfully warm. She sat there waiting, leaning slightly to her left, avoiding all contact with the man sitting relaxed in the saddle.

"Well?" she said when he didn't move on.

He twisted around to look at her. "I'm pleased you have such trust in gravity, ma'am, to keep you in place. But it might be wiser to hold on."

"To what?"

"Me."

Sara gulped down a thick swallow. "I don't think I ought to. It's hardly proper."

Even in the darkness she could see him roll his eyes heavenward. "I doubt there are any starchy matrons about. Unless you found one hiding in those bushes."

"If you insist," she said, taking a handful of his thick coat. "I knew this was going to be awkward."

"More awkward if you land in a ditch."

With that, he reached back and got hold of her right wrist, dragging her arm halfway around his waist.

"Now hold tight. We've wasted enough time, and I want my bed."

He immediately urged the horse into a canter—and Sara soon had both arms clasped around him to keep from getting jounced off. In another lifetime she had been something of a horsewoman, but that could hardly be compared to sitting sideways on a horse's backside without benefit of saddle or stirrup.

With her face pressed into his coat collar, she could detect the odor of the rum he'd been drinking, as well as a briary combination of horse, pipe tobacco and wool. His hair was long in back, and strands of it tickled her nose. She wondered what it would feel like to bury her face in those thick, silky strands—and immediately flung her head back. In her whole life, she'd never had such an odd inclination.

He eased the horse to a walk when they left the main road and entered a narrow track through a dense woodland. Sara took the opportunity to question him.

"What did you mean in the coach, when you said Amelie's governesses disappeared?"

"So you've finally decided to heed me?"

"I'm merely curious."

"It doesn't leave much to interpretation. They disappeared. One day they were at Tregallion—the next day they were gone. Two years apart this was."

"Did they run off, do you think? Perhaps they each had a suitor and eloped."

"One I might credit, but both of them? Not a chance. For one thing, unattached men are scarce in this district. Most of the tin and copper mines have closed, you see, and the young cockerels all go off to the cities to work." He turned to her, and she could have sworn he winked. "I hope you didn't come to Cornwall with hopes of catching a husband."

"I'm not even going to answer that."

"And where *did* you come from, if I may be so bold? Somewhere green and prosperous is my bet."

"Dorset," she said. "Very green, though not so prosperous." *No, not prosperous at all,* she thought, recalling the ultimate fate of Miss Bonnet's school.

"I've never been east of the Tamar," he said. "At least not until a few years ago."

"I'd never been west of the Tamar until yesterday. I'm afraid nobody prepared me for Cornwall."

He gave an abrupt laugh. "You make it sound as though you were entering the mouth of hell."

"Hell would be warmer," she observed.

"This isn't normal weather for early November," he said, as though obliged to defend his home county. "It's balmy in Cornwall most of the year-round, though it is windy. It's always windy here on the coast."

"Is that why you live inland? The boy at the inn—Georgie—said you live up on the moor."

"I do." He paused. "Just me and the sheep and an occasional ghostie. Abandoned mine shafts are very handy for disposing of bodies . . . and they do say a murdered man is more like to rise from his grave and walk the earth."

"Pah," she scoffed. "More hobgoblins. I warned you once that I am very difficult to frighten. I expect it's because I have no imagination."

He turned again to look at her. "Don't you? That will make for something of a novelty hereabouts. I often think Cornishmen are more fanciful than the Irish."

"I had noticed," she drawled.

His voice deepened. "Those things I told you in the coach weren't fancies. But you'll hear the tattle soon enough, when you come into Penwreath on market day. For your sake I hope the stories are wrong. But from my own dealings with the Brashears, I can tell you a few of them are God's truth."

"Every family closet has a skeleton or two," she pointed out reasonably.

"Skeletons?" he echoed. "No, the Brashears' sins are in the here and now. Walking around large as life."

"What sort of sins?" she pressed.

He chose that moment to turn mum.

"You know," she complained, unconsciously tightening her hold on his waist, "there's nothing worse than telling half a story."

"Half a story's better than none. Just keep your wits about you, my girl."

They'd come out of the wood and were now riding on a wide lane alongside a high stone wall. When they came to an imposing pair of wrought-iron gates, he drew up his horse. Sara eyed the gates with misgiving—their close-set bars were topped with narrow, businesslike spikes.

"That looks like a nasty piece of work. Are they meant to keep out the riffraff?" she asked in a teasing voice.

"No, to keep in saucy governesses," he shot back. "Riffraff isn't deterred by a wall or a gate. Any poacher worth his salt knows all the spots where the wall is crumbled or has been covered with a trellis of vines."

Her voice trembled slightly. "Never say I'm obligated to a poacher."

"Among other things," he muttered as he reached back and caught her tightly around the waist. Before she could protest this familiarity, he'd swung her to the ground.

"Sorry I can't take you to the front door. I'm not exactly a welcome visitor at Tregallion House. Truth is, the gamekeepers have orders to shoot me on sight."

Sara gasped. "That's beastly. I never heard of any landowner shooting poachers out of hand."

"It's not just the poaching," he said cryptically as he handed down her bag. "But you'll have the whole story before long. Just remember . . . don't believe everything you hear."

"I've been telling you that since we met," she reminded him.

"Oh, you can believe me. I rarely lie. It takes too much work."

"Well, thank you, Mr. Martyn. I won't keep you." She held up one hand in a farewell salute, and to her surprise he took it in his own.

When he leaned from the saddle and spoke, his voice had lost its drawling tone. "If you ever need a friend, ma'am, you go up to Needs Barrow and ask for Addie Spindle. Anyone can tell you the way."

She wondered why he wasn't offering himself as that friend in need. Then she recalled him saying he rarely put himself out for anyone.

"I'm sure I'll be fine," she said. "Governessing is fairly low in risk, last I heard."

"Then you haven't been listening."

He released her hand abruptly and turned his horse from the gate. Sara was sorry she'd annoyed him. After all, she was sure his warnings were well meant.

He was fifty feet away when she called out, "Thank you again. Oh . . . I never told you my name."

He reined his horse into a dancing circle and called back, "I've got your measure, ma'am. You're the daft woman from Dorset." He flicked the brim of his hat once and then rode off with a clatter along the hard, cold track.

"A rogue," Sara muttered as she hefted her bag and started for the gate. "Most definitely a rogue."

Chapter Two

*H*e might have warned her that the entrance drive to Tre-gallion was over a mile long, Sara thought irritably as she trudged through the darkness. Though what did it matter how far it was? She had no choice but to cover the distance since she couldn't have asked him to risk his neck to leave her at the front door.

A very odd sort of man, she decided. Concerned *and* surly, cautioning her one minute, taunting her the next. And a poacher, to boot. Lord knew what else he was involved in. Cornwall was infamous for its smugglers and wreckers—bloodthirsty men who lured ships onto the rocks to avail themselves of their cargo, mindless of innocent lives lost to the sea.

Still, she'd likely never see him again, so it wasn't worth troubling over. And at least she knew not to mention his name in the house. Nothing like arriving in the care of the family's avowed enemy. She'd keep that tidbit to herself.

After Gren Martyn rode off, a gatekeeper had finally answered her frantic tugging on the bell. He'd unlocked the enormous padlock on the gates and pushed them open. As she walked through, Sara had been struck by an eerie chill, the sort that skittered up your back for an instant, but left you shaken for whole minutes.

Blame her fanciful new acquaintance for that, she thought now, so full of ghosties and goblins and mysterious disappearances. She knew quite well that servants, even upper-class servants like governesses, often departed without notice.

Eventually she was able to make out the silhouette of the house up ahead, a low-slung Tudor affair of only two stories, with a few lights still burning on the ground floor. She crossed the cobbled courtyard to the front entrance, too weary to take much stock of the place. It appeared perfectly normal at first glance, which was all she could afford it.

Again, she had to ring several times before someone answered the bell. A youngish woman wearing a badly tied dressing gown and carrying a candlestick tugged the door open with a scowl. "So you've finally seen fit to join us."

Sara recoiled at her harsh tone. "I'm Sara Cobb, the new governess."

"And who else would you be?" the woman grumbled as she motioned her inside. "We'd given up waiting for you and all gone to bed."

Sara grew a bit miffed. "I waited for *you* . . . for your carriage, for over an hour at the Constant Star."

The woman, housemaid or housekeeper, looked down her nose. "You were to wait at the Royal William. Those were her ladyship's instructions."

Sara's mouth fell open. "How was I to know that?"

"I am sure Lady Brashear wrote to you of it. But you're here now, so it's all to the good. Come along, I'll show you where you are to sleep."

Sara wanted desperately to ease the hunger that burned in her stomach, but feared further riling the woman by asking for something from the kitchen. She'd gone to bed hungry before and hadn't been any the worse for it.

She nodded and followed the woman up a double-tiered staircase.

It seemed her long journey was not yet over; she found herself being led up and down a series of short staircases and along a number of narrow, low-ceilinged corridors.

"The schoolroom's in the east wing," her guide explained when Sara commented that the house was much larger inside than it appeared from the courtyard. "Her ladyship has had a room made up for you there."

They finally emerged into a large open space with a mullioned bay window facing to the south. Sara gauged it would be a sunny, cheerful room by daylight—if someone hadn't painted the walls a dark, somber gray.

The woman led her to a door in the wall opposite the window. When she opened it, Sara thought she was pointing out a supply closet—until she saw the narrow bed. That was it, just a bed. No night table, washstand or mirror. There wasn't even a window, since the room was situated off an interior wall.

"The nearest privy is closer to the central portion of the house," the woman said. "But I've kitted you out with this." Her toe tapped the discolored chamber pot sitting under the iron-frame bed.

Sara nodded, forcing herself to keep quiet, afraid to say even one word lest she give full vent to the horrified disbelief that clutched at her chest. Anyway, what could she say in the face of such blatant and utter disregard? That she had expected a few basic amenities . . . a decent room, a wardrobe for her clothing . . . a window, for God's sake?

Still, she reasoned, trying to make the best of things, she had the entire schoolroom at her disposal. Surely the Brashears would not mind if she fixed up a corner for herself.

"I'll leave you to get settled in now," the woman said. "We breakfast at six in the servants' hall."

Sara decided it was time to assert herself. "Governesses don't dine with the other servants . . . in the normal way of things." She attempted a composed smile to water down this minor rebellion. "After all, *my* duties don't begin until Miss Ileana has awakened."

"Suit yourself," the woman muttered. "But don't be expecting any of my girls to be traipsing all the way to the schoolroom to feed you. If you want breakfast, you'll fetch it yourself."

"You are the housekeeper, then?"

"Me and none else. Holcroft is my name. Been with the Brashears these four years."

"I'm sure we'll deal together very well," Sara said, holding out her hand.

Mrs. Holcroft looked down at it and then up into Sara's face. Sara could have sworn resentment simmered in her eyes. "That remains to be seen."

The housekeeper departed then, taking the candle with her, leaving Sara without a light in the shadowed schoolroom. She searched for a candle and tinderbox, but eventually gave up and undressed in the dark. She lay down on the narrow bed, resting her head on a hard lump of a pillow, tugging the thin woolen blanket over her. The humblest of the inns she'd stayed at during her journey had been more comfortable by far.

Not an auspicious beginning, she thought as she thumped on the pillow to make a hollow for her head. A missed connection, a pitiful closet of a bedroom and a hostile housekeeper. Oddly enough, the only bright spot in her entire day had been the unwitting kindness of a rogue.

Miss Bonnet had always said that life was full of little ironies, and as usual, she was right.

Gren Martyn approached his farm along a path carved in the heath, noting the cold chimney and dark windows. Somewhere on this wide moor a weary traveler was returning home to a warm hearth and the welcome embrace of his family. He, on the other hand, would have to build up a fire from scratch, and his only welcome would be from the scattering of wild goats that for some reason preferred the weeds in his yard to the ones growing on the moor. At least the darkness obscured the general disrepair of the place; he didn't need to be reminded that he was returning home to the local eyesore.

He saw to his horse in the small barn, then carried the lantern back to the house. Inside it was perniciously cold, and he doubted he had the energy or inclination to fiddle about with the tempermental flue. Finally he took to his bed, still clad in his coat and boots.

As exhausted as he felt, he lay there sleepless, staring around the room. Even in the diffused lantern light, the place was a disgrace. Piles of clothing lay over a scuffed wooden settle, unwashed crockery was strewn across the plank table, and clumps of mud littered the slate floor. His cupboard shelves held a jumble of open sacks: flour, cornmeal, sugar, tea. He was sure the resident mice had had few scruples helping themselves to his supplies during his absence.

Lately he'd spent more time in blasted Plymouth than in his own house. No wonder it never felt like coming home. And what had this latest trip gained him? Once again he'd come away with no new information, no fresh leads. His gaze strayed to the lone painting on the wall beyond his bed, a water-stained print of a three-masted ship sailing off a Cornish headland. Behind it lay the source of his woes—a single sheet of cheap paper that bore the deathbed testimony of the one person in the world who had ever looked after him. That paper was more than a testimony; it was a challenge, one that Gren found himself unable to walk away from.

For two and a half years, he had put his life and aspirations aside in order to follow the vague clues on that scrawled document, feeling some deep need to uncover the truth. His surroundings didn't matter, not compared to his ultimate goal. It was all temporary, he'd tell himself again and again. Once he found the answers he sought, once he'd seen justice served, he would leave this miserable farm behind. The moment couldn't come soon enough.

But what if it never came? What if more years passed and he still found himself unable to solve the riddle?

Maybe it was time to let it go and just move on. There were plenty of moments—like tonight—when he was convinced the whole story was rubbish, the confused mental ramblings of a man in dark despair. Unfortunately there was an equal number of times when the truth sprang from the page and inspired him anew.

No, he couldn't walk away just yet. But, God, he was weary of living in squalor, even if it was of his own devising. If it was pride that goaded him toward seeking that final justice, then where was the pride that kept a man from living like an animal?

He'd grown up in this one-room cottage, shared with his ill-matched parents and an older brother. His mother, in spite of his father's tendency to spend every spare coin at the local tavern, had never used poverty as an excuse for bad housekeeping. Water was free, she'd tell Gren, and soap was cheap. There had been flowers in the yard back then, and a window box full of geraniums had adorned the front window. Every spring it had been his chore to repair and whitewash the fence that enclosed the house. He wagered there was still a tub of the stuff stored in the barn rafters.

He tugged the ragged comforter up against his chin, wondering why he'd suddenly become possessed with domestic inclinations after so long. Was he, like the wind-scattered weeds in the yard, taking root here? That seemed unlikely, since he'd spent every spare minute of his youth scheming to get away.

It was long past time he stopped pretending his sojourn here was temporary. Would it be the end of the world if he settled in and fixed the place up a bit? Who knew, he might even have an occasional visitor then, a neighboring farmer stopping by to pass the time of day . . . a young lady from a nearby estate come to pay a call —

Gren sat up with a sour curse.

It was the woman who was behind the burr of dissatisfaction that was needling him. He saw that now. The chit on the coach, with her dark brows and prim mouth. Not pretty in the usual way, but possessed of the olive skin and languid eyes that lent a woman a near exotic beauty. French blood there somewhere, he thought. Well-spoken and proper, she was hardly the sort of female who'd ever give him a second glance. Or even if she did glance — and he suspected she had — she'd never let down her guard with a man she considered her inferior. That sort wasn't even good for an occasional tussle — they had too many expectations. Not like the willing serving maids he sported with, who understood that all he would ever offer was the pleasure of the moment.

Still, he couldn't shake the woman from his mind. She was walking into a quagmire in Tregallion House. A pity he'd had no solid evidence to lay before her, only rumor and speculation. And yet, in spite of his warnings, he'd ended up delivering her to the Brashears' gate — the very mouth of the lion's den. If he had any shred of conscience left, he might even be feeling a smidgen of guilt right about now.

But what was done could not be undone, as his mother was fond of saying. The prim little governess wasn't his responsibility any longer; he already had enough on his plate. His lost fawn would have to fend for herself in that place of secrets.

With another muffled curse, he leaned over and blew out the lantern. The reminders of all his neglected chores were now no more than faint shadows. It was far better that way.

Chapter Three

Sara was up and around surprisingly early the next morning. She'd left her door open and, just as she'd conjectured, volumes of sunlight spilled into the dark schoolroom. The bright rays had somehow found her dark cubby, so that when she stirred from sleep it was to find herself pooled in a honeyed glow.

After she dressed, she inspected her new domain, impressed that it was spotlessly clean. Mrs. Holcroft might be something of a female curmudgeon, but she clearly knew her way around a rag and a bucket. Two desks sat at the far end of the room, a larger one along the inner wall, and catercorner to it, a smaller one. More suited to a child, Sara thought, than a young lady of nearly eighteen. A freestanding blackboard stood canted in one corner, a low bookcase lay below the window, and beside it sat a large globe that appeared to date from the same era as the house.

The bookcase yielded a few mildewed volumes of history and geography—this last at least from a more recent century. The French text was a beginner's primer, hardly appropriate for Ileana, who, Sara had to admit, possessed a great aptitude for the language. No, all in all this was a sorry lot, and she lamented the loss of Miss Bonnet's wonderful library, which had gone under the gavel with all her other possessions.

Sara was thumbing through the solitary book on composition when her stomach began rumbling and would not stop. It was clearly time to face the rest of the household.

By fits and starts, she found her way back to the central

hall. After introducing herself to the footman on duty, she inquired the way to the kitchen.

"Her ladyship's been asking for you," he intoned.

"But surely I'm to be allowed some breakfast first," she said with a small frown.

"Follow me" was his only response, and when he led her back up the staircase, she realized she was to be denied sustenance yet again.

The portion of the house he guided her through was much grander than the east wing, the oak-paneled walls adorned with tapestries and oil paintings, the corridors lined with boule tables and marble statuary. Thick runners covered the floors and lit tapers appeared every two dozen feet. Sara thought of the dark rabbits' warrens that led to the schoolroom and felt as though she had been banished to some bleak hinterland.

The footman stopped before a carved door and knocked softly. "Miss Cobb to see you, ma'am." After a muffled reply, he opened the door and stepped aside for Sara to enter.

Lady Brashear sat writing at a fruitwood escritoire, backlit by the sun filtering through gauzy draperies.

"Please be seated," she said without looking up. "I'll be with you shortly."

Sara perched on the edge of a padded chair and studied her new employer. She was in dishabille, clad in a frothy muslin robe de chambre with a lace bonnet tied fetchingly over her blond ringlets. She had to be forty at least, yet her pale complexion showed nary a wrinkle and her fine-boned face bore no signs of the inevitable sagging. A classic beauty, Sara had labeled her at their previous meeting, just as her daughter was promising to become.

Beside the blotter, with its ornate inkwell and elegant oil lamp, sat a cup of hot chocolate. When the rich scent reached Sara, her mouth began to water. She prayed her stomach would keep quiet during the interview.

She felt a bit light-headed from lack of food and more than a bit disgruntled by the shabby treatment she'd received so far. Several of the other teachers had been former governesses, so Sara knew it was not usual for them to sleep in broom closets or conduct lessons with books fit for the dustbin. Sara had hopes that these problems would promptly be rectified.

Once she had completed her note, Lady Brashear folded it, sealed it with wax, and placed it into a leather box. Only then did she look up at Sara.

"We are not at all pleased with you this morning, Miss Cobb," she said without preamble. "Poor Tom Coachman spent over an hour last night waiting at the Royal William. Waiting for you. And on such a bitter cold night."

Sara opened her mouth to protest, but was forestalled by an abrupt wave of her ladyship's hand.

"The one thing I require of my servants is that they follow instructions. We do not have any commerce with the Constant Star. I clearly told you where you were expected to wait in my letter."

"There was no letter," Sara managed to squeak in.

"I sent it to Miss Bonnet's school last week."

"The school was closed up nearly two weeks ago, my lady. You ought to have realized that—Ileana's been home for more than a fortnight. I was staying with another of the teachers."

One pale brow rose. "Well, how was I to know that? You should have made arrangements to have your mail forwarded in that case."

Sara didn't bother to explain that she wasn't expecting any mail—for the simple reason that she hadn't anyone left to write to her.

"I am most sorry for the mix-up," she said earnestly. "I assure you I am quite good at following instructions. And to that point, perhaps you would care to discuss your intentions for Miss Brashear's schooling."

Her ladyship looked pensive for a moment, crossing her hands upon the blotter. They were bony and birdlike, discolored by several brownish spots. Sara felt a wicked thrill of satisfaction at the sight. Those hands gave away her new employer's true age as surely as any entry in the family Bible.

"My daughter is to have her comeout this spring, as you know. I believe we can dispense with the traditional areas of study. As the wife of a peer, Ileana won't require a head full of geography or astronomy. Calculating will be useful, since the lady of a manor must go over the weekly accounts with her housekeeper. French lessons will continue, of course, although I believe Ileana has virtually mastered the language. No, what I particularly require from you, Miss Cobb, is that you instill in my daughter a sense of . . . strict propriety. I inquired of the other teachers and was assured that you are a woman of firm character."

She fidgeted with her pen, her fingers tightening on the shaft. "I am not going to mince words with you. There's no point, since you will hear the servants' gossip before long. Ileana's sister was imprudent. To the point that we twice postponed her comeout. Then, during her season in London she formed a number of, shall we say, less-than-savory connections— fortune-hunters and the like. We were forced to return to Cornwall before her season was over. Alas, she was not discreet in her associations here either. Which led, I'm afraid, to her being . . . attacked by one of the local men."

"Attacked?" Sara echoed. She had a notion Lady Brashear was not referring to a beating, but to a more intimate assault.

"She was ruined, of course. Fortunately, one of her beaus from London came down here and offered to wed her. Sir Kenneth and I were that relieved. It would have scotched Ileana's chances otherwise. Thankfully, Amelie's husband removed her to Somerset."

Sara made a noise of commiseration.

"And so you will understand how imperative it is that no hint of scandal attaches itself to my younger daughter. You must watch over her, mold her and guide her."

Sara leaned forward. "Excuse me, my lady, but do I understand you correctly? You make it sound as though I am to stand guard over her. If so, it might be difficult. Your daughter is, and I am sure the other teachers would concur with me, a trifle headstrong."

Lady Brashear's mouth tightened. "Then you must find a way to curb that tendency. It was Amelie's undoing. I know Ileana does not care for you, Miss Cobb. She has been sulking in her room since she discovered you are to be her governess, and she's not once stopped pleading with us to withdraw our offer."

This hardly surprised Sara. "She does not need to like me, ma'am. But can you guarantee that she will heed me?"

Lady Brashear leveled a piercing stare at her. "I believe that is what we are paying *you* to accomplish."

Sara felt her dander rise and spoke out before she could stop herself. "I assume your elder daughter had governesses. Do you lay her disgrace at their doors, as well?"

Her ladyship first appeared affronted by this show of spirit. Then she smiled slowly. "Well done, Miss Cobb. If you can stand up to me, I believe you will have little trouble with my daughter. As for Amelie's governesses, unfortunately, Sir Kenneth and I made the mistake of choosing lively, attractive young women, thinking she would prefer the companionship of such. I fear they abetted her in her wild ways. You, on the other hand, appear to have a sedate, contemplative nature. And you've clearly had little traffic with the male sex, which is all to the good. I want Ileana kept away from men. Anyone whom my husband and I have not approved, which is to say, any man living in this district."

"Surely there are young men, neighbors, whom she will chance to meet in Penwreath. Is she to be allowed to talk to them?"

"There is only Tristan Spindle from Needs Barrow . . . and you needn't worry she'll want anything to do with him. They've been at odds since they were children."

Lady Brashear began to trim her pen point, and Sara understood that the interview was over.

"I will require a few things for the schoolroom," she said as she rose.

"Such as?"

"Books . . . for a start. The ones I found here are falling to pieces."

"Speak to Holcroft. Anything you can't find in Penwreath can be ordered from Plymouth."

"Very good, ma'am." Sara steeled herself and added, "I also wanted to mention, if I may make so bold, that my living quarters are rather austere. Perhaps Mrs. Holcroft did not understand your instructions regarding my accommodations."

A slight frown marred the smooth perfection of her ladyship's brow. "I believe she followed them implicitly. You are quartered next to the schoolroom, are you not? Trust me, Miss Cobb, it is for the best."

Her tone implied there were to be no arguments. Sara nodded meekly and said, "Will that be all?"

Her ladyship thought a moment. "Oh, yes, there is the matter of dining arrangements. We would prefer it if you took your meals in your room—that is, in the schoolroom. Unless we have guests, when you might be required to make up the numbers." She eyed Sara's plain brown gown. "I trust you have something suitable to wear in company."

Sara felt herself begin to blush. Her only dinner gown had to be more than eight years old, and it was held together by pins and the grace of God.

"No? Well, I will see what my dressmaker can find in the attic. I am afraid you are much too thick in the waist for any of my castoffs."

Sara was halfway to the door when Lady Brashear called out to her, "By the by, how did you get to Tregallion last night? Never tell me you walked all that way."

"I started walking, but a passing horseman took me up. He had been in the same coach from Plymouth."

"One of our local farmers perhaps?"

"I'm not sure what trade he followed. We were not exactly properly introduced." She edged toward the door.

"I am surprised you so blithely allowed yourself to be carried off by a total stranger."

"We'd spoken a little in the coach. He seemed . . . harmless."

Lady Brashear cocked her head. "Why don't you describe him? I'll have the cook make up a nice calf's-foot broth for him by way of thanks, and we'll send it over on Sunday."

"That's gracious of you, ma'am. But it was quite dark," Sara demurred. "He was not out of the common way . . . with rough clothing and a felt hat."

She had her hand on the door latch when Lady Brashear said, "You're keeping something from me, Sara Cobb. I don't tolerate secrets in my staff."

Sara had no choice but to face the reckoning. She turned

and bobbed a curtsy. "Please, my lady. I didn't want to distress you. The man warned me he is not well-liked in this house. I wasn't aware of that until he had taken me up . . . and it was so cold and such a long walk." She took a steadying breath. "His name was Grenville Martyn."

Twin spots of scarlet instantly appeared on Lady Brashear's pale cheeks. She rose from her writing table like an automaton and stiffly set down her pen. When she spoke, her voice trembled noticeably.

"If . . . if you ever mention that name again in this house, you will be dismissed without a reference. He is . . . he was . . . no, I owe you no explanations. I have made my wishes clear. You are to avoid him in Penwreath and never, ever to speak his name within my hearing."

"Yes, m'lady. As you wish."

Sara escaped through the door, stumbling along the hallway in a blind haze, certain she had just passed the worst twenty minutes of her life. However was she to stay on here, with a mistress who belittled and mortified her, who spoke to her as though she were a lackey . . . who thought she had a thick waist?

All the respect and deference that had been accorded her as a teacher had evaporated. While they had not treated her as a social equal, Sir Kenneth and Lady Brashear had spoken to her most pleasantly during their one encounter. Now that she no longer had the imposing presence of Miss Henrietta Bonnet behind her, it seemed she was a ripe target for bullying.

Somehow she made her way down the front staircase and found a door that opened onto another stairwell, which led to the kitchen level. Food was now the last thing on her mind, but she would have killed for a cup of tea. She went stumbling down the steps, missed one near the bottom and ended up flinging into the kitchen.

The cook, a strapping female Goliath with a mop of wild russet hair beneath her mobcap, looked up in alarm from her chopping. A monumental scowl twisted her wide mouth.

"Who are you to be invading my kitchen without so much as a by-your-leave?"

"Sara Cobb," she choked out. "The new governess."

"You're from upstairs," the cook proclaimed darkly, "and not welcome in this part of the house."

Sara opened her mouth to defend herself, but she was shaking so badly she couldn't get any words out. Instead she thrust past the woman, fleeing out an arched door that led to a cobbled yard where wash hung. She ran among the drying sheets, looking for something, anything, to hold on to. Tears were streaming down her face as she tried in vain to gulp back her sobs.

Clinging to a wooden laundry post, she finally gave vent to the grief and shock that had been brewing inside her for nearly three weeks. Bad enough to have lost a dear friend, but now to discover that her imagined haven had turned out to be a harsh prison where not one soul spoke to her with any trace of kindness . . . It was almost beyond enduring.

She was scrubbing her eyes with the edge of a sheet when a large shadow loomed over her.

"Been having a word with our lady, have you?"

The cook stood before her, hands splayed on her wide hips. Sara was surprised to see a twinkle of amusement in her eyes. "Nay, you're not the first to turn watering pot after speaking with Lady Brashear. Half the housemaids in Tregallion—and not a few of the footmen—have shed tears at my table. Come inside now, and I'll make you some tea. And leave that sheet alone. Our washerwoman's already got more work than she can handle."

Sara hung back. "You said you didn't want me in there."

The cook scoffed. "Startled me, you did, tripping into the room so sudden like, and me with my meat cleaver like to chop off a finger or two. You come now. . . ."

Sara gave one final sniffle and followed the cook back to her domain. The woman coaxed her to a chair at the long plank table.

"Upstairs folk rarely come down here," she said as she carried a massive kettle over to the table and poured hot water into a pot along with a scoop of loose tea. "I attend her ladyship in her morning parlor to go over the menu each day. It's better that way, since I won't brook any interference in how I run things." She gave Sara a sly look. "And her ladyship does have a knack for interfering."

"Everything I did or said was wrong," Sara moaned, not caring that she didn't know this woman from Eve, "even when I was blameless. How is one to work for such a person?"

The giantess laid one finger aside her nose. "By agreeing with her most amiably . . . and then going off and doing precisely what you like. Here, drink this now. And by the look of you, you could stand a scone or two."

Sara nodded numbly. "I haven't eaten since breakfast yesterday."

The cook's eyes flashed with a martial light. "Typical of the Holcroft creature not to offer you even a crumb when you arrived. But she rarely eats a bite herself. Lives off her own vitriol, that one."

She plunked a tray of food in front of Sara. Raisin scones spread with clotted cream, ham sliced into delicate slivers, warm kippers.

"This is . . . wonderful," Sara sputtered between bites and sips, her appetite now fully restored. "Thank you, Mrs.—"

"May Belle True," her savior announced. "May, queen of the kitchen."

"I will be your most loyal subject," Sara proclaimed, "if you feed me like this at every meal"—she hesitated—"though perhaps I ought to watch what I eat from here on. Lady Brashear told me I have a thick waist."

May Belle made a rude noise. "Her ladyship judges everyone by her own severe standards. Always been rail-thin, even as a girl. She had Miss Amelie on potatoes and vinegar the instant the girl started to fill out her gowns a bit too much, though it wasn't my good food that caused it."

The cook paused and frowned slightly. "But that's nothing you need to know, little Miss Cobb. All water over the dam, as my da used to say. You just finish up your meal while I get on with Sir Kenneth's luncheon—and don't fret yourself about your waist. A man likes a handful of flesh when he reaches for a woman, and don't I know it."

She patted her own impressively corseted middle, then

went back to hacking at a joint of beef, wielding the cleaver like a maniac.

Sara calmed down after a time, convincing herself that hunger had magnified the wretchedness of her interview with Lady Brashear. They'd merely got off on the wrong foot. She recalled now that the woman had actually complimented Sara when she stood up to her. Perhaps Lady Brashear was one of those combative people who provoked, not out of malice, but out of a simple need to brangle.

When she returned to the schoolroom the door was open. She was sure she had shut it before she left. Her bedroom door was also ajar, and she could see someone in the tiny space.

It was Ileana, going through her belongings, which were still packed in her travel bag. The girl looked over her shoulder as Sara approached, but made no attempt to disguise what she was doing.

"Those are my things," Sara said indignantly. "You'd no right to open my bag."

Ileana shrugged. "You needn't worry that I'll steal anything. I vow our scullery maid has finer gowns."

"Nevertheless," Sara insisted, "it's an invasion of my privacy. You are welcome to use the schoolroom any time you like, but this is my bedroom. Please respect that."

Ileana flounced out, if such a thing were possible in that small space, and began to stroll around the larger room. "I've only come here to tell you that I am not going to cooperate—I've done with books and studying. They can't make me. *You* certainly can't make me."

"Your mother isn't so concerned with your schooling, you might be interested to hear. She wants me to guide you in deportment and manners."

The girl made a rude face. "That's the last thing I require."

Sara leaned against the door frame and folded her arms. "So you believe you are ready to go out into the world, a polished young lady?"

"Precisely," she said with an arch smile. "At least there's nothing I could learn from a dried-up old spinster like you. Now if Mama had hired Miss Gimble or Miss Tate, I might have been willing to put up with this nonsense for another few months. They knew a deal about the fashions in London and all the *on-dits* of the *ton*. I doubt you were ever outside of Dorset."

"It might surprise you where I've been."

"I don't care if you've been to see the Queen," Ileana declared. "I am to marry a peer, if Mama has any say, and it's a mystery to me why she hired a little nobody to groom me for the role."

"Perhaps the little nobody is the only one who will be honest with you about your flaws. Peers are notoriously averse to willful misses with bad tempers and irritating—and completely misplaced—airs of self-consequence."

Ileana's jaw dropped. "How dare you! How dare you say such things to me? You are a servant in this house. A *servant!*"

Sara moved farther into the room. "*That* is the first thing you need to learn. A lady, a true lady, does not belittle those below her. Furthermore, it's true I am here to serve you, but to do that effectively, I must be in charge of you." She gave a rueful grin. "A tricky business, as you must see."

"I don't see!" Ileana cried plaintively. "I spent six years in that horrid school, watched over, inspected, chided for every little misdeed, and I won't be treated that way any longer. Especially not in my own home." She put her chin up. "I am not a child."

"Then stop behaving as one. These outbursts are not attractive."

"I don't care what you think is attractive. I happen to know that gentlemen appreciate a bit of spirit in a young lady."

"Spirit, yes. Spitefulness and spoiled behavior, definitely no." Sara moved to the bookcase. "Now as for your lessons, I'm afraid we've no books but these . . . relics. So until I can order some from Plymouth, I suggest we begin with an essay."

Ileana backed toward the door. "Oh, no. I didn't come here for lessons. I thought I made that clear. Short of prying me from my bedroom, you won't get me in here again."

"I believe your mother might have something to say on that score."

The girl narrowed her eyes. "It's just like a prosy little nun like you to go running to Mama. But I tell you, she won't like it. She'll believe you're not doing your job properly and dismiss you."

Since Lady Brashear had virtually implied this very thing, Sara awarded her daughter a hit direct. She meshed her hands before her, gazing intently at the girl. "And you won't care that your thoughtless behavior results in an innocent person being cast out?"

"Why should I care?"

Sara nodded her head slowly. "I was wrong. I can see that you'll make an excellent bride for some lord. You haven't a thought for a single soul in the world but yourself, you feel no sense of responsibility or remorse, and you speak without thinking—like a child in leading strings. Yes, I vow the peers of London will be lining up to court such a selfish, heartless, undiplomatic young lady."

Ileana looked as though she were going to explode. Instead she strode over to the blackboard and slammed it to the ground. There was a startling *crrrck!* as the slate shattered into a hundred jagged shards.

Sara forced herself not to flinch. "The patronesses at Almack's would have enjoyed seeing that. Perhaps you can hire yourself out in London as a sort of comical entertainment."

The girl flashed her one final look of inchoate fury and stormed from the room. Sara bent to pick up the scattered bits of slate, wondering who had won that encounter—or if it even mattered. It felt as though they had both lost.

Chapter Four

*I*leana made good on her threat. For four days she did not come to the schoolroom. Sara lived in fear that her ladyship would call her in for a progress report, but each day passed without the dreaded summons. For the first few mornings, Sara went to Ileana's bedroom and knocked on the door.

"It's time for your lessons, Miss Brashear," she would say in a firm voice.

"Go to the devil," Ileana would respond.

Totally charming, Sara thought. Gutter language and defiant rudeness in one delectable package. The girl would barely last one week in London before she was forbidden all the best homes. Lady Brashear would be lucky to wed her to a fishmonger after that.

Sara repeated her visit each afternoon, with similar results. She'd even tried the door once, out of exasperation, but found it locked. She began sliding notes under the threshold, lists of the things Ileana would need to know to get on in society. On her last attempt, she found a pile of shredded paper lying on the carpet in front of the door. That was when she gave up the siege. She'd have to think of another way to lure Ileana into the schoolroom. Blackmail was not beyond her at this point, if only she could think of some way to coerce the girl. But she had no leverage.

To pass the time, Sara began helping May Belle in the kitchen. The cook was short staffed due to an early incursion of the winter influenza, and Sara enjoyed working beside the enormous hearth, which had to be the warmest spot in the otherwise badly heated house.

She'd given her order for books and supplies to Mrs. Holcroft, who'd read it and snorted, "Why not order the whole blessed bookstore?"

"There are only twenty titles on the list," Sara started to say, and then stopped herself. She owed no explanations for doing her job properly, least of all to this woman. "Please see that they are sent here promptly," she said in a chilly voice.

Mrs. Holcroft went away grumbling, and Sara felt a little frisson of victory.

That same afternoon, Miss Prake, Lady Brashear's dressmaker, came to Sara with several dinner gowns. They might have been outmoded, but they were far finer than anything she had possessed in years.

"Velvet," Miss Prake said, spreading them out on the window seat, "since it's come on so cold. I know muslin and silk are all the crack in London, but those ladies don't have to contend with the damp winds of Cornwall."

"Were these Lady Brashear's gowns?" Sara asked, recalling that comment about her waist.

"They were Miss Amelie's. She was about your size, miss, though a bit taller. The family does quite a lot of entertaining over the winter, so I decided I'd best make up two."

Sara thought they were both lovely, one a soft blue-gray with pearl buttons halfway up the sleeves and a scalloped neckline, the other a rich amber, with darker beadwork along the bodice and a delightful tassel of corded silk that draped over the skirt.

"Necklines have plunged since these were made up," Miss Prake observed, "but I could lower them in a trice."

"Oh, no," Sara said quickly. "I've no evening shawl to keep me warm . . . the higher the better."

Miss Prake cast her an assessing glance. "If I may say, miss, it is a shame to hide your bosom. Unlike you, Miss Amelie was rather amply endowed . . . not at all the style, alas."

Wonderful, Sara muttered to herself. A thick waist *and* an underendowed bosom. Still, the gowns were a treat, the first nice things she had received at Tregallion, not counting her budding friendship with May Belle True.

The next day, Miss Prake returned for a fitting. Since there was no mirror in the schoolroom, Sara had to trust the dressmaker's opinion. "You'll look fine as five pence," she assured her after Sara had tried on both gowns. "Now if there was only something to be done with your hair."

"My hair?" Sara raised a hand to the two braids that were coiled at the nape of her neck.

"I'm sure that style is fine for a governess, but Lady Brashear will expect something more elegant at the dinner table. I can send her ladyship's dresser to you . . . a wizard with her shears, that one. Though I fear there's little can be done with the color."

Sara knew her hair was an unremarkable shade—dirt brown, in plain English. But when uncoiled from its braids, it was thick and lustrous, her one small vanity. No one was coming near her with shears, wizard or not.

Once Miss Prake left to work on the gowns, Sara was faced with another long day with little to do. She still hadn't left the house, nor had she mustered up the courage to enter the library. A book or two would have made her days tolerable, but she knew from May Belle that Sir Kenneth haunted the place. She still hadn't met the master of Tregallion, not surprising since she rarely ventured out of the schoolroom. But May Belle had told her he was an odd sort of gentleman, who on one hand required the house servants to attend group prayers after supper, yet was also something of a terror among the housemaids. Sara had also got the impression from May Belle that he was carrying on with the sour Mrs. Holcroft—and that the previous governesses had likewise suffered from his familiarities. This, she reasoned, must have been what Grenville Martyn meant to warn her about.

So she kept well away from the library, even if it meant spending hours writing in her journal or staring out the schoolroom windows at the distant gray sea. With no real duties to perform, time weighed heavily on her, and she often found herself daydreaming about Mr. Martyn, wondering if she would ever see him again. He had not tried to be engaging, quite the opposite, yet she'd been drawn to him in spite of it.

A sad reflection of how barren her life had become, she reflected dismally, to find herself beguiled by a tattered, taunting poacher.

Perhaps it was nothing more than basic physical attraction. Not that she'd ever experienced such a thing in her life. The few young men she'd met during her comeout had never sparked the least bit of yearning in her bosom. Now here she was mooning over a blue-eyed scoundrel . . . well, not exactly mooning, but far more distracted than she ought to be.

She determined to focus all her energies on Ileana and to stop wasting her thoughts on Mr. Martyn. Even in the unlikely event that he reciprocated her interest, he was hardly the sort of man she could imagine sharing her life with.

In her youth, not so long past, she'd dreamed of being wooed by a high-minded man of letters. She had never aspired to a titled husband, even though her own family tree contained a few baronets and one distant viscount. No, she'd have been quite content to find a mate of intelligence and wit. A pity the *ton* had been singularly lacking in candidates with those qualifications. Of course, the fact that the instant she was out in company she became tongue-tied and prone to severe blushes seriously impeded her chances of discovering such a paragon. Even the brightest of them found it nearly impossible to converse with a stammering beet root.

Yet she'd had no trouble whatever talking to Mr. Martyn, who should have been far more intimidating than the well-bred young gentlemen she'd encountered in London. What was it about the man that made him so approachable?

On the evening of her fourth day at Tregallion, May Belle invited her to share some sherry in her parlor. After two glasses of the cordial—and warmed into uncharacteristic mellowness by the blazing fire—Sara asked her friend the one question that had been plaguing her since her arrival.

"I met a man on the coach from Plymouth," she began, purposely examining her toes toasting on the fender. This was not a conversation conducive to eye contact. "He ended up taking me to Tregallion on his horse."

"That was a blessing. As I recall, it was uncommon cold the night you arrived."

"Unfortunately, when I mentioned him to Lady Brashear she turned quite pale and threatened to dismiss me if I ever spoke his name again. I—I've just been wondering what he did that was so dreadful."

May Belle took a healthy swallow from her glass, then set it aside. She leaned forward from her chair—Sara distinctly heard her corset creak—and shook her head. "I take it you're speaking of Grenville Martyn. He's a silver-tongued rascal and no mistake. Been having his way with women since he was breeched. Men, on the other hand, tend to give him a wide berth."

"The landlord at the Constant Star was quite amiable toward him."

"That's because they're cousins of a sort. And Lather Pitt is not so squeaky clean. Those cellars of his have been used to store smuggled goods since the days of Drake."

"And is Mr. Martyn also a smuggler?"

"Not that I know of. Poacher is more like it, though it's not only birds he steals. Unwary husbands are like to find him poaching in their own beds."

Sara's brow furrowed. "That still doesn't explain Lady Brashear's reaction. Unless he made overtures to her."

"It wasn't *her*," May Belle chuffed. "No, he went hunting after younger, plumper game than that dried-up old hen."

Her eyes narrowed. It was precisely as she had feared. "Amelie?"

"So you know of her disgrace?"

"Lady Brashear was frank with me; she didn't want me to hear the story from the servants. But she left out most of the details."

"So now you're asking one of the servants."

"Please, May Belle, you must know you are my friend. My only friend in this sorry place. The thing is, I—I was struck by Mr. Martyn's kindness to me. It's difficult to equate that with everyone else's aversion to him."

May Belle shot her a sly grin. "You sure it wasn't his wicked blue eyes that struck you?"

"I barely noticed his appearance," she lied boldly. "But I need to understand what he did that was so wrong."

"Why? So you can put him from your mind?"

Sara realized this was the exact truth. "Perhaps. I admit I can't help thinking of him from time to time. I have had very little exposure to rogues . . . and they do have a certain dark appeal."

"That one more than most. But he's from a wild family and was bound for trouble practically from birth." She heaved a deep sigh. "They say 'like harks to like,' Sara Cobb, so it shouldn't have surprised anyone that Miss Amelie, freshly returned from London with a whisper of scandal at her heels, would be drawn to the local rakehell."

"Yet Lady Brashear said *he* attacked her."

"I fancy Amelie flirted with him, perhaps even allowed him a few liberties. But her breeding wouldn't let her consort with such a base-born fellow—these Brashear women think very highly of themselves, in case you haven't noticed—and the upshot was that she teased him once too often."

"And he . . . had his way with her?"

"So she claimed. Gren Martyn claimed otherwise, which is why he is not this moment festering in the hulks off Plymouth. He had witnesses who vouched for him, among them Adeline Spindle of Needs Barrow."

"Lady Brashear mentioned the Spindles. They are not, I take it, a laboring family."

"County gentry fallen on hard times. Their late father lost all his money in failed mining ventures. But Addie's voice kept Gren from prison. She swore on oath that he was at her home, repairing one of their outbuildings the night Amelie was attacked."

"And you believe Miss Spindle was lying?"

"I can't think why Amelie would lie. No reason to put herself through the stress of a magistrate's investigation, not to mention enduring the scorn of her family, if she hadn't something to tell."

Sara mulled this over. It made little sense that a libertine would resort to violence. Any experienced seducer would have no trouble bending a callow young woman to his will, especially one as impetuous as Amelie Brashear. It was more likely she'd been a willing party, only goaded by her conscience *after* the fact to lay the blame at the man's door.

When she pointed this out to the cook, that a man with Gren Martyn's wicked tongue hardly needed to use force, May Belle nodded. "The same thing occurred to me. But I expect you know little of the ways of men. A girl can flirt and tease for only so long before a man loses patience. There's an unpleasant name for such a girl—not that it excuses a man who takes matters to an extreme."

"I can understand now why Lady Brashear reacted as she did," Sara said after some reflection. "It must be a thorn in her side, knowing Mr. Martyn is still about in the neighborhood— a constant reminder of the family's disgrace."

"That it is. And say what you will against her character, her ladyship's kept her chin up and managed to soldier on . . . still goes to church regular and attends all the local fetes."

"Is the story widely known in the district?"

"Who can say? Sir Kenneth believes he managed to keep most of the details within the family. I wager the most the locals know is that Gren Martyn was taken to gaol for attacking a woman—and released within a fortnight. Whether he's spoken of it or not is anyone's guess."

"He told me not to believe everything I heard about him. But I suspect every man who's ever been behind bars makes similar protestations of innocence." She frowned as she weighed these two warring factors.

May Belle eyed her over the rim of her glass. "I see you straining to find points in his favor. Or at least trying to justify his behavior. But there's another thing you ought to know before you let down your guard with such a fellow."

"I'm n-not about to do that . . ." Sara stuttered. "Truly I'm not."

"The bad blood between the Brashears and Gren Martyn goes back nearly three years. Gren had reason to strike out at this family, you see, and he knew in his clever heart that a scandal would be the worst sort of blow to them."

"What was this reason?"

May Belle's eyes narrowed. "Sir Kenneth hanged his older brother."

Sara half rose from her chair. "What?"

The cook nodded. "Or as good as hanged him. Three years past, Jacob Martyn was taken for poaching. Sir Kenneth is a crony of Lord Denby, our local magistrate, and he somehow convinced his lordship that Jacob was a horse thief, as well. Jacob was sent to the assizes in Bodmin, and with such serious charges confirmed by Sir Kenneth's testimony, the judge had no choice but to order his execution. The ladies of Penwreath all but declared a public day of mourning."

Sara was trying to dispel the image of this other Martyn, another handsome, cozening rogue, going to his death. And there was that rash Gren Martyn making no bones about poaching on the grounds of Tregallion. "I imagine Sir Kenneth wishes he could arrange the same fate for Jacob's younger brother," she murmured.

"The day is not long off," May Belle declared. "Gren can't seem to stay away from Tregallion Wood."

Sara wished it weren't so. For some reason, in spite of all the evidence against him, admitted out of his own mouth, she couldn't bear to think of him dangling from a gibbet.

When a log shattered in the fireplace, May Belle recalled that she had to be up at sunrise. Sara thanked her for the cordial—and for the information she had shared—before heading off to her room.

As she was crossing the front hall, Sara heard someone on the landing above her. It was a man, tall and robust, wearing a fitted velvet banyan. Sir Kenneth Brashear in the flesh.

He leaned over the banister to observe her but said nothing. Sara didn't know whether to address him or not, but she had no intention of scurrying away like a frightened rabbit. They stared at each other for a moment, then he broke the awkward silence. "Ah, Miss Cobb, the errant governess, I presume."

"Sir Kenneth," she said, with a nod of her head. She had a fleeting notion she had interrupted him on an excursion to the housekeeper's bedroom.

To her dismay, he started down the stairs, the light from his double candlestick making his long shadow dance on the far wall.

"Let me have a look at you then," he said as he approached her.

Up close, he smelled of port wine and hair pomade. He was fully as handsome as his wife—tawny haired, with a finely sculpted nose and heavy-lidded eyes, his mouth large but well-shaped.

Sara suffered his scrutiny in painful silence. She nearly gasped when he set a hand on her shoulder. "You've snagged a cobweb," he said easily, as he brushed his palm down her arm. "Been creeping about in my cellars, have you?"

Sara shook her head almost violently. "Certainly not. I was passing the time with your cook."

"Ah, the magnificent May Belle. I wager she could make two of you, though I trust she'll soon fatten you up properly. You look as though a stiff breeze would blow you away."

"I assure you, sir, I do not go hungry."

He eyed her provocatively, stroking the tips of his fingers over his wide mouth. "Perhaps you're one of those women with a delicate appetite."

Sara had no skill at countering innuendo. It was one of the reasons she had been such a dismal failure in London.

"Which makes sense," he continued, "since you appear quite sylphlike."

Sara decided this was not a good time to point out her thick waist. His eyes were already roving over her body.

"Will that be all, Sir Kenneth?" she said with as much ice as she could muster. It wasn't difficult; the front hall was frigid.

"Run off, then," he said with a wave of his hand. "Though you'll discover it's wise to keep on my good side."

"I have every intention of proving myself quite satisfactory to you," she said briskly, "as a governess. I bid you good night, sir."

She sailed away, head up, even while she seethed at his overt and inappropriate conduct. Still, he'd not been as intimidating as she'd expected after hearing May Belle's stories, just cloyingly lecherous. Rather like a panting, fawning spaniel who needed to have his nose smacked.

She ought to be amused that he'd accused her of creeping about in his cellar. She had in fact been creeping about, but in the attics—under the instigation of May Belle. The cook pronounced it a scandal that her room was so barren, and she had taken Sara up into the attics several times. Her meager bedroom now possessed a small wall mirror, a shelf with a row of pegs below it, and a ceramic plant stand she'd wedged next to her bed to use as a night table. There was also a thick featherbed and down pillow that May Belle had "borrowed" from one of the guest rooms.

As she drew on her nightgown, Sara was struck by the thought that all this business of getting settled in might have been for naught. If Ileana continued to ignore her, Lady Brashear was bound to hear of it, and then there would be hell to pay. Sara wondered if she shouldn't begin advertising for another position. She would, of course, omit any mention of working for the Brashears. It wasn't precisely a lie—she'd done virtually no governessing as yet.

She would be saddened to lose her friend and fellow conspirator in the kitchen, but would not be sorry to leave the neighborhood where Gren Martyn dwelled so close by. He still preyed upon her thoughts, and she cursed herself for behaving like a besotted schoolgirl, to be smitten with a man after so little contact. He'd probably never given her another thought.

"There," she told herself harshly, "focus on that. He's doubtless chasing after some local siren at this moment. He is certainly not mooning about over a dowdy spinster with a thick waist and no discernible bosom."

Chapter Five

The next morning, Sara was gazing mournfully out the schoolroom window, when she saw Ileana and a groom ride by. They were heading toward the ornamental lake that spread out to the left of the drive. Here was her chance, at last, to accost the girl away from the house. Sara quickly tugged on her pelisse and went racing through the east wing.

The sunlit sky was a pale blue overhead, the wind no more than a light breeze. Sara breathed a prayer of thanks for this as she hurried across the courtyard and down the drive.

The lake lay between a copse of stately oaks and a sprawling woodland, its banks an angled carpet of sheared grass. She hurried along there, wondering where the riders had gone. It was only when she was halfway around the lake that she noticed a trail leading into the woods. The ground there had been recently churned up by hooves.

With a sigh, she headed down the trail, wishing she'd spent some time walking the property during the past week. She had no idea how large this wood might be or how many paths might run through it. It seemed her plan of running Ileana to earth was not going to be as simple as she'd hoped.

At least it was a pleasure to be outside again. In Dorset, walking had been one of her chief delights, a passion she had shared with her employer. It was a total mystery to Sara how a doughty woman like Henrietta Bonnet, who could hike from dawn till sundown, keeping up a nonstop discourse on plant and animal life, could have in actuality been ailing.

Sara meandered along, stopping every so often to peer at some odd bit of tree trunk or a stray bird's feather, dearly missing her learned companion. She'd gone a fair distance into the wood when she began to sense someone or something keeping pace with her in the thick cover beside the trail. It wasn't a noise or motion that alerted her, more a sort of primal awareness that she was no longer alone.

"Who's there?" she called out sharply—and immediately felt foolish.

Until she heard a rustling in front of her, and a dark-garbed figure stepped from the bushes onto the path. It was Gren Martyn, wearing a wide, leering smile.

"Very good," he said, applauding softly. "They ought to make you a gamekeeper."

Sara's first reaction was a shiver of apprehension. This man had possibly done unspeakable things to Amelie Brashear. Then steady reason intruded, reminding her that if he'd intended her any mischief, he'd had ample opportunity to act on it the night they met. Instead, he had been almost solicitous.

Her second reaction was one of anger at his foolhardiness.

"Are you mad?" she uttered. "Ileana and her groom are in this wood."

He shrugged. "They've been and gone. The young lady rides like she has little regard for her life—or anyone else's." He gazed a moment in the direction where the riders had passed. "A wild piece, that one. I'm surprised you haven't had a more calming effect on her."

"I've had *no* effect on her," Sara muttered, and then noting the speculative expression on his face, added, "And don't you dare think of setting your sights on Ileana. I've heard all about your intrigue with Amelie."

He sighed melodramatically. "As I knew you would. I suppose you will damn me now, along with all the rest of the Brashears."

"I am not in any position to judge you."

"Now there's a novel reaction. What if I told you it was all true?"

She glowered at him. "I would think you were bamming me. But true or not, I want nothing to do with you."

She hiked up her skirt with both hands and began walking swiftly away from him.

He sauntered after her. "I came here to see you, you know," he called out. "Risked life and limb to see how you were faring. I've been here every day since you arrived, hoping you'd venture into the wood. I was imagining they had you chained to the dungeon wall by now."

Sara slowed her pace, but did not turn completely around. "As you can see, I am in fine fettle."

Meanwhile, her heart was rapidly going *trip-a-trip-a-trip*. Had he really come to see her? Or was he simply turning a chance meeting into something that reflected well on him? She stole a glance at the game bag at his hip. It was suspiciously plump. So much for his avowed concern—he'd been poaching.

"And how goes the governessing?"

Sara winced. "I was a classroom teacher, so there's been a slight period of adjustment."

"One student or a dozen, I don't see that it makes much difference. So what did you mean when you said you've had no effect on Ileana?"

"I was merely making an idle comment."

"Now you're bamming me. . . ."

She spun to face him. "You are a very nettlesome man, Gren Martyn. The truth is, Miss Brashear has refused to enter the schoolroom. Barring the first day, when I caught her rifling through my bag. Once her mother learns of this defection, I shall be turned out of the house."

He whistled a long, low note. "And there is nothing you can do to force her?"

"Short of carrying her bodily to the schoolroom, no."

"I'd be happy to help out in that department. She's a tasty bundle for all that she rides like a madwoman."

Sara growled and started walking again.

He didn't say anything for a time, and she hoped he had given up and vanished back into the foliage. But when she came to a branching of the trail, he spoke up from close behind her. "Follow the left-hand fork. . . ."

Sara purposely headed to the right. In a few paces he caught up with her and took hold of her arm.

"Let go of me!"

"Hush," he said. "There's a pretty, dappled glade in the other direction—just the sort of place females favor."

And silver-tongued poachers . . .

"Don't you understand?" she pleaded as he coaxed her along the path. "My position here hangs by the merest thread. If I were to be seen walking with you, talking to you, I would be cast off without a reference."

"They're likely to do that anyway, from what you just told me. But if you come along with me, I might put in a word for you with the Spindles. Trust me, you'd much rather work for Addie Spindle than the festering Brashears."

She stopped and turned. "Does Addie Spindle require a governess?"

He scratched thoughtfully at the dark bristle on his chin. "Not at present. But if she were to marry, there's no telling how many sprats she might pop out."

"Oh, you are hopeless," Sara cried. "I thought for a moment you might actually be trying to help me. But how could I forget that you never put yourself out for anyone?"

The grin eased from his lean face. "You really are worried."

"Of course I'm worried. I haven't two shillings to rub together. And if I lose this position, I will most likely starve."

To her surprise, he shifted away from her and settled on a fallen log. "I'm sorry. I didn't realize your situation was so precarious." He gazed up at her, and she was surprised by the knot of concern on his face. "I should have seen it that first night. You didn't even have enough money to pay for a cup of tea, did you?"

Sara shook her head. "Or to rent the landlord's gig."

"What happened to you? I mean, your clothing is old, but it's cut from fine cloth, and you were clearly well educated and brought up respectable."

Sara didn't know how to respond. It really wasn't any of his business, and so she told him.

He braced his arms on either side and gazed up at the canopy of tree limbs meshed overhead. "Seems to me you've learned a great deal about Gren Martyn. Only fair that I learn something about you."

"Why?" she asked bluntly.

"Let's just say I feel a bit proprietary about you. After warning you about the place, I ended up bringing you here. So I need to know that you're not in a bad way. It's obvious to me that something's upset you. Something more than Ileana's mutiny, I wager."

"It's nothing . . . nothing I care to speak about."

He reached out and got hold of her hand. "Tell me. At least tell me how a well-born young lady ended up toiling for these upstarts." His eyes flashed. "I'll badger you mercilessly if you don't."

"Oh, very well," she said, lowering herself to the log beside him. "Though it's hardly a remarkable tale. For the past five years, I've been teaching at a school for young ladies. The headmistress had been my own governess years before. My . . . my family suffered a number of financial reverses, and when my parents died, I was forced to work for my bread."

"I'm not going to sympathize with you on that score," he chided her gently. "It's been my lot and my family's lot for generations."

"I know," she said. "It was just a bit of a shock at first. But Miss Bonnet was the best of employers and a very dear friend."

"Then why are you not still among the green fields of Dorset?"

"Miss Bonnet died," she uttered bleakly. "She had just turned forty, and no one knew her heart was weak." She'd pulled a leaf from a nearby shrub and now began to shred it between her fingers. "She left me the school in her will. Beyond my grief, I was thrilled at the prospect of carrying on her work. For about three days, that is. Until the debt collectors arrived."

Gren Martyn *tsk*ed softly. "There's always a worm inside the windfall."

"More like two dozen worms. Turns out my wise, prudent Miss Bonnet had been living on tick for years. Her debts ate up everything, including my own small savings."

He craned forward to look at her. "Surely it wasn't up to you to satisfy her creditors."

"I wanted her name to be clear of any stigma. I needed to give her that."

He sat in silence for a time, eventually removing the shredded remains of a second leaf from her fingers. "Easy now. No need to ravage the landscape. You'll strip away all my favorite hiding places."

Sara grinned. "And you called *me* daft. I'm not the one sitting in a forbidden wood, where at any moment a gamekeeper might take off the best part of my skull."

He flicked one finger over her chin. "What *is* the best part of my skull, ma'am? I've heard the ladies fancy my eyes, but I've always thought I had a rather fetching nose." He tipped his head up in a highly affected manner, and Sara chuckled.

"There," he said, "that's more like it. I'll play the buffoon for you, Sara Cobb, if it will make you laugh. Anything to lighten the load from those serious eyebrows of yours."

Sara felt herself being enticed and did not fight it. It was such a lovely novelty to banter with an attentive, attractive man. She easily convinced herself that he hadn't once done or said anything improper. Instead, he had listened to her as a friend—a simple act that had somehow consoled her.

"I was a very good teacher," she said, half to herself. "A pity Ileana Brashear never thought so. Behind my back, she called me Sour Sara and Miss Crab."

"And you probably called her Ill-bred Ileana, the brash Brashear."

Sara gave a gurgle of protesting laughter. "I never did, though I wish I'd thought of it. It's very apt."

He was looking at her, those deep-water eyes fixed and intent. "You'll have other students, Sara Cobb. If it's teaching you've set your heart on, you'll find the clever minds you require."

"Will I?" she said a little forlornly. "This situation has me doubting and second-guessing myself. If I fail at this, I wonder if I will have the confidence to teach again." She gave him a wan smile. "Miss Bonnet always told me I clutched too tight to the present to ever see what the future might hold."

"Unfortunately, *your* future held *her* debts. But she had a point. It's akin to riding—if you're timid, you hold the reins too tight, and you never move forward, never get where you need to go."

"Speaking of needing to go, I should get back to the house." She rose from her rustic perch, brushing the leaf bits from her gown. "I had a foolish notion of tracking Ileana and trying to reason with her. Away from Tregallion, you see, where her mother or father would not overhear us."

"She's long gone," he said as he got to his feet and then stretched, flexing one arm above his head. His coat gapped, and Sara tried not to notice the lean planes of his stomach below his snug vest.

"There are miles of trails through these woods," he added, "not to mention a path that runs along the sea cliffs. Though I've never yet heard of a governess who had to hunt her pupils down like a bloodhound. Are you sure you wouldn't rather look for another post?"

Her eyes narrowed. "Still trying to be rid of me, I see."

"I wasn't jesting when I said I feel uneasy about you staying here."

"And yet you won't give me any of the details."

"Perhaps I don't have all the details. . . ."

"Well, until you do, I'm bound to keep after Ileana. For pride's sake, if nothing else."

"Then I think you'd better try another tack with her."

"Meaning what?"

"Meaning you need someone else to intervene. Someone close to her. And I know just the person."

Sara nearly tugged on his sleeve. "Who?"

He offered her a smug grin. "Her sister."

Sara's mouth hardened into severe frown. "Never tell me you are on cordial terms with the woman you . . . you . . ."

"Raped? Or is that word too raw for you?" He turned away from her, sinking his hands deep into his coat pockets. The anger rising off him was nearly palpable.

"I'm sorry," she said quickly. "You would hardly be on any terms with her if that were true. But you've got to admit this is all very confusing."

He glanced over his shoulder. "You'll figure it out one day. I might even expect an apology when that occurs. I will tell you this—Amelie and I were friends as children. That might help you sort it out."

Sara was more perplexed than ever, especially since it appeared that his former friend's father had been instrumental in hanging his brother. But she wasn't going to bring that up now. Enough wounds had been bared.

She touched him once on the arm because she couldn't leave without some sign of acknowledgement. He didn't seem to notice.

He did call out, however, when she was a dozen yards away. "I'll write to Amelie. Ileana will be back in the schoolroom within a few days. I promise."

When Sara shifted around to thank him, he was gone, lost in the dense cover of shrubs and bracken.

As she was retracing her steps along the trail, she heard movement off to her right. Sir Kenneth, accompanied by a gamekeeper leading a brace of spaniels, was making his way through a dense thicket. Her first instinct was to hide, but then she realized the men were heading directly toward the spot where she had last seen Gren Martyn. Since she had no way of knowing how far away he was, she decided she'd better delay them.

Gritting her teeth, she called out loudly, "Sir Kenneth! Halloo! Over here, Sir Kenneth."

He did not appear pleased as he came thrusting through the greenery. "Stop that caterwauling," he growled. "Bless me if you haven't scared away every gamecock for miles."

"Sorry," she said. "But I am so relieved to see you. I was looking for Ileana."

The gamekeeper had caught up with them, and the spaniels were now capering around her skirts. She bent down to rough up their ears.

"I haven't seen her," Sir Kenneth muttered. "And stop agitating my dogs."

Sara stood up. "I didn't mean to interrupt your hunt. I thought I saw your daughter ride this way, but I seem to have got turned around in the wood. If you could just point the way to the house."

At Sir Kenneth's orders, the gamekeeper walked her down to where the trail forked. Sara could barely contain her smile. A canny, woods-wise man like Gren Martyn would have had plenty of time to make his escape. Sara felt as though she were a fledgling outlaw herself—and the thought did not trouble her one bit.

Gren Martyn watched the entire exchange from his leafy perch in a tall beech tree. The instant he'd heard the two men thrashing through the underbrush, rather like a pair of ungainly bulls, he had climbed up to safety. He'd been more than amused by Sara Cobb's ruse to draw Sir Kenneth away from his hiding place—he'd been downright surprised. He hadn't thought her capable of such duplicity. It was something of a revelation—and it made him more determined than ever to help her with Ileana.

For all that he bragged he went out of his way for no man, he'd rarely met a woman who had ever gone out of her way for him—save for availing themselves of the obvious pleasures he could furnish. None had ever tried to cosset him or soothe him. Certainly none had ever thrown herself between him and approaching danger. Those other women, well, he couldn't exactly blame them, since he gave such a strong impression of never needing anyone. And the truth was, he hadn't needed the intervention of Sara Cobb. Those foolish, goggle-eyed spaniels hadn't been bred to tree their prey, and so unless he had actually fallen from his branch onto Sir Kenneth's head, the man would have passed below him with no idea he was up there.

No, Gren decided, he hadn't needed her assistance at all. Yet being the beneficiary of it made him feel oddly pleased.

The next day was Sunday, and Sara received word from Mrs. Holcroft that she was expected to attend church with the family. This was a wrinkle she had not anticipated. It was going to be tricky being in company with both Ileana and her mother without giving away that there had been no hint of lessons.

She needn't have worried. She made the journey to Penwreath in the utility coach with May Belle and Mrs. Holcroft and, once in the small stone church, she took her place with them several rows behind the Brashears. May Belle promptly fell asleep, while Mrs. Holcroft sat upright, stiff as a poker, clutching her prayerbook. Sara wondered at her piety, considering she was probably carrying on with the master of the house.

Even though Mr. Ivey, the aged vicar, was an inspiring speaker, Sara spent most of the sermon studying the congregation, shopkeepers and local gentry by the look of them. In the row opposite her own, a young woman with auburn ringlets was seated beside a tall, dark-haired young man. Sara noticed her elbowing him in the ribs whenever he started to nod off. They were alike enough to be siblings, and she suspected this was Addie Spindle and her brother, Tristan.

When the service ended, Miss Spindle stood up and turned to speak to an elderly couple behind her. Sara was dismayed to discover she was unusually pretty, with large blue eyes and a charming cleft to her chin. A pang of jealousy ripped through her. She knew she was being idiotic, yet she couldn't help wondering what sort of connection the girl had with Gren Martyn. Surely there wasn't anything amorous between them, but that didn't stop her from feeling blue-deviled.

Mr. Spindle was also something of a stellar specimen, with an angular, open face and an impressive pair of shoulders. Sara doubted Ileana would find a peer in London with such a pleasing countenance. She had just come to this conclusion when Ileana herself drifted into view along the aisle.

"Miss Cobb," she said with syrupy bonhomie. "I do hope you enjoyed the sermon. I assure you, Mr. Ivey outdid himself. I told Mama that you of all people would value the parable of the wise and foolish virgins"—she half turned to Lady Brashear, who was directly behind her—"did I not, Mama?"

"A lesson there for both of us," Sara said with equal sweetness of tone.

But she was simmering. She hated being brought unwillingly into this farce. But Ileana and her mother had moved on, and Sara now found herself facing the auburn-haired young woman.

"Miss Cobb? You must allow me to introduce myself. Adeline Spindle. And this great clunch is my brother, Tristan. Tris," she hissed. "Pay attention."

Her brother had his glaring gaze fixed on Ileana Brashear, who had stopped in the doorway to speak with the vicar.

"Sorry," he said affably. "Pleasure, ma'am. Or should I say, condolences. I don't envy anyone who's got the keeping of that hoyden."

Miss Spindle set a hand on Sara's sleeve. "If you've got the afternoon free, my brother and I were wondering if you'd like to come to Needs Barrow and take lunch with us."

"We were?" Tristan murmured.

The invitation also took Sara by surprise. It was not an overture she expected from a member of the local gentry. "Thank you for your kind offer. But today I really need to get back to Tregallion." She smiled awkwardly. "Perhaps another time."

"Of course," Miss Spindle said. "I simply thought you might like to see something of the neighborhood. After nearly a week in Tregallion, I wouldn't blame you if you wanted to kick up your heels a bit."

"If you've any sense, Miss Cobb," her brother uttered, "you won't let Addie cozen you. She just wants to hear all the tattle from Tregallion."

Sara grinned. "Next week would be better—for tattle. I've already made plans for this afternoon."

Once they returned to Tregallion, Sara went walking in the woods. It was foolish to deny that she hoped to meet up with Gren Martyn again. Shamefully, it was the chief reason she had refused Adeline Spindle's offer. After wandering the trails for nearly an hour without seeing another human being, she decided poachers must take the Sabbath off.

The one benefit of her fool's errand was that she discovered the path along the sea cliffs. She came out of the woods, lured by the sound of the surf, and found herself standing at the edge of a clearing, the summit of a high limestone headland. It was a stark space, open to the elements, full of the inevitable rock piles and peppered with a few wind-stunted bushes. The sea below crashed onto a tumble of boulders, the sound surging up the cliff face like the raucous clash of cymbals.

Sara stood peering over the edge for some time, mesmerized by the violent churning of the water. The more sense she got of Cornwall, of its bleak, primitive landscapes and its changeable moods, the more she began to perceive it as foreign soil, as though it had broken lose from some barren, distant land and drifted across the sea until it nestled up against the welcoming green shores of England.

And yet she couldn't honestly say she disliked it. Everything was so markedly different from Dorset, and not just the terrain. There was the singsong lilt that marked the Cornishman's speech, the swarthy complexions of many of the villagers, the mealy-colored moor ponies they rode, the hearty meat pies they called pasties. The things that set these people apart from the rest of England intrigued her.

There was a wild promise in this place, one that whispered to her, beckoned to her. It seemed highly unlikely that tame, timid little Sara Cobb could have yearned for something beyond the borders of placid Dorset, yet she did. She realized that now. And she further determined that even if she were released by the Brashears, she would do her utmost to remain in Cornwall.

When she returned to the house, she came upon Sir Kenneth in the courtyard, about to set out on horseback. He waved her to his side.

"Ah, Miss Cobb. I see our good Cornish air has put the apples back in your cheeks." He motioned her closer, and said in a low tone, "Sorry if I was gruff with you yesterday. In truth, my mood had soured long before you appeared. We couldn't scare up a single partridge or pheasant. . . . It was as though a troop of cavalry had beaten the bushes ahead of us."

Or one lone poacher, she reflected silently.

As if he had intuited her thoughts, he added, "My gamekeeper, Mathers, found a number of wire snares down in that hollow where I met up with you. If those infernal poachers don't stay out of my woods, I'll have no choice but to drag out the mantraps."

Sara winced. "That seems unnecessarily harsh, Sir Kenneth. Surely you can spare an odd bird or two."

He scowled down at her as though she had been spouting

treason. "They're *my* birds, ma'am. I do not care to spare even one of them."

She watched him ride off on his gleaming bay horse, a fine figure in his black riding cloak and gray beaver hat. A pity he was so typically territorial. It was common knowledge that many landowners dined well while their people starved; it must be especially true in this part of England, where so much of the industry had disappeared. How could a man who professed to be a Christian begrudge another man the means to feed his family? And to use mantraps, with their broad iron jaws that could sever a limb, to deter them? It was unthinkable.

She must find some way to warn Gren Martyn to stop his visits to Tregallion and to spread the word to any other locals who might also be inclined to poach there. For all she knew, half of Penwreath could have been wandering in those woods—they were that dense. It was no wonder the gamekeepers couldn't keep track of the whole estate.

She'd seen two of them as she was returning from the sea cliff, strapping fellows in canvas coats and leather gaiters, one of them leading a brawny, buff mastiff. Staying clear of men, with their dulled faculties, might be easy for a skilled poacher, but she wondered how Gren Martyn managed to evade the keen senses of a dog.

Probably charms them into submission, a wry inner voice responded.

Tuesday morning Sara had returned from breakfasting with May Belle and was sketching the sea cliffs in her journal when there was a scratching at the door. She looked up in surprise. No one, save an occasional housemaid with bedding, ever came there.

She called out, "Enter," and was nearly shocked off her chair by the sight of Ileana Brashear.

The girl came sauntering in, crossed the room and perched on the edge of the smaller desk.

"I'm bored," she announced. "It's very tedious to stay in my room every day with nothing to do."

Sara decided to go gently. "I'm not exactly thrilled to sit here for hours staring out the window, regardless of the fine view. Although I did happen to see you riding out the other day."

"Mama went to visit Mrs. Abernathy, the doctor's wife. I barely made it home before her."

"I gather you don't want her to know you've been skipping your lessons."

"Of course not. I'd be in the suds for certain. You might not credit this, but she's got a horrid temper when she's riled."

Sara fervently hoped she would never have to experience this in the flesh. Icy disapproval was bad enough.

"So," Sara said, rising slowly from her chair so as not to startle her student into flight, "what shall we do with ourselves to while away the time?"

Ileana shrugged. "I don't suppose you know any card games."

"Nary a one," Sara lied. "Or if I did, I've forgotten them. What do you say we engage in a bit of playacting?"

"You mean like pantomime?"

"No, more like charades. I will suggest a scene and you can act it out."

The girl mulled this over, then asked warily, "This isn't a lesson, is it?"

"Not precisely. Think of it as a trial run. You'll be placed into all sorts of unfamiliar situations in London, and it would help if we could anticipate some of them."

"It can't be that complicated," she grumbled.

"How do you formally address the mother of a married duke?" Sara inquired. "How do you inscribe a letter to the wife of an archbishop? How many times may you dance with the same man at a party?" Sara recalled Gren Martyn's comments on the girl's horsemanship. "What is the acceptable pace for riding in Hyde Park?"

Ileana stood up, her brow creased in disbelief. "Does any of that truly matter?"

"More than you can ever imagine. Put the wrong nose out of joint, say something indelicate to the wrong hostess, and you will find yourself cut from society in a twinkling. The door will swing shut, and you will be left standing on the outside."

Ileana made a pretext of tossing her head. "Amelie never paid attention to such things. Papa is wealthy and Mama is the granddaughter of a baron. Surely those things weigh more than silly rules and stuffy regulations."

"Very well, discover this all for yourself. And end up coming home before two months are out, just as Amelie did." She added slyly, "Perhaps Mr. Spindle will offer for you in that case."

"Even desperation wouldn't make me consider Tristan Spindle," she declared. "He is the greatest clodpole imaginable, always pottering around with the disgusting, slimy things he dredges from the sea."

"So he is a naturalist."

"That's how he refers to himself, but I believe he has never outgrown a little boy's need to be grubbing about with snakes and snails and polliwogs."

"Has Mr. Spindle been to London?"

"I expect so. He was away at Oxford until last year. Now he just hangs about on the rocks below Needs Barrow, in his shirt-sleeves without his boots or stockings and— Oh, why am I even speaking about him? He is nobody of consequence."

Like me, Sara nearly said.

"So what do you want me to do?" Ileana asked in a tone that Sara might have dared to call eager. "Shall I need a fan or a feathered headdress? Mama has one in the back of her dressing room. . . . It must be all of three feet high."

"I think we can dispense with the headdress," Sara said dryly. "You won't need to wear feathers except when you are presented to the queen. The style in London these days is for young girls to wear silk flowers or pearls in their hair."

Ileana ran a hand over her rippling toffee-colored hair, which was caught up in a simple chignon. "Pearls . . . yes. I have a lovely strand that Papa gave me last year."

By the time they stopped for luncheon, Ileana had mastered the intricacies of Almack's, had memorized the names of the patronesses and had finally been made to understand why waltzing was frowned upon until permission was granted. It occurred to Sara—in between bouts of elation that her career as a governess was not about to end in ignoble failure—that Ileana would need someone to teach her to dance. A young man who'd been to London and attended Oxford might do nicely, since she didn't imagine dancing instructors were thick on the ground in rural Cornwall.

Sara heated a bit of soup in the small fireplace, still unable to keep a foolish grin from her face.

This was Gren Martyn's doing, she knew without question. Ileana hadn't grown bored. She had been bullied into compliance. As only an older sister could effectively do.

Sara had to find some way to thank him. And there was also the matter of warning him about the mantraps. Did she dare visit him at his home? After a morning spent warning Ileana of all the social improprieties a young lady might unwittingly commit, could she herself perform such a brazen act?

It was pointless to ponder; now that Ileana had returned to the classroom, Sara would likely never get the chance.

Chapter Six

*L*ater in the week, Ileana announced that her mother was taking her to Plymouth for a few days of shopping. Sara saw this as an omen. She'd be at liberty until the girl returned and so made up her mind that a brief visit to a new friend—male or not—wasn't completely debauched. She asked May Belle whom she should speak to about a horse for riding. The cook gave her a long look before telling her to ask for Seth Pethrick in the stables.

"Always willing to do a favor for me, Seth is. Especially since I make up a special horse blister he favors. I've a fresh bottle here you can take out to him."

Seth, it turned out, was an ancient groom, his face more leathery than the saddle he was polishing on a wooden stand. "I'll give you Sadie," he said after Sara presented her tribute and explained her request. "She belonged to Miss Amelie. Poor old girl is grown quite fat for lack of riding."

Sara's initial startled notion was that he was referring to the elder Brashear daughter, of whom no one spoke well—until he led a virtual dumpling of a large pony from a stall.

"I was thinking of riding up onto Bodmin moor," Sara said idly while he tacked the mare.

"Moor's not hard to find," he said. "You just follow the main road west until the land starts to rise on your right. Any of the trails will take you to Bodmin."

"Is there a farm or homestead up there where I could ask directions in case I lose my way?"

He thought a minute. "There be the Martyn farm, over past Beebe's Brook," he said, then frowned. "But you don't want to

have no truck with Gren Martyn. I'll send one of the grooms
to ride with you, an you like. There's boggy places up there
can suck a horse right down if you leave the path."

"That's really not necessary," she said quickly. "I don't plan
to go far. I'll just have to see where the road takes me."

It had been years since she'd been in the saddle, not counting that jouncing ride behind Gren Martyn. Sadie had soured
from too long in the barn and fought the bit all the way down
the drive, going backward more often than forward. Sara
thought peevishly that she'd have made better time crawling
on all fours. She devoutly hoped Seth hadn't watched her
progress—or lack thereof—from the stable door. He'd likely
never saddle another mount for her, horse blister or no horse
blister.

Once they neared the front gate, where the tempting sounds
and scents of her stable no longer lured her, Sadie settled
down, proving to have a stomach-jarring trot and a delightful
slow canter.

Sara found the main road with no trouble—at the turning
lay the large pile of rocks Georgie Hobblyn had mentioned.
Reining the mare to the west, she set off at a brisk pace, admiring the rugged severity of the landscape. She passed a number of abandoned cottages, their yards littered with broken
farm implements and dead bracken.

The day was overcast, but the air had a balmy texture.
She'd been afraid her pelisse might not prove warm enough,
but after ten minutes of riding, she'd had to open the top two
buttons.

She crossed over a small stone bridge, where a wide stream
burbled its way to the sea, and then began looking for a trail
inland. The character of the terrain to her right had changed
noticeably, from flat, rocky fields interspersed with small
groves of trees, to heath-covered embankments that rose away
from the level of the road. This was the edge of Bodmin—a
place long fabled as the home of outlaws and renegades. "And
an occasional poacher," she added under her breath.

A little way beyond the bridge she turned onto a narrow, rising trail carved into the spongy mass of heath. She gambled

that this was the way to the Martyn farm and was rewarded when, after a little time, she rode over a small hill and saw chimney smoke in the distance, wafting straight up into the still air. Since the homestead was set in a hollow, Sara had no idea how much of a true farm it might be. She somehow couldn't imagine Gren Martyn milking a goat or slopping the pigs. For all his shabby clothing, he possessed a sort of raffish glamour that made it impossible to picture him performing menial chores.

She had a more complete view of the moorland now, and could make out a number of craggy tors and dark, mysterious crevices. There were also swampy patches with hillocks of wild grass sprouting in their midst—the bogs Seth had warned her to avoid.

She followed the winding track across the November-sere moor until she reached the hollow. Below her she now spied a low house of wattle and daub, and behind it a timbered barn and several smaller outbuildings. The closer she got, the more she prayed this was not Gren Martyn's home. The place was a shambles. If not for the smoke rising from the chimney, she'd have assumed it was another abandoned cottage.

After dismounting beyond the littered front yard, she tied the mare to a bush, since the fence posts were all crumbling with rot. The path to the door was grown over with dead weeds, and the front stoop was a chunk of hewn granite that bore what appeared to be the detritus of generations of men who spent their lives tromping in manure.

She hiked up her skirt to protect the hem before stepping onto the stone, and then knocked softly. Once, twice, three times she knocked. A fire might be burning in the hearth, but there didn't appear to be anyone within. She tried looking through the front window, but it was begrimed with dried rain splatters on the outside and a cloudy layer of soot on the inside.

She moved away from the house and stood gazing around at the rest of the farm. Mud heaves hardened by the cold seemed to be the general effect, softening into large brown puddles in some places now that the weather had eased. Sara picked her way carefully across the yard until she reached the barn. A few scrawny chickens ran toward her expectantly, and then promptly all ran away, fluttering into the low branches of a stunted pine tree. A small herd of goats was browsing on the hillside behind the house, but no other animals were evident, though there was a small turnout containing a pile of soggy hay.

The interior of the barn was low-ceilinged and murky, and holding tight to every bit of the cold that had beset the district earlier in the week. There were three stalls, one of them relatively clean, with fresh straw laid out on the wooden flooring. Across an aisle littered with dirty straw, a gig shrouded in cobwebs sat beside a wooden feed bin. She pried the slanted lid open and at once smelled the rich odor of fresh sweet feed—oats, grain, and molasses.

She stood a moment inhaling the well-remembered scent, all the while wondering why the horse was missing. No one left home with a fire burning; it just wasn't practical.

The large shed beyond the barn was padlocked. Through the window Sara was able to make out a heavy plank table strewn with tools and lengths of wood propped against the far wall. Some sort of workshop, she guessed.

She was scrubbing at the grimy window with her handkerchief when a man came striding around the corner of the building.

She squawked loudly, and he grunted in surprise. They stood staring at each other for long seconds before he growled, "What in blazes are you doing here?"

It wasn't until he'd spoken that Sara knew for sure it was Gren Martyn. He was covered head to foot with mud, as if he'd been rolling in a wallow.

Sara took an involuntary step backward. "I . . . wanted to thank you."

His frown didn't fade; if anything it grew more ominous. "Sweet Jesus, you startled ten years off my life," he muttered. "Creeping about like that . . . and if taking me unawares wasn't bad enough, you've no idea what a shock it was to see Sadie tied to the gate."

Of course, she thought dismally, he'd have recognized Amelie's horse. She'd probably ridden here for their assignations. Oh God, what if he thought she'd come here with a similar purpose in mind? What ever had possessed her to think this was a harmless notion?

"I'm sorry," she murmured, still retreating. "I didn't mean to trespass."

She turned and hurried away from him, setting a straight course toward the mare, the mud sucking at her boots as she crossed the largest of the puddles. She was fumbling with the reins, cursing a knot that would not come lose, when he caught up with her.

"Wait," he said breathlessly, his hand staying her from untying the reins. "I'm in a bear of a mood today. It's not your fault. You just wandered in range."

"And I intend to wander right out again," she retorted, slapping his hand away.

He put both his hands behind him and looked amused. "I've got mud on your sleeve," he observed.

"I'll survive." She had the reins free now and was tugging the mare along the track, looking for a place to mount. The rickety fence rails were not an option and, this being the Cornish moors, there wasn't a convenient tree stump within a hundred miles. And she certainly wasn't going to ask *him* for a boost into the saddle.

Gren hadn't moved from beside the gate, but he was still watching her closely. "What were you going to thank me for?" he called out.

"It doesn't matter," she said. And then she recalled the other part of her mission, that she needed to warn him about the mantraps. It would serve him right if he found himself caught in those great mauling jaws. She'd think of that image every night before she fell asleep. Gren Martyn, trapped, powerless . . . bloodied and in pain. No, it was too great a fine to levy merely because he had been rude and unwelcoming.

With a sigh, she turned back toward the gate. "There *is* one other thing—"

"Then you'll stay? At least let me make it up to you for being so testy."

"I can't linger," she said. "I actually came riding out to see the moor."

"I can show you the moor. Truth is, I've a few deliveries to make up on Bodmin, if you give me the chance to get cleaned up."

Sara doubted there was enough soap and water in all the kingdom. Not to mention, he was giving off the rank odor of an outhouse.

He opened the rickety gate. "Best bring Sadie into the barn."

"Where is your horse?" she asked as she followed behind him.

"Loose on Bodmin. . . . My hay's gone moldy, so I'm letting him forage on wild grass."

"Aren't you afraid he'll run off?"

He cast her a long look. "What? And leave this paradise behind?"

Sara's cheek drew in. "Yes, I see your point. I take it he is fond of mud."

"Can't get enough of the stuff," he responded with a wink as he closed Sadie in the clean stall. The mare immediately buried her nose in the empty feed trough and grunted in disappointment.

Gren turned to Sara, leaning one hip on the slatted stall door. "So how did you happen to find me, Miss Cobb?"

She shrugged. "Blind luck, I suppose."

"So you didn't actually come looking for me."

"I told you, I came out to see the moor. When I saw the smoke rising from your chimney, I followed it here." She paused, then added sweetly, "I thought it might be the home of a pleasant person who would offer me a bit of country hospitality."

He made a rude noise. "Yes, and pigs will fly."

"Although, now that I've found you, I want to thank you for interceding with Amelie."

"So the truant's returned to the schoolroom?"

She nodded. "It never pays to underestimate the power of an older sister. I truly appreciate you writing to her."

He shrugged. "And once again it's me who's responsible for keeping you here. I wonder what it would take to make you go away."

Her eyes narrowed. "Maybe learning the truth about Tregallion House?"

"I'd give five years of my life to know that."

As they were crossing the sorry, littered yard, Sara halted. Some imp inside her overrode all her good sense, forcing her to speak her mind. "I know you probably don't want to hear this, but this place has the makings of a decent farm."

"I never intended to set up as a farmer," he said gruffly.

"Oh yes, poaching is so much more . . . rewarding. The thing of it is, you don't have to live in squalor, even if you never lift a hoe or till a field."

"Maybe I prefer it like this." His blue eyes were stony as he glared at her from that mask of drying mud. "I don't ever have visitors—"

"Not since Amelie stopped coming here," she said in an undertone.

"—so what's the point of fixing the place up?"

"It's your home."

"It's my brother's home," he said. "You've probably heard by now, how he was hanged."

She nodded once.

"He left it to me. I didn't want it, didn't want to be tied down in this mud hole. But I've some unfinished business in this neighborhood, so it suits me . . . for now."

He stalked across the yard, wondering at the uncanny way of women—how they got it into their heads a fellow needed reforming practically the *instant* he'd decided for himself that it was time to mend fences. Literally, in his case. And now if he repaired so much as a loose hinge, the baggage would begin preening insufferably and fully think herself behind it.

"Wait out there," he said as they came up to the rickety fence. "I won't be but a tick."

She found herself unable to look away when he tugged his shirt off and went to the hand pump at the side of the house. After dousing himself all over, he slathered a brick of yellow soap over his arms, neck and face. When he rinsed off, crouching before the spigot so the water sluiced over his back, the mud and filth streamed off him.

Sara was intrigued by the smoothly contoured muscles of

his arms and shoulders and long, tapered torso. Who could have guessed that such perfection hid beneath his ragged clothing? It was akin to finding a Greek statue wrapped in a moth-eaten lap rug. She was so entranced, she forgot to look away when he finally stood up.

Gren knew an admiring female glance when one was cast in his direction, especially when the onlooker's ears turned a delightful pink. He met her eyes and was surprised when she did not blush or look away.

"I suppose I should thank you for not mentioning, while listing my shortcomings, that I smelled like a pig wallow."

She wrinkled her nose. "I wasn't sure what that odor was."

He was about to tell her that he had, in fact, been cleaning out the noisome pig sty, in preparation for a pair of shoats a neighbor had offered him. But he decided it was none of her business.

"You're not likely to forget it now" was all he said.

He went inside, stripped off the rest of his wet clothing and toweled dry with a length of sacking. He tugged on a pair of cleanish breeches and a darned shirt, followed by a moleskin vest and his one decent pair of riding boots. He took his woolen jacket from the peg by the door and was slipping his arms into it as he went outside.

Sara Cobb looked up from scratching the ears of one of the goats.

"Better," she said. "Cleaner."

He headed back to the barn, nearly chuckling. The prim little governess clearly preferred him half-naked—and wet—to fully clothed. It was a stimulating notion, and one he probably shouldn't dwell on.

"What are you delivering up on Bodmin?" she asked, trailing after him.

"What do you think a poacher delivers? Fine fat pheasants and plump partridges."

"Courtesy of Sir Kenneth Brashear?"

"Among others. Though I must say, his gamekeepers do a top-notch job of keeping his birds in good fettle."

Once inside the barn, he nodded to a half dozen birds hanging, tail up, from the lower rafters. "Far more than I can eat myself, so I've worked out a system of barter. I get butter and cheese, a loaf of bread, the occasional gooseberry pie. And my neighbors get meat for their stew kettles, those who might not see meat for a month or longer."

Sara realized there was a rightness in his actions that had nothing to do with temporal law.

The woodlands belonged to the gentry, so gamebirds rarely strayed onto the common land. Deer were scarce on the moor, she imagined, and so aside from fish or rabbits, or the occasional aged hen, the locals had few sources of meat.

Gren Martyn, by risking his freedom, possibly even his life, kept his neighbors decently fed while he profited only in a few simple staples. She didn't know what she'd thought he did with the birds he poached—sold them to the innkeepers of Penwreath for gold or some such nonsense.

He led Sadie out of the stall and, without asking permission, lifted Sara onto the side saddle. After he'd placed several birds in a sack and snatched a bridle from the wall, they made their way up a winding path behind the house, clear up onto the wide expanse of moorland that lay virtually at his back door. At the crest of the hill, he gave a shrill whistle between his teeth. Seconds later, a dark form emerged from a distant hollow and came racing toward him over the springy peat.

"See," he said, laughing up at her. "Cap hasn't deserted me yet."

"Such devotion in the face of mud and moldy hay is truly admirable."

"Let us not forget the bribe," he said, pulling a large carrot from his back pocket.

He broke off the tip and offered it to Sadie as Cap came dancing up to them, eyes a bit wild, his coat rough with stickleburs and briars. Gren brushed a hand along his neck, smoothing out his tangled mane while he fed him the treat. When he slipped the bridle over his head, the beast barely noticed.

In her youth, Sara had been around horses a great deal; she'd seen how men of kindness and patience treated them, and so she admired the way he soothed the animal. A rough man, but with a very gentle touch.

Something skittered along the edge of her spine, making her look away from him with a guilty frown.

Gren boosted himself easily onto Cap's back, still calming the restive horse with his voice.

"No saddle?" Sara said.

He shook his head. "Lather Pitt put him out to hire while I was in Plymouth. Some hamhanded young buck harnessed him up all wrong and left him with a canker on his withers. What's the matter?" he taunted her. "Afraid I'll fall off, and you'll have to doctor me for a broken head?"

"It's not likely to be your head you fall on," she observed tartly.

He flashed a grin, and the next instant bolted off across the turf, curled low over the gelding's neck, moving easily with his rocking motion.

"Show-off," Sara muttered as she kicked Sadie into her ungraceful, jarring trot.

They rode in easy silence for a time, Sara taking in the broad vistas spreading around her. This was ancient ground, she couldn't help thinking, primeval and pagan. It took hardy, determined men and women to cleave a living out of such unforgiving terrain.

And yet it was hardly barren. Life burgeoned here, even in the bleak throes of November. Hedge and nettle thrived, as did heather, sedge, and a variety of wiry grasses. Though there were no towering trees, and the growing things clung close to the ground, there was a rich tapestry of undulating shapes. She thought of Tristan Spindle. Little wonder a boy growing up in such a place should find himself transfixed by the world of nature. This countryside invariably drew you down for a closer look.

"Did you grow up here?" she asked Gren as they waded into a wide stream.

"Aye, I did," he said.

"I envy you," she said with a small sigh.

He turned, his expression puzzled. "I doubt Cornwall can hold a candle to Dorset. I've heard tell it's a pretty shire."

"Pretty, but so very tame. This is a wild, unearthly place. . . ."

He *tsk*ed slowly. "And you say you've no imagination. Just look at you now, waxing romantic over the poorest, bleakest, *muddiest* patch of God's earth."

Sara's eyes darkened. "It may be all those things, but it's also very compelling. I didn't realize there were places like this left in England, places that hadn't been groomed and pruned and landscaped into submission."

He stopped in midstream to let Cap drink, leaning back along the horse's spine as he appraised her. "I said it before. You're daft."

"Do you hate it so much, then, that you can't see the beauty?"

He hitched one shoulder. "I see it fine. On a sunny day in June, when the heather's all in bloom and the shadows of the clouds trace over the hillsides . . . and a goshawk rides the currents above the tors. It speaks to me then, I suppose. I'm only surprised it speaks to you on a dull November afternoon."

Sara was a little miffed by his choice of words. So far, this had been her least dull afternoon in recent memory. But then she reminded herself he was speaking of the weather, not the company. She hoped.

They left the stream and went up a steep embankment. A small farm lay on the other side. It wasn't in much better repair than Gren's holding, but the woman who came out into the yard at least wore a smile. She was past the first bloom of youth, but had retained a certain beauty, in the freshness of her complexion and the crisp curl of her hair. Gren introduced her as Rosamund Grambler. Two waifish young boys had followed her from the house; they now clung to her skirts and gazed up at Sara with wide eyes . . . hungry eyes.

"How's Jackie faring?" Gren asked the woman.

She shook her head slowly. "As well as a body can expect. He do have a bit of his strength back, but I fear it'll be months before he can look for work."

He handed down two birds, a pheasant and a partridge. Mrs. Grambler clutched at Cap's bridle. "I can't tell you, Gren, what this means."

"It means that layabout husband of yours will get back on

his feet betimes, and stop making you sorry you didn't run off
with me when you had the chance."

The woman grinned at that. "As if I ever looked at anyone
but my Jackie Grambler. Still, you be a good man, Gren Martyn, for all your wicked ways."

"Then you best pray for me, Rose. And pray for Sir Kenneth's fine birds . . . ah, but not for his festering gamekeepers."

When they rode away, Gren still had two birds in his sack,
but had received no items of barter. Sara pointed this out to
him.

"I take whatever they can spare. If they can't spare anything, I know they'll make up for it another time. Rosamund is
running the farm herself these days, as you no doubt gathered."

"What happened to her husband?"

"He was caught in a mine cave-in. Got out alive, but barely.
Seven other men weren't so lucky."

"And the mining company doesn't see to its workers?"

He pulled up his horse and goggled at her. "What distant
land have you come from to ask such foolish questions? The
owners only care about able-bodied men, not those half crip-
pled. Jackie Grambler will never see the inside of a mine
again. Not that that isn't a blessing of sorts. He won't die in another cave-in or drown when the shaft floods."

"I thought you said the mines had closed."

"Not all of them. Sir Kenneth and Lord Denby have kept a
few open, though most of copper and tin has played out. It
forces the men to dig deeper, you see, and then there's more
chance of a tunnel collapsing or water flooding in."

"It all sounds like a dreadful business," she muttered.

"It's the business that put Cornwall on the map," he said
brusquely. "We'd be nothing to the rest of England but a lump
of rock and a clod of peat if it weren't for those mines. But
badly run or well run, any trade that sends men to work far
below the ground is bound to be risky. The miners know that.
They also know it's the only way to earn a decent living in
Cornwall."

"A necessary evil, is what you're telling me."

"It's what these people have done for centuries. In other
parts of England, they farm the land. We harvest what lies

below. My father used to say, 'Most men aren't truly dead till they're six feet under, but a Cornishman's not truly alive until he's fifty feet in the ground.'"

Sara heard something in his voice, the distinct note of hard-won experience.

"How many years did *you* work underground?" she ventured.

He acknowledged her insight with a tight smile. "Four years, from the time I was nine. I was a pit boy, dragging the empty carts down into the tunnels."

"And how did you escape that life?"

He shifted away from her probing eyes. "What does it matter? The main thing is, I got out. I still dream about it, still wake up dreading the mornings, when you rise in the dark and trudge to the mine in the dark, and go down into a blacker darkness than you can possibly imagine. And then, at the end of the day, you drag yourself home in the dark. And never once, for days on end, do you ever see the sun." His fingers fisted on the reins. "No, Jackie Grambler may have no work and no prospects, but it's still a lucky man who can get shed of that place."

They soon came to another farm, this one a bit more prosperous. An elderly couple greeted them; Gren introduced them as Mr. and Mrs. Curry.

"You the new girl from over Tregallion way?" the man asked Sara as his wife hurried into the house to fetch her items of barter.

Sara nodded. "I'm Miss Brashear's governess."

Mr. Curry seemed to work this information over with his jaw. Then he spat once and muttered, "I say bad cess to them Brashears. Though no offense to you, miss."

Gren took him aside, darting looks of amusement at Sara, and handed over a small bag. Sara now recalled that this was the farmer whose cattle he'd brought to market. When the old man try to press a few coins into his hand, Gren shook his head and backed away. Odd behavior, she reflected, for a man who didn't put himself out for anyone.

On the way back to his farm, Gren took her along a different route.

"I thought you might like to see this," he said as he pointed out a clutch of buildings on the horizon, the tallest of them sending out a plume of dense black smoke. Behind the complex lay a virtual mountain of dark rocks.

"That's Wheal Prosper," he said, "one of Sir Kenneth's tin mines. Inside that high building is the pump engine. It runs day and night to keep water out of the shafts."

"And what is that great heap behind it?"

"Slag." He said the word like a curse. "The rock left over after the ore's been separated. I hear tell that in Wales, mountains of coal slag come down sometimes and bury entire villages."

"Ugly," she said as they rode off. "I had no idea mining was such an ugly business."

"But lucrative," he pointed out. "At least it was during the last century. Now it's failing, just like everything else around it."

They'd gone only a short distance when she veered Sadie into Cap's path. "No, hold up a minute. I just figured something out. You believe that Cornwall is dying, don't you? That it's a lost cause."

She stared at him, but he made no move to deny or affirm her accusation. "The mines played out . . . the young people leaving. Only the landowners, with their gated homes and vast acres, are prospering. It explains why you don't feel any need to keep up your own farm. Why bother if everything around you is wasting away?"

"Why, indeed?" he drawled, still not meeting her eyes.

She reached for his arm, her fingers curling around his wrist. "But I feel such strength in this place . . . such possibility. Oh, I know you are going to tell me that I am an outsider, and daft to boot, but listen to me, Gren Martyn. You can't give up, not yet. I saw how these people look to you—the one man who snaps his fingers at the landowners and takes their birds from under their noses. It is a minor rebellion, to be sure, but it means you are standing up to them. To the mine owners, to the men who take and take and give very little back."

He grunted disparagingly. "You've gone beyond daft if you're painting me as some sort of latter-day Robin Hood. I poach because it's what I do well, and I trade my birds for food."

"You could do more," she said. "You could *be* more. For yourself and for the Rose Gramblers and the Currys. You put the heart in them, Gren. Stop frowning at me that way. I saw it for myself."

He tugged away from her, his face twisted. "I don't care about any of them. It's nothing more than commerce to me. And once I've completed my business here, I will be off, as far from Cornwall as a man can go."

She gasped when he reached out and caught her chin hard in his fingers. "And mark me, Sara Cobb, your serious eyebrows and stern little mouth won't keep me from going."

She swatted his hand away. "It won't be me who'll grieve when you go—I promise you that. It will be all the people you've aided."

Beebe's Brook was meandering along beside them and she realized his farm was just over the next hill. "I know my way back from here," she said between her teeth, reining Sadie abruptly away from him. "You needn't trouble yourself over me any longer."

To her amazement, the mare complied when Sara asked for a ground-eating gallop. They slowed a little as they crested the rise, but, much as she longed to, Sara didn't turn around to see if Gren Martyn was still watching her. She was nearly at the gates of Tregallion when it occurred to her she hadn't warned him about the mantraps. In her present mood, she swore she didn't care if he was ground to mincemeat by those wicked iron jaws.

Gren did watch her ride off, a thundercloud hovering on his brow.

The last, the very last thing he needed in his life was a needling woman to act as his conscience. What gall she had to come to his home and criticize him, to prod at him. As though her life was so picture perfect, the threadbare little governess without a shilling to her name. And that speech about him being a source of inspiration to his neighbors . . . utter nonsense.

He knew full well where he fit into the scheme of things in Penwreath—he was the local ne'er-do-well, blatant poacher of gamebirds, brother of a convicted, executed horse thief, seducer of women and general layabout. What did it matter that he occasionally gave Rosamund Grambler a pheasant free and clear or that he brought the Currys' cattle to market in Plymouth? Those minor benevolences didn't make him a blasted saint, and they certainly weren't going to alter the prevailing opinion of his character.

And the one thing he *did* have to his credit—his dogged quest to clear his brother's name—most of Penwreath, including Sara Cobb, knew nothing about.

As he set Cap down the hill toward his farm, Gren's angry resentment lessened a little and turned instead to apprehension. It was obvious Sara Cobb had been stretching to find some good in him, a highly troubling notion. When a respectable woman started seeking redeeming qualities in a man who possessed very few, she was either wits to let or she was forming an infatuation. That was the last thing he could afford right now.

The plain truth was, he felt increasingly drawn to her. He saw beyond the straitlaced clothing, the severely controlled coils of hair. She lamented that she had no imagination, but he had enough for both of them, enough to envision her fully unbound and uncoiled.

She was a plain woman only by intent. Nature had fashioned her far more lavishly than she conveyed, and so what Gren saw was not the bland facade, but each signal attribute—the fine skin and elegant bones, the Latinate eyes and lustrous hair, the slender form with endowments ample enough to stir his pulse. He'd liked the look of her from the start and it was an attraction that had only strengthened with familiarity.

Besides, when a woman could wax passionate about the beauty of the moorland, about the needs of the people of Penwreath, there was no telling how much passion she could muster under the hands of a knowing man. The possibilities took his breath away.

Nevertheless, there was no point dwelling on it. Sara Cobb, he reminded himself sternly, was not the dallying sort. She had no idea how dangerous it was to come to his farm and throw herself into his path. His conscience and restraint were practically nonexistent when it came to following his baser appetites.

As much as he relished the thought of making her his latest conquest, he had an even greater fear of the complications that would ensue. He'd already been jailed once for taking liberties with a lady. This time it might actually be the truth.

Far better if when he saw her again—and this was a foregone assumption—he made damn sure she developed a healthy aversion to Gren Martyn. Repelling women wasn't his long suit, but a fellow was never too old to learn a few new tricks.

Chapter Seven

*I*leana continued to attend her lessons, usually with the saintly suffering air of a medieval martyr. Nevertheless, Sara felt they were making progress. Mornings were focused on deportment and social etiquette; afternoons were spent in French conversation. Sara even managed to sneak in a bit of geography now and again, after Ileana expressed interest in the progress of the war on the Iberian Peninsula.

The girl still found the rules of the *ton* tiresome, but she was finally coming to understand how paramount it was for young ladies new on the town to follow every last one.

"If you take," Sara explained, "the hostesses will soon turn a more permissive eye."

"Of course I will *take*," Ileana protested. "Mama says I am by far the prettiest girl in Cornwall."

Gazing at her assessingly, Sara murmured, "It *is* rather a pity about that spot forming on your chin."

The girl's eyes widened in horror. She leaped up from the window seat and raced across to Sara's room, where she peered into the small mirror.

"Sorry," she said sheepishly when she came out. "I forgot I wasn't to go in there. But you have to admit this is something of an emergency. Though for the life of me, I didn't see a single spot."

"Perhaps I was mistaken."

Ileana eyed her suspiciously. "Were you tweaking me?"

Sara sucked in one cheek. "Maybe just a little. You do tend to puff yourself up. And while I'd have to be blind not to acknowledge that you are a very pretty girl, it takes more than looks to succeed in London. Sometimes the pretty girls sit on the sidelines while the plain girls have their pick of partners."

"That makes no sense."

"There are other things besides physical beauty that attract men—charm, animation, graciousness, the ability to draw others into conversation. That last might be the most useful skill of all. Not all the men in London are full of address and polish. Some need a bit of coaxing."

Ileana pondered this, her fair brows drawn down.

"Didn't your sister talk to you about her season in London?"

Ileana huffed. "She was forbidden to talk about it. I even smuggled a bag of comfits into her room one night, trying to bribe her. She threw her hairbrush at me. I don't know what happened to Amelie while she was there, but when she returned, she was a completely different person."

"In what way?"

"For years before her comeout, she was so excited by the prospect. When I was home from school, she'd sit on my bed at night and tell me about all the glittering members of the *ton* she hoped to meet, about all the dashing officers and elegant lords she would dance with. She vowed she would see every play and attend every ball."

"I suppose she rather overdid it."

The girl sprawled back against the embrasure of the window seat. "When she came home she was so . . . secretive. She kept her door locked, though I often heard her crying. And then she started sneaking out at night. To visit that wretched Grenville Martyn, it turns out." She shot a sharp look at Sara. "I suppose you've heard of him. Our local reprobate. Though what she saw in such an uncouth fellow I will never know."

Sara knew exactly what Amelie had seen in him, but kept her own besotted thoughts to herself. Instead, she inquired gently, "So you feel as though you lost her when she went to London?"

"I did lose her," Ileana declared. "Even now that she's settled down, married and with a baby, she only ever writes when she wants to ring a peal over me."

Sara felt a smattering of guilt, since she'd instigated Amelie's most recent peal.

"Perhaps she doesn't want you to make the same mistakes she made. One could say she's being protective of you."

"It's a bore. She went from being my dearest friend to a total stranger. And now she's set herself up as my judge and jury." Her fist thumped down onto the cushion. "Oh, I don't know why I'm telling you all this. I don't even like you."

Sara knew why. "I think you're a little afraid to go to London. Even with your parents there, it must sound fairly daunting."

"Lot of good my parents did keeping watch over Amelie," she grumbled. "Ah, but I'm not going to come home in disgrace." She flicked her fingers in a graceful parody of her mother. "I vow I'll send every fortune hunter away with a flea in his ear and encourage only the most respectable men."

"Providing you can tell the difference," Sara pointed out dryly. "They don't exactly wear signs around their necks."

That Sunday at church, Miss Spindle was seated without her brother. After the service, she again invited Sara to Needs Barrow and this time Sara accepted.

"I hope your brother is not unwell," Sara said as they made their way along the coast road in Miss Spindle's gig.

"No, just playing truant. The weather's turned so warm today. . . . And there's a disgusting film of red algae in the cove and on the rocks below our house. Tris was nearly beside himself with excitement this morning."

"What will he do with it—the algae?"

Addie Spindle made a face. "You cannot imagine. He will study it under a microscope, try to grow bits of it in a dish . . . and probably attempt to eat it."

Sara chuckled. "Not very scientific, is he?"

"No, I believe he is actually quite scientific. You might not credit it, but other men of science pay him for the things he collects. Because of the ocean currents, all sorts of exotic flora and fauna wash up on these beaches. Tris found a rare shell last month that will probably keep us in coal all winter."

"Amazing," Sara said. "So he gets to potter about and is

compensated for it. I'd say that's the description of a near perfect world."

Addie nodded. "That's what Tris always says. That he's the luckiest of men." She paused and pointed with her whip. "Oh look, there's Needs Barrow now."

Sara peered beyond the roadside shrubs to the house nestled below them. The small manor of whitewashed bricks, with its red tile roof and wide stone terrace, might have been a Mediterranean villa—except that it was perched above a typically Cornish cove of jagged rocks and surging gray water.

Addie drove into a small stableyard where a groom ran to the horse's head. "Would you like your luncheon now," she asked, "or would you rather walk down to the cove and see how Sir Isaac is doing?"

"Let's visit the cove while the sun is still shining. One thing I've learned about Cornish weather—it changes every five minutes."

They made their way down a narrow path that had been carved between granite outcroppings. There was no proper beach, only a tumble of boulders forming a wedge-shaped breakwater. Sara spied Tristan—minus boots and stockings just as Ileana had predicted—clambering over the top of the breakwater. He was speaking to someone out of sight below him.

"Bring the net in closer," he called out. "I want some of the stuff with the bloom on it."

Addie raised her eyebrows. "Ooh, the algae is blooming. I can hardly wait."

Sara chuckled—and nearly slid off the large rock she'd just negotiated.

Finally the two women stood looking down at Tristan, who was currently crouched over a number of glass jars. The second man was thigh-deep in the water, facing away from them as he skimmed a large flat net over the surface, collecting patches of the small red plants that floated there.

"Well done," Tristan said as his helper turned and handed up the net.

Sara nearly cried out in surprise. It was Gren Martyn. He looked up at the two women, shading his eyes with one hand.

"Well, if it isn't the little busybody from Tregallion," he said. "Come to rearrange the furniture or clean out the barn?"

"Gren!" said Addie with a chiding laugh. "It's not like you to be rude."

"Oh, isn't it?" Sara muttered. She ignored Gren Martyn's smirk and smiled widely at Tristan. "Good day to you, Mr. Spindle. I am come to see your remarkable algae."

"Look," he said, pointing to the wire carrier at his feet. "I've got jars and jars of the stuff." He held one up. "Good thing Gren came by earlier to do some fishing. I put him to work when the cold water got too much for me."

"They'll both have the grippe by nightfall," Addie predicted. "Not that it won't be exactly what they deserve. That water's got to be frigid."

"It's not so bad," Gren said as he scrambled up onto the rocks.

Sara tried not to notice that he was soaked nearly to the waist. Bad enough that his lean, muscular calves were bare.

"Though I *will* expect one of you ladies to massage the life back into my poor, cold limbs."

He'd been looking at Sara as he spoke, but it was Addie who answered. "Don't worry about getting warmed up. We'll put you in the barn with Nelly the cow. I recall that's how they used to revive the pilchard fishermen after a storm at sea. Nothing like cuddling large livestock to get your blood flowing."

Gren's eyes danced. "You are a cruel woman, Adeline Spindle."

"Cruel but just," she said. "Now Miss Cobb and I have admired your rather poisonous-looking algae long enough. We are going back to the house before we lose our appetites."

Tristan was gazing off into the distance. "I rather fancy it *is* poisonous." He pointed to the edge of the rocks, where a half-dozen fish floated belly up in the surf. "I'll have to make note of that in my journal."

"Lovely," Addie grumbled as she and Sara moved away. "Just another day of fun and frolic at Needs Barrow. You must think we are all demented."

Sara paused halfway over a steeply canted rock. "No. Not a

bit. I recently lost a dear older friend who would have adored your brother. She couldn't go three feet during a country walk without stopping to examine a weed or sketch a tree knot in her journal. I promise you, your brother's eccentricity is more welcome than you can possibly know."

Addie squeezed her wrist. "I am so glad. I'd given up on ever having a female friend in the neighborhood. They are all attracted to my brother's manly beauty . . . and then promptly go running when he starts talking nonstop about pupae and cilium."

"I don't find that sort of talk off-putting at all." Sara glanced back at Tristan. He and Gren Martyn had their heads together, studying something in one of the glass bottles. The two were so similar in height and frame and general aspect, they might have been brothers.

"Though you needn't worry I'll set my cap at him," she added.

"That's a relief," Addie said with a sigh.

Sara must have looked taken aback, because Addie quickly amended, "Oh, I've nothing at all against you, Miss Cobb. But he's already formed a tendre. I don't think he even realizes it, but sisters know these things. It's hopeless really, poor lamb."

A young serving maid met them in the hallway and took their outer garments. Sara was left to wander around the small parlor while Addie went to see about lunch. The room was comfortable and pleasant, even though most of the furnishings were threadbare. The sunlight spilled in through the mullioned windows, gleaming off a collection of rock crystals displayed on a beautifully carved mantel shelf. She was examining one, wondering at the perfection of the facets, when Gren Martyn came through the door.

"Tristan's gone to get cleaned up."

Sara eyed his damp breeches and salt-stained vest. "And what about you?"

"This is as clean as I get," he said with a careless shrug. "I hope you don't mind sitting down to your meal with a water-logged poacher."

"I didn't know you were on such cordial terms with the Spindles."

He moved to one of the two shabby sofas and perched on the arm. "We go back a ways, the three of us. Actually Amelie was also part of our little confederacy. You'll find that in Cornwall the lines of class are a bit more . . . blurred than in other parts of the country."

"I wasn't implying anything against you," she said as she carefully set the crystal on its stand. She turned to face him, clasping her hands at her waist. "Actually I'm glad you're here. I've been thinking that I owe you an apology."

A grin twisted his mouth and his eyes gleamed expectantly. "This should be good."

"I was completely off the mark the other day when I criticized you," she said. "I really don't know what made me think I had the right to tell you how to conduct your life."

"So it's fine with you that I live in a pig wallow?"

Sara felt her ears begin to burn. Curse the man for making things harder than they already were. "It's none of my business. It was unforgiveably meddlesome for me to speak to you in such a way."

He tipped his head back as he regarded her. "You know, there's an odd thing I've noticed. The people who are worst at managing their own lives are invariably the ones who feel the greatest need to manage others." He stroked his fingers along the horn buttons on his vest, but never took his eyes off her. "Why do you think that is, Miss Cobb?"

She thought for a time, then said, "Frustration?"

It earned her an abrupt laugh. "Now there's an honest reply. And I tend to agree with you. So much easier to sort out someone else's tangle than your own when life's not going your way." He sketched a graceful motion with his hand and said in a low, silky voice, "Then again, some frustrations have very interesting outcomes. For instance, if you were to come to my farm some night and allow me to work on a few of yours."

His smile was a calculated leer that stung Sara to the quick. She suddenly felt more distant from him than any time during their tiff on the moor.

"Why are you baiting me?" she snapped. "There's no need to insult me with innuendo—I thought we were on our way to becoming friends."

He raised one brow. "Friends? What makes you think I require something as paltry as a friend, Miss Cobb? You are very green indeed if you think a man of my character cultivates women as friends."

"I daresay Miss Spindle is a friend to you."

"Addie?" He glanced toward the door. "No, Addie is no friend of mine. More like an annoying cocklebur one can't get shed of."

She took a step toward him. "Why are you being so beastly? Three days ago you were a rather decent companion for an afternoon. Today you are behaving like a knave."

He rose from his perch and came across the carpet. "I want you gone from Penwreath, Miss Cobb. Nothing's changed since I spoke those warnings to you in the coach. And I certainly don't want to be the lure that keeps you here. Ah, you blush. So am I right in thinking you have a soft spot for old Gren Martyn?"

Sara pulled herself together. "*If* I were to care for you—and I tell you that possibility is quite remote at this point—it would not be in the way you are suggesting."

"There's only one way a woman cares for a man who's not her kin. You can waltz around the truth all you want, but that won't change anything. And I'll tell you how I knew. It's because the instant a woman sets her sights on a fellow, she starts trying to change him, to improve him all out of recognition. Just as you did."

"That's not why I did it," she protested hotly. "I'm a teacher, if you will recall. It's my job to instruct others, to show them how to go on. Besides I've already apologized for meddling. Though I see now that I was wrong to think you could ever be more than a poacher, more than a shiftless idler."

"Good," he said. "You're coming around. Not that I ever volunteered to be your pupil, Miss Crab. If the tables were turned, however, I wager I could instruct *you* very nicely in how to go on."

He came dangerously close and, short of backing into the blazing fireplace, Sara had nowhere to go. She trod heavily on his toes—highly strategic, since his feet were still bare—and when he danced back with a yelp of surprise, she moved quickly around him and out of the parlor.

She took a moment in the hallway to compose herself, pressing icy fingers to her burning cheeks. The man must have caught some rare red-algae fever; how else was she to explain his provoking behavior?

Tristan Spindle ought to note *that* in his journal.

Gren sprawled back onto the sofa nearest the fire, stretching his feet as close to the flames as he dared. Lord, he wondered if he'd ever get the feeling back in his frozen toes. Curse that Tristan for setting him to work when he'd planned a pleasant morning of fishing in the cove.

At least he'd got Miss Cobb sorted out. His stray kitten would have to find another tomcat to moon after. He could put her out of his mind now, not worry about her turning up at the farm, not fret that thoughts of her would keep him up nights, wondering how that prim little mouth would melt under an onslaught of kisses or how those piercing eyes would grow mysterious and dark with passion. No, he was sure she'd scurry off back to Tregallion and strike out every line in her diary with his name in it.

As for himself, he'd have her banished from his thoughts in no time. Innocence had never appealed to him; if anything it acted as a deterrent. Why waste time seducing the unwilling, when the willing were so much more entertaining?

Not that Sara Cobb wasn't entertaining company; he had to give her that. So serious at times, and yet an ironic amusement danced in her eyes when she thought no one was looking. But he was always looking where she was concerned. Ever since that first day in the coach, he'd barely been able to look away. So contained, he'd thought. So tightly reined. It occurred to him that a man, another sort of man, might take great pleasure in breaking through that guard, freeing that confined spirit. Another sort of man might win her trust, gain her love even. And then watch her blossom like the moor on an April morning. But not Gren Martyn. He was not the man fated to awaken Sara Cobb to senses she didn't yet know she possessed.

It was a blessedly freeing notion. Or at least it should have been.

Once the feeling had returned to his lower limbs, he went out to the hallway. Cilla, the maid, was there, daydreaming by the hall window.

"Tell Miss Addie I've decided not to stay for lunch," he said as he collected his boots and woolen stockings from the cubby below the hall tree. "I seem to have lost my appetite."

She bobbed her head. "It's no wonder, Mr. Gren. I seen the foul mess in those jars Mr. Tristan carried up to his study. Looked like bloody murder had been done."

Sara relaxed once she learned Gren Martyn had decided to forgo lunch. She wasn't sure she could have sat across from him and not lobbed cutlery at his head. Addie kept up a pleasant stream of conversation throughout the meal, describing their neighbors in Penwreath to Sara, while Tristan nattered on about his algae. When Sara idly mentioned that she was in need of a dance instructor for Ileana and asked if he might volunteer, he shook his head. "No disrespect, Miss Cobb, but I wouldn't go within ten feet of that girl. The last time we were together, she did something quite unforgivable, something so—"

"She broke his nautilus," Addie interrupted with a tiny snort. "A chambered nautilus shell. He'd wanted one forever and Papa had sent for it all the way from America."

"It was the rarest thing I'd ever owned up to that time," he explained.

"Good Lord, Tris, this happened when you were sixteen and she was only twelve. I really think it's time you let it go."

"She dropped it," he said to Sara, "and then she stepped on it. Twice."

"I'm not going to defend her," Sara said with great feeling. "She broke my favorite vase. I used to fill it with wildflowers and set it on my desk in the classroom. Once, when I took her to task for something, she picked it up and hurled it against the wall. She then blithely told me to send the bill to her father." She paused a moment. "But I will also tell you this—I believe she is very unhappy. Her sister has virtually abandoned her, and from what I can tell, her parents act as though she isn't even in the house. It seems she calls attention to herself any way she can."

"Amelie wasn't much different," Addie said in a thoughtful voice. "Our governess used to say she was hell-bent on destruction. Her own."

"With a little abetting from Gren Martyn," Sara couldn't keep from murmuring.

Addie drew back. "No, Miss Cobb. That's not the way of it. I'd forgotten that that's what you'd hear at Tregallion House. Someday when you know Gren better, you'll hear the true story from him. It's not my place or Tristan's to explain it to you."

"But you vouched for him in court."

"Of course I did. But more than that I am not at liberty to say. Just don't judge Gren by the common tattle. Amelie has finally found some happiness and peace, and a good part of that is his doing."

Sara shook her head. "There's no point in my trying to figure it out, Addie. I'm just not that interested in Gren Martyn's secrets."

Tristan drove her home in the gig, and she did her utmost to convince him to help out with Ileana.

"She needs companions her own age," she explained. "She fancies me something of a relic, if you want the truth, though I am barely seven years her senior. Whereas, you are closer to her in age. I think she even admires you a little, Tristan . . . that you went off to Oxford and spent time in London. It would be a kindness. She's like a princess in a castle, with everything she could possibly want at her fingertips—except the one thing she really needs."

"A good thrashing?"

"Well, that too," Sara concurred with a chuckle. "But you can't still be holding that shell business against her. Children break things by accident all the time."

"It wasn't an accident," he said between his teeth. "After she did it, she looked up at me and said quite coolly, 'I don't want you to have prettier things than me. You are no one of consequence.'" He looked away from her. "I never told Addie that part. It was hateful."

"It's not you she hates. I sometimes think she hates herself."

He huffed out a breath. "That conceited little baggage?"

"Come on, Tristan," she pleaded. "I've made some initial cracks in her defenses. She was actually pleasant to me the other day, when she was talking about Amelie. I should think a clever *scientific* young man like you could wind her around his finger."

He pulled up the gig and glared at her amiably. "Blast it, Miss Cobb. You must have been taking cozening lessons from my sister. Very well, I will teach the minx to dance. But I warn you, she's not going to like it one bit."

Chapter Eight

Sara awoke in a hazy, distracted mood—one she couldn't shake. Her mind refused to focus on anything and she ended up dismissing Ileana early. She spent the rest of the afternoon on the window seat, gazing at the sea and thinking about Gren Martyn. He'd been insufferably rude to her yesterday, but she'd come away with the suspicion that the entire encounter had been a tad overplayed. Surely she hadn't said or done anything that required him to hold her at arm's length, yet he'd made a point of thrusting her away. There was no reason on earth a notorious libertine would feel threatened by *her*.

None of it made sense and she was a fool to waste her time dwelling on the matter. If they happened to meet again, she would treat him like the merest acquaintance. Still, it continued to infuriate her that he fancied himself the lure that kept her here, the arrogant coxcomb. No matter that there was a smidgen of truth to it.

A knock on the door sent all thought of Gren Martyn fleeing away—Mrs. Holcroft waited on the other side, wearing her usual pinched frown.

"Sir Kenneth requests that you begin attending servants' prayers after supper."

Sara had no idea what to say. She could think of few things less appealing than standing about every evening while her employer read the Bible.

"Perhaps Sir Kenneth does not understand my position in the household," she said with a bit of temper. "Governesses are not precisely servants."

"Those are his orders."

"Did Miss Amelie's governesses attend the prayer sessions?"

"Not that I recall, but they might have fared better in the long run if they had."

"And what exactly happened to them . . . *in the long run?*" She stared at the housekeeper. "Because, you see, Mrs. Holcroft, I have heard that they both disappeared from this house. You wouldn't know anything about that, would you?"

"No more than you do, Miss Cobb. Now shall I tell Sir Kenneth you will be down?"

"Yes," she said. "Though I do it under protest."

Smug victory flickered in the woman's eyes. "We meet in the back parlor at eight." Sara shut the door, feeling as though her sanctuary had been sullied. How dared that wretched creature come here and lord it over her? And what possible reason could Sir Kenneth have for requiring her to attend?

She had her answer at eight that night.

Sir Kenneth stood before the hearth with the servants ranged in a semi-circle around him. May Belle was conspicuously absent, but every other member of the indoor staff was present, from the lowest skivvy to Lady Brashear's dressmaker. And Mrs. Holcroft, of course, standing practically at Sir Kenneth's elbow.

Sara was unlucky enough to be positioned directly across from him, and it was obvious he was watching her whenever he wasn't reading from the Book of Ezekiel. No, not watching, ogling. His gaze roamed over her body each time he looked up and it made her flesh crawl.

She'd long ago stopped dwelling on the ominous warnings Gren Martyn had uttered that first day. Now they all came back to her—the nasty character of Tregallion House, the foul odor that rose from the place. She knew exactly what he'd meant now, as the master of the house quoted scripture in a deep round voice and leered at her shamelessly.

After they'd recited the Lord's Prayer aloud, he dismissed the staff. Sara tried to make a hasty exit, but he caught up with her and blocked the doorway. "Stay a moment, Miss Cobb."

"It's been a tiring day," she said. "And I need to go over tomorrow's lessons."

"Tish, tish. Ileana won't mind if you skip an occasional lesson. Though I must say, you've done very well with her. She's almost conversing like a sensible adult these days. And her mother tells me she hasn't sulked over anything for a whole week."

"I'm pleased you and Lady Brashear find my work satisfactory." She eyed the doorway with longing.

"Your Miss Bonnet was quite complimentary about you when we visited her school. She told us something of your past, how she had once been your governess."

"Yes, that is true."

"And that your family suffered a number of reverses, followed by the loss of both parents. So sad . . ."

"Sir Kenneth, I cannot see what—"

"And there were no other relatives who could have offered you a home?"

"No. Neither of my parents had siblings."

"So you are alone in the world." He'd said it with a warm look of commiseration, but Sara's hackles had risen up as though he was threatening her with a knife.

"Not so alone," she said with a touch of spirit. "I have made friends in the district. Miss Spindle and her brother, for instance."

He slid an arm around her shoulder. "And of course you have us now. We will watch over you, Miss Cobb, and see that you prosper."

"Thank you, Sir Kenneth." She dipped out from beneath his arm and turned to face him. "That is most gratifying."

"Of course," he added, "how much you prosper depends upon how much you please me. You must prove that you are deserving."

She managed to say, "No one's ever faulted me for lack of enterprise."

He smiled, his heavy-lipped mouth curling up at one side. "I am of an enterprising nature myself. It appears we are kindred spirits . . . eh, Miss Cobb?"

He was closing in again. Sara felt the bile rise in her throat. "I really must be going. Good night, sir."

Before he could prevent it, she had thrust her way past him.

She turned and fled down the hall, not feeling safe until she was in May Belle's parlor.

"It was horrid!" she cried in a shaking voice as she paced in front of the fire. "He put his arm around me and told me I would prosper here if *he* thought I deserved it, his voice just dripping butter the whole time."

She shuddered at the memory of those oily insinuating words.

"Worst of all, I have an uncanny feeling he intends to set me up in place of Mrs. Holcroft." Her fingers dug into the folds her skirt. "Dear God, I swear I never once encouraged the man."

"His kind doesn't require much encouraging," May Belle observed. "And you are a taking little thing, Sara Cobb. You cast the Holcroft viper quite in the shade."

"But what of his wife?" Sara nearly wailed. "Lady Brashear is exquisite. I doubt she has an equal west of the Tamar. The man is a lunatic."

"I know you've been sheltered from a good deal of life, off in your school for young ladies. P'raps it's time you understood that the gentry rarely keep company with their own spouses. And not only the gentlemen, neither. I've heard that Lady Brashear had a young man in London years ago . . . a violin player who performed with her at parties. Only he wasn't just fiddling in the parlor, if you get my drift. And Sir Kenneth's had a string of mistresses. Why do you think he's always riding off to Plymouth? It's not for the cockfights or the card games at the Red Lion."

"I'm hardly shocked that he is an adulterer, May Belle. I'm not that naive. I just don't want him to think he can be one with me."

"Then you've got to bring him to the sticking point—and then tell him no."

She spun to face her friend. "I do know one thing. I am not returning to that farce of a prayer meeting. I vow, every time he ogled me, I kept waiting for lightning to strike the mantel behind him."

The cook grinned. "That would solve your problem."

Sara finally sank into a chair. "Before Ileana agreed to her lessons, I was thinking of seeking another position. I suppose I could still advertise, but it seems such a shame now that she's finally coming to trust me."

"Then just tell him no," she said again. "He can't very well force himself on you. Lady Brashear would be bound to intervene in that case."

"And no doubt find some way to blame me," Sara grumbled.

Sara barely slept that night and awoke with a pounding headache. She was relieved when Ileana's maid arrived with a note explaining that she had caught a head cold and would be staying in bed.

"*With* the improving novel you gave me yesterday," she'd added in a postscript, "so you needn't think me a total scapegrace."

Sara smiled. Incredible as it seemed, she was actually growing fond of the girl. Wouldn't it be a miracle if the two of them actually came out of this as friends?

Friends . . . there was that word again. The word she had thrown at Gren Martyn—and he had summarily tossed back at her. He'd implied that it was a pale inferior thing, at least between a man and a woman. He'd further protested that Addie Spindle was not his friend, which made her what exactly? It was impossible to imagine that bright bemused young lady involved in a sordid intrigue. Furthermore, Gren's manner around her had hardly been loverlike. As for Addie, she had behaved toward him exactly like an old family friend—or a sister—teasing him the way she did Tristan.

Perhaps May Belle had the right of it. Sara had spent too much of her life sequestered in Miss Bonnet's school. She had few clues about how men and women interacted in the real world. How ironic that she was giving Ileana lessons how to win a husband, she who'd never had a proper beau in her whole life.

She decided to take Sadie out to the sea cliff, hoping the brisk, salty air would clear the cobwebs from her head. Seth again saddled the mare for her, but when Sara tried to pass the time with him, he seemed distracted.

"Is something wrong?"

"Ach, it be a world of worry, young miss. My great niece went off to Plymouth these two weeks past to take a position in one of the larger posting houses, the West Wind. She'd heard tell of an advertisement what was posted in the Royal William here in Penwreath. It sounded like a fair berth." His mouth trembled. "But she never got there. Promised to send a message home after she arrived, but more'n a week went by with no word. Her poor mother went there only yesterday, but they say she never turned up. Our sweet Bessie's gone missing and the Lord only knows where she may be."

Sara gnawed the edge of her lip, feeling a creeping sense of unease. "You must speak to Sir Kenneth. I am sure he or Lord Denby will be able to trace her. She's probably found another posting and just hasn't sent word to her mother."

"I pray you've got the right of it, miss. These be wicked times for innocent lambs. A young girl is hardly safe in her own backyard."

Sara rode out feeling surrounded by a dismal pall. Seth's distressing story, combined with her own tense situation, removed any possibility of her enjoying the ride. Still, the fresh air was invigorating, and once she reached the sea cliff, the steady rise and fall of the waves did ease her a bit. She tethered Sadie to a clump of bushes and went to sit at the very edge of the drop-off, where she could watch the sea spend itself upon the rocks.

Once upon a time her life had been placid and predictable. —she had been restless and often bored. Now she felt herself in the midst of a maelstrom. No longer even remotely bored, but still oddly restless. She'd at least stopped holding so tight to the present; Henrietta Bonnet would be proud of that. She saw a future, for the next few months at any rate, where she grew into an easier accord with Ileana, became fast friends with the Spindles and where she somehow managed to adeptly refuse Sir Kenneth's overtures without jeopardizing her position.

She purposely did not dwell on where a certain blue-eyed poacher fit into that equation. She was concentrating on her *future*, and he'd surely have no part in that. It was a pity, though, that she hadn't spent enough time with him to have acquired a tiny bit of a past. Not a fall from grace, certainly, but a light flirtation might not have gone amiss. It would have furnished her with something shivery and romantic to look back on in her waning years.

"Thinking about me?"

Sara scooted around so quickly, she nearly tumbled off the cliff. Gren Martyn was standing beside Sadie, running his hand along her shoulder.

"You ought to appear in a puff of smoke," she told him. "It would complete the startling effect."

"I'll work on it," he said as he came across the clearing.

She noticed that once again his game bag was full. He slung it off his shoulder as he settled beside her. "Though there's little trickery involved. You left a trail a blind man could follow." When she didn't respond, he prodded her with his elbow. "So is Ileana shirking today?"

"No, she has the grippe. I am the one shirking, actually. I ought to be preparing our lesson for tomorrow."

She started to get to her feet, but he caught her hand and tugged her down again. "Don't run away, Sara."

"Why shouldn't I?" she asked a bit crossly. "Isn't that what you intended I do at Needs Barrow? Keep out of range of your fatal charm? Although, I must tell you, you're not nearly as charming as you think, Mr. Martyn."

"Hmmm . . . you're full of sauce this morning."

"I'm not accustomed to being warned off by scoundrels, for one thing. I offered you my friendship and you ground it underfoot, for another. So yes, I am feeling peppery."

"I suppose I did sound a bit . . . arrogant. But I was just trying to warn you—"

She grunted. "That's all you ever do."

"—that you're in over your head here. In a number of ways. With me, with the Brashears."

"And you don't want me to discover these supposed dangers for myself?"

"I only wanted to tell you that I handled things badly on Sunday. I was actually flattered that you considered yourself my friend. But it's never that simple. Not with me."

"What do you mean?"

He turned to gaze at the Channel beyond them, his eyes following a distant merchantman beating into the wind. "When I was young," he said, "I wanted to go to sea. My brother absolutely forbade it. Worse than the mines, he assured me. Bad rations, questionable company and utterly foul conditions. At least with the mines, you slept at home in your own bed."

"So he looked after you."

"Mmm. Once our parents were gone—they both died while I was a boy. But Jacob mistrusted people. I'm not sure why. He worked for himself all his life, wanted nothing to do with other men. Solitary, I guess you would say. There were times I think he could barely tolerate having me around."

"I can sympathize," she said with a swift grin.

"Yes . . . I am a trial. Anyway, once I left the mines, I fell in with a group of smugglers. Found out that everything he'd warned me about the sea was true. After that, he sent me away. Far away. He'd apprenticed me to a craftsman because he wanted me to have a respectable trade—one that didn't involve poaching or smuggling. I stayed there, learning that trade, for nearly six years. And the whole time, I can't say I made even one friend. My master was never more to me than that, for all he was a fair, decent man." He shifted around to look at her. "So you see, Sara, I am not very good at this business of friendship. There are only five people on this earth I ever trusted—and one of them is dead."

"Your brother?"

"Yes, and the others are Addie and Tris, my cousin Lather Pitt and Amelie Brashear."

"And you're not sure you can trust me."

"Women do not inspire a great deal of confidence, if you want the plain truth."

"Yet two of those you just mentioned are women."

"Friendships formed in childhood, when the two sexes haven't yet drawn the lines of battle. We swore a blood pact, and I've still no reason to believe either one of them would betray me."

"And I would?"

"Not intentionally. But I can't forget that you work for a

man who considers himself my enemy. If given the option of turning on me or losing your position, I wonder how you would choose."

"This is all nonsense," she burst out. "You make it sound as though you are deep in some political intrigue, when in fact you are merely a poacher who thumbs his nose at the local gentry."

"There is a great deal more to it than that, Sara."

She rolled her eyes and recited in a singsong voice, "And if you trusted me, you could tell me. Honestly, this is growing very tiresome. The cook at Tregallion once accused women of being the worst teases, but you take the prize. Either tell me what's really going on or stop talking in riddles. I've already got enough on my mind, what with Sir Kenneth making sheep's eyes at me and the groom's niece disappearing."

She expected *some* response to either of those leading comments, but he merely continued staring down at the outgoing tide.

Finally he muttered, "You keep Brashear at a distance. He's one of the chief reasons I warned you not to work at the house."

"I can handle Sir Kenneth," she assured him with false bravado. "But what of the groom's niece? Any sage advice on that little problem? No, wait," she said darkly. "I forgot. You don't bother about anyone but yourself. So a farm girl gone missing in Plymouth isn't going to—"

He got hold of her wrist, clamping down hard. "I know all about Bessie Pethrick," he growled softly. "I'd need a heart of stone not to care when a neighbor's seventeen-year-old daughter disappears." Gren's eyes had gone a deep troubled gray. "She's the sixth girl from Penwreath who's vanished this year. And they were all bound for Plymouth when it happened."

Sara took a moment to assimilate this startling piece of information. "That's dreadful. Where do you think they went?"

"Where all foolish country girls end up if they don't keep a level head. In brothels."

Sara drew back. "Is that what you really believe? That they decided on a whim to give up respectable posts as house maids or serving girls and take up a life of vice?"

"They didn't decide anything. I keep forgetting how clois-
tered you were. They are lured into it, promised fine positions
with good wages. Instead, they find themselves drugged and
eventually coerced. I must have met a dozen whores who tell
the same tale."

"I just bet you have." When she saw anger spark in his eyes,
she quickly touched his sleeve. "No, sorry, that was ill-timed.
But tell me, is the business that's keeping you here something
to do with these missing girls?"

He nodded. "I *can* admit that much."

"Are you trying to find where they've gone? Or who took
them?"

"I'm not saying anything else. It's best not to involve you.
Just keep your wits about you, as I advised that first night."

She gave a low, self-deprecating laugh. "Why? Do you
imagine they'd come after me, the dowdy little governess?"

"I'd come after you, Sara."

She blinked twice as a bolt of heat shot through her.

He was watching her openly, not a bit shaken for having
said something so . . . naked. But it had shaken her to the core.
It was impossible to look away from that intense blue gaze,
impossible to form a single word. Not even when his arm
snaked out and tugged her against him. Her head snapped
back, then was forced back even farther when he kissed her.

Surprise immediately gave way to dismay, and she went
rigid in his arms. It wasn't from fear, however, but from un-
certainty. For all her book learning, Sara hadn't a clue of how
to kiss back. It might be the most humiliating moment of her
life.

Gren murmured her name and a few words of reassurance
against her lips, which were clenched tight.

Relax! Sara ordered herself. *Before he stops.*

Gren drew back a little, his eyes puzzled, questioning. His
hands shifted up to cup her face, thumbs caressing the hollow
of each cheek. He held her gaze as he tilted his head and kissed
her again, mouth slightly agape. She felt him breathe out
against her lips, a warm sigh, then breathe in, a gentle suction.
Her eyes drifted closed, her mouth relaxed, and she eased at
last into a proper kiss.

Shifting her into the crook of his arm, he increased the pressure of his mouth, his kisses warm, honeyed and arousing. All her senses came roaring back then; her awkwardness vanished, replaced by a rush of desire. Sara had both arms around him now, hands splayed on his shoulders. She'd seen those shoulders bared, glistening with a sheen of water, and had hungered to touch them. That recollection now freed something deep inside her. She arched up, pressing shamelessly against his chest, feeling his arm tighten around her like an iron band.

Then suddenly he retreated, dropping both arms and shifting away from her.

"Damn," he muttered under his breath. "I had no intention of ever doing that."

Disappointment washed over Sara. She wanted to shout at him, to insist that this was *exactly* what she wanted. After a moment of strained silence, however, she realized he'd offered her a reprieve. If a few kisses had the power to inflame her beyond any thoughts of propriety, she'd have surely been consumed if he'd gone any further. Gren had sensed that and, surprisingly, had disentangled himself.

She said grudgingly, "I suppose I should thank you for drawing back."

He gave a mirthless laugh. "Now you know why I can't be friends with you. A man doesn't go about kissing his friends. . . . And that's nearly all I think about when I'm with you. Hell, it's all I think about lately even when I'm not with you."

Sara lowered her head, fighting off a thrill of jubilation. "I think about it too," she whispered hoarsely. "But you're right that it wouldn't be wise to do it again."

She touched the ragged cuff of his shirt. In spite of her resolve she needed to make some contact with him. "And yet maybe we can still salvage something here, Gren Martyn. I will be *your* friend, should you ever need one. There's no law that says friendship has to be reciprocated."

He cocked his head to stare at her. "Daft, as usual." He'd not spoken with his usual careless drawl. His tone was almost fond.

They sat without speaking after that, gazing out to sea, but tension still crackled in the air between them. Sara had to find some way to restore their former accord, if only to stop the awful churning in her stomach.

"Where did you go when your brother sent you away?" she asked lightly, as though she were picking up the thread of a recently lapsed conversation.

After a moment he said, "To New York. I returned to England a year before the war started."

"But you told me you'd never been out of Cornwall until recently."

"I said I'd never been *east* of the Tamar. I've been considerably west of it though."

"I should have guessed. You don't speak like most other Cornishmen. So how did you find it, living in America?"

"So full of questions, Miss Cobb," he teased, though his eyes were still guarded. "In truth, it's not much different from England—the very rich and the very poor with most people somewhere in between."

"I gather you received an education there."

He nodded. "My master insisted on it. He didn't want any clotheads working in his shop."

Sara was about to ask what trade he'd been following when the deep baying of a large dog sounded from the woods beyond the clearing.

"It's the gamekeepers!" she cried. "They've got a fearful mastiff, Gren. You must go at once."

He rose swiftly and shouldered his game bag, his gaze swinging across the clearing. "Not into those woods," he muttered.

Before Sara could object, he'd scrambled over the edge of the cliff, clinging to the rocks by his fingertips as he made his way out of sight.

"If you slip, you'll fall to your death," she hissed down at him.

He looked up at her, eyes now snapping with light. "Will you wear the willow for your poacher, Sara Cobb?"

"This is no time for jesting. Just stay out of sight until I get rid of them."

She hurried across the gravel-spattered clearing, obscuring

any traces of his hobnail boots with one toe. When the two gamekeepers and their dog came thrusting out of the trees, she was sitting under a wind-stunted evergreen with her knees tucked up, studying a spray of wild grass.

She looked up in feigned surprise.

"Seen anything of a poacher, miss? A man with a net and snares?" the elder of the two asked her. The younger man was busy keeping the mastiff from lunging across the clearing.

"I'd hardly be sitting here so calmly if there was a stranger roaming along the cliff," she pointed out.

"Brawly smells something over there," the younger man said, pointing to the drop-off. "Look, sir, he's fairly turning inside out to get at it."

Sara wrinkled her nose delicately. "It's a dead seagull. And not recently dead, either. Which is why I am sitting here and not closer to the water."

"Best hold 'im back, Fielding. . . . Have you forgotten last week when he got into that festering deer carcass?" The man sketched a salute to Sara. "Sorry to 'ave troubled you, miss. Still, you might not want to linger in the woods today. We found the fellow's tracks on the bridle trail quite nearby."

Sara's breathing returned to normal only after they'd been gone for five minutes. She rose then and hurried over to the cliff edge.

Gren Martyn was gone.

She peered down at the tumble of rocks forty feet below her, praying she wouldn't see a broken body splayed there. With the tide receding, there was little surf to carry a body away, so if he had fallen he'd still be there. Which he was not.

"Damn you, Gren," she grumbled. "Every time I'm with you, I end up with palpitations. And not always the good sort, either."

He'd doubtless been climbing these cliffs since he was a boy, she reasoned, and it was more likely he'd scuttled, crablike, along the rocks until he found a safe place to come up.

Still, she sat there fretting. Just like the man to disappear and not give a thought to how she would react. Then she noticed a fluttering of blue against the chalky gray rocks not far below her. It was Gren's open neckerchief, spread beneath a loose stone. Stretching out on her belly, Sara reached over the edge and tugged it loose. As love tokens went it wasn't much, she thought as she tucked it into the front of her pelisse, just a square of homespun laundered to the texture of flannel. But as a reminder that he had thought to reassure her before he moved on, it was most satisfactory.

Halfway to the house, she turned the mare toward the front gate. She still had the rest of the afternoon to herself and decided that it was time she had a proper look at Penwreath.

Chapter Nine

*T*he village consisted of a High Street with several commercial lanes running off it at right angles. The Constant Star, ancient and vine laced, lay at the east end of the village, while the larger Royal William, of spotless whitewashed brick, was situated in the bustling town center. The latter was Sara's destination; she handed Sadie off to an ostler in the stableyard and went inside. The center hallway was wide, carpeted with a thick floral runner as befit a prosperous hostelry. At the far end sat a gleaming wooden counter with a pigeonhole rack on the wall beside it.

There was no one at the counter, so Sara was at liberty to examine the notices posted below the rack. Handbills describing horse sales and livestock auctions seemed to be in the majority. There was, however, one advertisement for chambermaids in Plymouth:

RESPECTABLE WAGES AND DECENT LIVING QUARTERS.
APPLY AT THE WEST WIND ON HAMILTON STREET.

It looked innocent enough. She doubted the landlord of the West Wind had any idea that his handbill was luring young girls into the hands of vice peddlers.

Sara cast a quick look over her shoulder. A low buzz of conversation was coming from the adjoining dining parlor, but there didn't seem to be anyone near the hall. She quickly tugged the notice off the wall, folded it once and thrust it into her pocket.

"Can I help you, miss?"

Sara spun around, praying that her fatal tendency to blush didn't betray her. The landlord, tall and stern-faced, was standing in the open archway of the dining room.

"I'm the governess from Tregallion House," she managed to say smoothly. "Miss Brashear is looking for a trap pony—" She sketched a wave at the horse sale notices.

"Tell her to try Jenks's farm. He has a Dartmoor mare that might do her very nicely."

She thanked him, and then forced herself to make an unhurried exit.

Once again, she had no coins to offer the young ostler, so she bestowed a wide smile on him. This seemed to satisfy the lad all out of proportion.

It was occurring to Sara, as she rode off in the direction of the church, that she might not be so graceless or plain-featured as she'd always thought. Today a rather delicious man had kissed her, and just now a mere smile had lit up the face of a strapping young groom.

Fine thoughts to be entertaining when she was about to pay a call on the vicar, she muttered dampeningly.

She found the Reverend Mr. Ivey in his walled garden, spreading straw over the base of his rose bushes. Several still carried the last remnants of flowers. A hardy strain, Sara thought, to flourish in such a topsy-turvy climate. He greeted her with a genial smile, asking after the health of her employers. She commented knowingly on his garden—Miss Bonnet had been a tireless tender of flowers—and then got to the point of her visit.

The vicar listened to her soberly, nodding his head every so often. Finally he took Sara's arm and led her toward his small manse. "Come inside," he said. "I've some rosehip wine I'd like you to try. It will give me a chance to think over your problem."

When Sara returned to the stable at Tregallion, Seth seemed even more downcast. She pondered telling him that she'd removed the troublesome handbill from the Royal William. But there was little point; it had come too late to do his Bessie any good.

She wandered the rows of stalls for a time, admiring the sleek necks and wise eyes of the horses—and mentally rehearsing her part in the upcoming confrontation. Finally she decided she was being a spineless coward and went striding determinedly off to the house.

Sir Kenneth was reading in his library, as she'd hoped. It was a lovely room, with burnished walnut paneling and the satisfying scent of leather bindings, but Sara barely noticed. He rose as she came in and she tried to ignore the way his eyes lit up. It was one thing to enliven the face of a young groom and quite another to arouse open lust in one's employer.

"I have a request, Sir Kenneth," she said, keeping her fretful hands behind her. "It has to do with the nightly prayer meeting."

His mouth tightened, but he said nothing.

"You see," she continued. "I have never been comfortable with public displays of piety. Of course, when one is in church, praying aloud is quite acceptable. But doing so in a parlor full of people just seems so . . . Methodist."

She silently thanked the vicar, who had initially expressed that same sentiment.

"I hope I am not the one who made you uncomfortable," he said.

"The whole notion makes me uncomfortable," she prevaricated. "I came upon the vicar in his garden today, and he assured me that one's manner of prayer is strictly a personal preference."

"So you spoke to Ivey," he muttered, not seeming at all pleased. "For the most part, he's a doddering fool. Still, I suppose I shall have to defer to him on matters spiritual." He shifted closer to her. "Perhaps, Miss Cobb, you would prefer it if you and I prayed together in here. That would certainly be less public."

Sara's heart turned cold. She had never considered this possibility. "But hardly proper," she quickly pointed out.

"I would be the best judge of that."

Sara saw she was going to have to be more forthright. She paced away from him and then back. "I believe some plain speaking is required, Sir Kenneth. Your wife hired me for my good character, hoping I would be a calming influence on your daughter. Any whisper of impropriety on my part would jeopardize my situation here."

"And you think I would not put in a word for you, were that to happen?"

She drew in a deep breath. "Just more fuel to the fire, I'm afraid, when a wife believes a servant has caught the eye of her husband. I wouldn't want to do *anything* that might foster such an impression."

His tawny brows creased in bewilderment. "Have *I* given you that impression?"

Yes! she wanted to wail. The wretch was trying to make her feel like an overly imaginative spinster.

"Last night you said I would prosper if I pleased you. It seemed an odd wording."

He gave a gruff laugh. "Dear girl, you misunderstood me. I was simply speaking of setting you up with a gentleman once Ileana is launched. I know some very fine fellows who would leap at the chance to take you under their wing. You'd like that, wouldn't you? Someone who could offer you a secure and pleasant future and see to all your needs. Now calm yourself. I am sorry if I caused you even a moment's grief."

Sara still gazed at him suspiciously.

"We take care of our own, here at Tregallion House," he added. "You'll see, Miss Cobb. You will be very happily situated come spring. And yes, you may forgo evening prayers until you feel more at ease with the staff."

Muttering something that might have been "thank you," Sara nodded once and went from the room. She still had her position, but for some reason did not feel very reassured.

On Wednesday morning, Sara brought Ileana down to the music room. Tristan Spindle was waiting there as arranged. The girl frowned when she saw him, but there was not the eruption of temper Sara feared. As the dance lesson commenced, she was beginning to congratulate herself on finally drumming some manners into her pupil—until it became evident that Ileana was gleefully doing the exact opposite of everything Tristan told her.

"No, you great *paperwit*!" he cried as she sailed away from him for the tenth time during their faux quadrille. "I said go left. *Left*!"

"Sorry," Ileana said with a dimpled smile. "I thought you said right."

"She's unreachable," he muttered as he came up to Sara. "You see it, don't you?"

She thought a moment. "Waltz with her," she said. "You do know how to waltz, don't you?"

"Of course I do, but I fail to see how—"

Sara leaned forward. "You lead, she follows. It's the only dance where you can control her absolutely."

Tristan appeared uncertain, but when she went to the piano and began playing a lilting tune in three-quarter time, he stalked over to Ileana, caught her roughly around the waist and hauled her onto the floor.

His mouth was set, his eyes burned with a martial light, and he was holding her far too close for propriety . . . but, ah, how they waltzed! Sara could have sworn the girl's feet barely touched the floor as he spun her around and around. Sara was halfway through the tune when she was struck by the certainty that Ileana was the object of Tristan's infatuation. The willful child who had crushed his favorite possession had apparently also stolen his heart. Poor Tris!

When Sara stopped playing, he gave Ileana one final whirl, then came to an abrupt halt and firmly put her from him. Ileana just stood there, glassy-eyed and weaving.

"There," he stormed quietly, his fingers still clenched on her upper arms. "That is how a man dances with a woman. And if you'd stop your childish shilly-shallying and your idiotic May games, why then who knows? He might even do it again someday."

Sara watched with dismay as he strode out of the room. So much for dance lessons.

"As if I give a fig!" Ileana called out after him.

But she'd spoken in the shaken whispery voice of a forlorn, frightened little girl.

*   *   *

Ileana had gone off in a huff after her dance lesson, and Sara was now drowsing on the window seat, imagining herself waltzing with Gren Martyn. If the callow Tristan Spindle had mustered up enough heat to dazzle Ileana, Sara could only imagine the inferno her poacher could kindle.

Not that he'd ever waltzed a step in his life, she reminded herself. Somehow the image of him doing a country clog dance was far less enticing, and therefore was the vision she *should* be focusing on. But she refused to give in to hard reality, not with the sunlight flickering like fairy fire upon the distant sea and the great billowing cumulus clouds sailing across the sky like the armada of a mighty conqueror.

When a brisk knock broke the spell, she got grudgingly up from the window seat and went to the door.

"Her ladyship wants to see you in the back parlor," a young maid informed her.

Sara quickly tidied her hair in the tiny mirror and followed the girl to the west wing.

Today Lady Brashear was in lemon sarcenet, a perfect counterpoint to the azure-striped silk of the sofa where she was seated. She waved Sara to a spindly chair that had been drawn up facing her.

"I have been remiss in not meeting with you sooner," her ladyship said. "But we entertain a great deal over the winter, and I have been distracted by my plans for a number of dinner parties."

This isn't going to be so bad, Sara thought. The woman sounded almost cordial.

"If I *had* met with you," Lady Brashear continued, her voice grown flinty, "I might have seen how misdirected you are as a teacher."

Sara's head jolted up. "Excuse me?"

The woman held out a book. It was the novel Ileana had been reading while she had the grippe. "What do you call this, Miss Cobb?"

"It is called *Clarissa* . . . by Samuel Richardson."

"Don't be impertinent," she snapped. "I can read the title for myself. I was referring to the fact that it is a novel."

Sara tamped down her frustration. "A very edifying novel, as I pointed out to your daughter."

"Edifying? I hardly consider the exploits of a fallen woman edifying. You see I *am* familiar with the story, Miss Cobb. I believe it was a favorite of Amelie's."

Sara winced. How was she to know the disgraced daughter had read Richardson?

"It is hardly one of Mrs. Radcliffe's lurid melodramas, ma'am. And I thought—"

"What?"

"I thought it wouldn't hurt Ileana to discover the pitfalls that await any imprudent young lady. I believe literature is full of life lessons we can learn without having to experience them ourselves."

Lady Brashear visibly thought this over, then shook her head. "Exposing my daughter to vice, even on the printed page, is not why we hired you. I am distressed and disappointed beyond words."

Sara felt all the confidence she'd built up over the past week begin to erode. "There is a deal of vice in London," she said in rebuttal. "If Ileana goes there unprepared, she will be at the mercy of every glib opportunist she meets. Or, at the very least, she will be shocked and frightened. I only thought to expose her to some of the reality she will be facing."

Lady Brashear chose not to respond to Sara's logic. Instead, she launched into a new attack. "There is also the matter of Tristan Spindle. Ileana came to me in tears this afternoon, telling me of how you forced her to dance with him, a young man she detests."

Sara bristled. "He was doing me a favor. The dance lessons at Miss Bonnet's school were very provincial, I'm afraid, and I thought Mr. Spindle would be up on all the latest steps."

"He is not exactly a welcome visitor here. As you will recall, his sister testified for that . . . man."

Sara forced herself to speak calmly. "Again, I believe your daughter needs to spend time with others her age. Else she will be thrown into the marriage mart without a clue of how to behave in mixed company. Surely you must see that, Lady Brashear. And you yourself informed me that Mr. Spindle is the only acceptable young gentleman in the neighborhood. He is hardly accountable for any unpleasantness that occurred between Amelie and that man."

Her ladyship sniffed. "You are very quick to defend yourself with these clever arguments, Miss Cobb. But that doesn't alter my initial opinion of your methods. You are to school my daughter in deportment and French, and nothing more. We will see to a dancing instructor once we reach London." She gave a brittle laugh. "Why, to hear you talk, a person would think London society was depraved on a par with ancient Rome. Yet I imagine you know very little of it. You did not take, as I recall. So how could you have the tiniest clue how a beautiful girl like Ileana will go on?"

Sara felt her chin go up of its own volition. "Amelie is my clue, ma'am. It's clear that no one cared enough to warn her about cozening libertines or desperate fortune hunters. She may have read *Clarissa*, but I venture to say she did not comprehend one whit of its underlying message. I merely wish to keep Ileana from being another victim of ignorance."

Her ladyship frowned as she rose. "You will adhere to my instructions or you will be dismissed."

She was still holding the book, but kept it at arm's length, as befit such a loathsome object. Sara nearly cried out when the woman moved to the hearth and tossed the volume onto the burning coals.

"So much for your *literature*, Miss Cobb."

Sara went directly to Ileana's room. The door was locked, so she scouted through the halls until she found a housemaid with a key. This time she knocked once, and then thrust the door open.

Ileana was seated at her writing desk. She looked up in shock when she saw Sara striding through the door.

"You little traitor," Sara uttered as she crossed the carpet. "Running to your mother like an infant. You come to me when you are sad or blue-deviled and expect me to lend a friendly ear. Well, let me tell you, this is not how a friend behaves."

Once she got closer, Sara realized the girl had been crying.

Great crimson welts stood out on her pale cheeks, and her swollen eyes were rimmed with red.

"You brought him here!" Ileana cried. "He hates me! I am sure you knew that."

I thought I did, Sara mused, until I saw how he looked at you, how he danced with you.

"I trusted you," Ileana added raggedly. "And you betrayed me. Is *that* how a friend behaves?"

"I'm sorry you saw it that way," Sara said in a gentler tone. "I only wanted you to grow accustomed to being in company with young men, since you haven't any brothers or male cousins about. I had the same problem, you see. No experience at bantering or flirting. So when I got to London—"

"You had a season?" Ileana asked with a wet sniffle of surprise.

"Why do you suppose your parents hired me? Do you think a green governess from Dorset would have known all the intricacies of the *ton*?"

"I don't suppose I ever did think about it. You seem to know everything—even about places you've never been. I assumed you'd got all your information about London from a book."

Sara smiled crookedly. "I am not quite that retentive . . . or omniscient."

"I suppose you're also angry that I showed Mama the novel you gave me."

"Your mother burned it," Sara said baldly. "*After* she pinned my ears back."

Ileana started crying even harder. "I am so sorry," she gulped. "I—I was angry at you . . . and . . . and I wanted to hurt you. I forgot how she can be so . . . so—"

"Icy?"

Ileana nodded. "And cutting. She always makes me feel like an absolute insect."

"Yes," Sara said. "I am feeling distinctly carpet beetle-ish at this moment."

Ileana gave a stuttering chuckle. "You shouldn't be nice to me, Miss Cobb. I played you a wicked turn."

"I'm still here," she said simply. "I imagine her ladyship's too busy right now with her dinner party plans to search out another governess."

"I don't want another governess," Ileana protested, and then startled Sara when she flew from her chair and wrapped her arms around her. "I want my own Miss Crab."

Sara tugged lightly on the girl's disarrayed hair. "Then the next time you are cross with me, Miss Brash Brashear, come to me with your complaints."

"I will," Ileana promised.

Sara was nearly back at the schoolroom before she realized this was the first time she'd not gone running to May Belle with a problem, but had confronted it head-on. A fair indicator that she was finally starting to handle things for herself at Tregallion House—Sir Kenneth put neatly in his place, Ileana in charity with her again, and Lady Brashear . . . well, two out of three, Sara reckoned, wasn't bad. She doubted anyone ever had the last word with her ladyship.

Chapter Ten

That Saturday brought the first of the Brashears' dinner parties. It was to be a small gathering of local dignitaries, including the mayor, the doctor, and the vicar. Sara had not been asked to join in the festivities.

She lay in bed that night eyeing the two lovely gowns hanging on the back of her bedroom door and wondering if she'd ever get to wear them. Her unguarded thoughts drifted to Gren Martyn . . . and whether he would approve of her in velvet. She immediately stifled these wayward musings. He'd not be allowed within a mile of the house during a dinner party. Or any other time, she thought. And a very good thing that was.

The next morning after church, Adeline again invited Sara for lunch. While Addie and Tris were distracted by the vicar, Ileana caught Sara by the arm and drew her aside.

"I wish you wouldn't go," she whispered. "I know they are your friends now, but Mama is so disapproving. I heard her talking to Father, and neither of them like it."

"The Spindles are hardly social outcasts," Sara pointed out. "And this is my afternoon off. I am at liberty to see whom I please."

The girl nodded sullenly. "I was hoping we could go riding together."

"We can ride tomorrow. You can tell your mother we're practicing for Rotten Row."

Ileana still didn't move away. "I don't know if Addie's told you," she said darkly, "but *he's* forever hanging about at Needs Barrow. My maid is walking out with the Spindles' groom. She's seen him there."

"I take it you are referring to Grenville Martyn."

Ileana gave a low hiss. "Of course. I don't like to think what would happen if you were to run into him."

He'd probably irritate me beyond words, Sara reflected.

"I believe I am safe," she drawled. "Mr. Spindle would protect me."

"That clodpole?" Ileana scoffed. "He's more likely to have his nose in a beaker of foul-smelling chemicals."

Sara had a sudden inspiration. "Why don't you come with me? No, don't start huffing and puffing. I take it they are the only respectable young people in the district. Isn't it time you mended fences with them?"

"*I* am not the one who broke off all contact," she said with great heat. "It was that toplofty boy who sent me away and told me never to come back."

"And that was, what? Six years ago? He can't bear that much of a grudge if he offered to teach you to dance?"

This did not serve to convince Ileana. She declared she would rather have a tooth pulled than spend even a minute in the company of Tristan Spindle, which got Sara thinking, as the Spindles' open carriage tooled along the coast road, that such heat on Ileana's part was hardly the result of total indifference. Maybe Tris had a chance with the girl after all.

Gren Martyn did not appear that afternoon, leaving Sara simultaneously relieved and disappointed. The Spindles did their best to entertain her, showing off Tris's various collections, with Addie making sly, teasing remarks whenever his enthusiasm carried him away. Which was frequently.

Tris drove her home again. As their carriage passed the lane to the Martyn farm, Sara said abruptly, "I'll get out here, if you don't mind. I think I need some time on the moor to walk off that rather fine lunch."

He glanced over his shoulder to the track in the heath and she feared he knew exactly what she intended. "Be careful," he said as she climbed down. "Quagmires out there, you know."

"You have no idea," she murmured.

He was turning the gig around when she called out on impulse, "I was wondering, Tristan, if you would you mind very much if I invited Ileana to come with me some Sunday?"

He thought a moment, his eyes fixed on a distant point, then looked down at her. "Very well. But only if she promises not to break anything."

Oh, Tris, I fear she's already put a sizeable crack in your heart.

Sara was winded by the time she reached the hill above Gren's farm. There was no smoke rising from the chimney today, but she could hear the din of hammering, the noise reverberating off the sloping sides of the hollow. She strode down the turf incline and went along the muddy lane. The fence rails were new, she noted. Not new wood, but sturdy old planks that had been crisply whitewashed. The mud heaves in the front yard had been graded, and there was now a path of yellow pebbles leading to the polished stoop. The front window gleamed and the door appeared to have suffered a fresh coat of paint.

Well, pigs will *fly*, she thought. No wonder she hadn't seen anything of him during her daily walks in the wood.

She found him in the shed, constructing what appeared to be a gate.

"Working on the Sabbath?" she said from the doorway.

He looked around, not seeming a bit surprised at the sight of her. "Don't say a word," he drawled as he set down a wooden level. "Not one word."

"Not even to compliment you?"

"Just so you know, I was fully intending to make some repairs before you started in haranguing me. I figured I'd better. The way things are going with that little business matter, I'm likely to be here until my dotage."

She leaned her shoulder against the door frame. "And that would be such a bad thing?"

"I happen to have plans, Miss Cobb. Unlike you, I itch to be out of the present and well into my future."

"Then why not put that business aside and just go?"

"It has occurred to me. But not one other soul seems to be troubling himself over the matter. You'd think the vicar in Penwreath or Lord Denby would light a fire under the local constables. Denby has the blunt to hire a whole battalion of Bow Street Runners."

"Perhaps no one's brought it to his attention."

He shook his head. "One of his own kitchen maids disappeared. A flighty little goose, she was, but she didn't deserve to be carried off."

Sara traced her finger over a fine piece of fruitwood veneer that was leaning beside her. "Have you thought of going to Plymouth, to the newspapers there? Get a public outcry going? In Dorset we had a landowner who kept increasing his tenants' rents to pay off his gaming debts. Before long, those poor people were being evicted left and right. Miss Bonnet wrote a number of editorials for our little paper, and the whole neighborhood ended up marching to the man's estate and demanding he let the cottagers return to their homes."

"That's called a riot, Miss Cobb. You're lucky the militia wasn't brought in."

"We were very peaceful," she said primly.

"We had the militia here last year when the mines started closing. The people of Penwreath marched on Tregallion House to protest, but Sir Kenneth had been forewarned. He'd put armed men at every gate. The villagers were so angry and frustrated, someone climbed the wall in the night and set fire to his carriage house."

She cocked one eye. "Someone?"

He grinned. "I'm not naming any names."

"How about Grenville Martyn and Lather Pitt?"

He shrugged. "Mere rumors. You know how they spread."

She stood there gazing up at his face, wondering at his brazen disregard for the law, and at the same time understanding that, in his own way, Gren Martyn was a better neighbor, a better human being, than the falsely pious Sir Kenneth or his hypocritical wife.

"What?" he said, coming forward rather than retreating from her scrutiny.

"You're an interesting man, Gren. And I don't necessarily mean that as a compliment."

"I could return the sentiment," he said, looking at her

through his furled brows. "Interesting and irritating. Rather like a rare tropical disease."

Sara laughed outright. "Shall I need to dose you with quinine?"

"No," he said, all his glibness suddenly gone. "There are some things a man needs to experience full out.

Sara tried for a light response—the open hunger in his eyes was too disturbing. "From what I've heard about you, you'll be immune soon enough."

He reached out one hand and traced the back of it over her cheek. "I don't know about that."

Sara felt her throat constrict. She suspected he was merely flirting with her—*full out*, to use his own words. But there was something else there, some vague promise in his gaze that was stirring up tiny embers of hope inside her.

Don't, she warned herself sternly. *He is a first-rate dallier, and you're an idiot if you believe even one word.*

"I nearly forgot. . . . I have something to give you," she said, hoping to break the tension between them.

"My neckerchief?"

Sara smiled to herself. His token was tucked away in her trinket box and there it would stay.

"No, this." She opened her reticule and drew out the handbill she'd stolen. She had been carrying it about with her, hoping to run into him.

"I went right into the Royal William and pulled it down," she boasted as she passed it over. "Nearly got caught. Even if the landlord of West Wind is not working with the procurers, this notice is dangerous. I thought taking it would prevent any more local girls from heading off to Plymouth,"

He sighed. "There are probably dozens of these, one at every inn along the coast. But at least you've protected the Penwreath girls for now. It wouldn't have occurred to me to do it."

She fought down a blush. "One thing puzzles me, though. How many farm girls would actually see this? Even if they knew how to read, what reason would they have for going into the inn?"

"They wouldn't need to read it. If only one person in the

village saw it and remarked on it to a neighbor, before long all of Penwreath would know there was work to be had in Plymouth."

"So, in effect, the whole village is responsible for sending Bessie off to her fate."

He nodded grimly. "You might say that."

"Then perhaps you could use that guilt to make them *do* something. Or to help you, at the very least. It seems to me, the more people you enlist, the greater your chance of catching these men."

"Except that the men are not in Penwreath. They work out of Truro and Plymouth and Bodmin . . . and only God knows how many other coaching towns."

Sara sighed deeply. "Talk about quagmires. I'm surprised you don't just stay in Plymouth then—you'd have a far better chance of catching them."

"And what would I live on?" he said with a frown. "What little I make comes from my birds."

Not *your* birds, she almost said. "You could hire yourself out as a carpenter," she suggested, motioning to the gate. It appeared sturdy and well-made. "You appear to know your way around a hammer and saw. I gather this is what you were apprenticed as in America."

He started to say something, but then scowled. "There are few hereabout with money to pay for a man's good labor," he pointed out. "And I thought you weren't going to meddle in my life."

"But—"

"Trust me, the less you know this business, the better. And now I need to get back to work."

Sara's heart sank. She managed to say lamely, "All I came for, really, was to give you the handbill."

He'd begun fiddling with the gate again and didn't even turn around when she left.

She cursed herself as she crossed the farmyard and headed for the lane. Once again she had angered him with her well-meant suggestions. What possessed her to think she could sway him into a lawful life? And more importantly, why should his choice of occupation matter to her? It was probably better this way, to be sent packing before she got even more attached to him. Much better, much safer, much—

"Hold up, Sara," he called. He was standing by the corner of the barn. "Let me get Cap and I'll give you a ride to Tregallion."

"Where have I heard that before?" she called back, her heart singing now. Odd, how the sun shined or set based on his attentions.

"I've got to see Lather in the village about ordering some lumber," he said when he came riding toward her. "I think it's time the chickens had a proper coop."

"And the goats?"

"The goats are squatters," he muttered as he swung her up behind him.

"You are a harsh landlord, Mr. Martyn," she said severely. "It would serve you right if I organized a mob of outraged barnyard animals to march on your farm and burn it to the ground."

He shifted around, his blue eyes dancing. "Promise?" he drawled.

She pinched him hard in the side until his laughter echoed through the hollow.

It came to Sara then, as she leaned her cheek against the strong, comforting blade of Gren's shoulder, that she was falling in love with him. Not a schoolgirl's notion of ideal love, but rather the sort that made her relish a man's laughter as much as his kisses, that saw every one of his flaws and allowed her to value him and care for him in spite of them.

They didn't say anything more during the short ride back. Sara kept her arms tight around him, even though he never urged the horse beyond a walk. She found herself pressing into his woolen coat until her whole upper body was molded to him. Brazen, she knew, but she couldn't help it. He felt solid and supple, his muscles wonderfully hard against her soft curves. There was more than novelty to the sensation—she feared she would crave that contact for the rest of her life. Ah, but he was a man itching to get on with his future, where she would have no part. That thought alone made her tighten her hold on him until she wondered how he could breathe.

Instead of taking her to the main entrance, Gren veered off before they reached the estate, winding through the woods on an overgrown trail.

"I'm taking you to the old wood carters' gate," he said. "There's no gatekeeper and the lock's been broken for donkey's years. I thought this would be more . . . discreet. You can follow the wagon ruts back to the house."

When they reached the rusted iron gate, he pulled up his horse. She felt his spine stiffen and reluctantly lowered her arms back. He didn't say anything for a time and she was aware that his whole body had tensed.

"Don't come to me again, Sara," he said without looking at her.

She didn't need to see his face to know that it was drawn into a tight frown. "No?" The word came out like a whimper.

"I've kept away. I expect you to do the same."

So, she thought, *that was that.* She'd meddled once too often and driven him off for good.

"Very well," she said raggedly, preparing to slide to the ground.

He did turn then, and grasped her by the wrist. "You *do* understand why, don't you?"

The misery in her eyes must have told him how very much she understood. But instead of looking at her with contempt, his own eyes blazed.

"Dammit," he growled under his breath.

In one fluid motion he'd caught her by the waist and swung her before him. The next instant his arms were locked around her and he was kissing her fiercely. Her lips, her cheeks, her throat. He thrust her bonnet back and kissed her brow and the tiny seam of skin where her hair was parted. She was drowning in his kisses, her breath stolen from her by the rapid pace of his assault.

When he claimed her mouth again, she clung to him, returning his kiss, mouth open and hungry. He groaned and then his tongue flicked against hers, deep and hot. She nearly swooned as heat soared up from deep in her belly.

"Sara," he crooned, nuzzling his rough chin along the line

of her jaw. "Don't you see? This is why. . . . This is exactly why."

He'd disengaged himself and lowered her to the ground before she could prevent it. She stood there reeling, clutching onto a handful of Cap's thick mane.

"We've got to stop this now. Because there isn't a prayer that it can work. You . . . me. You're gentry and I'm low-born . . . lower than you know."

"You said in Cornwall the lines are blurred."

"Blurred, but not invisible."

There was such finality in his voice. She waited, expecting him to ride away, but he sat there studying her, his expression almost angry.

Well then, she'd at least have her say.

"I don't care about any of that," she said, trying to keep a sob from her voice. "I don't know why you stir me as you do or why you are stirred by me, for that matter. But I do know that you are not one notch lower than me, not in any way."

He made no response. If anything, his jaw grew more taut.

"Of course you have the right to ride off and leave me—but don't use your class as an excuse."

He shrugged. "You're a complication I can't afford right now."

Sara nodded, even though the words had cut deep. "That's better. More honest."

"I didn't intend to hurt you." His gaze shifted away. "All I really wanted was to seduce you. But, as I said, it got complicated."

"No harm done," she said, trying to bolster herself with a show of pride. "A few kisses, a minor dalliance. The truth is, I never expected any different from you. Or anything more." She offered him an airy smile. "I'm afraid your reputation precedes you."

"Then consider yourself lucky to have escaped."

"Perhaps I do."

"It's far better this way." He leaned down, as he had that first day, and touched her chin. "And you'll be fine."

She wanted to toss her head like Ileana and let him see how

little he meant to her. Instead, she found herself whispering, "Watch out for yourself, Gren Martyn."

He collected his reins, his expression one of stern resolve. "I always do."

She didn't watch him ride off; she was too busy clinging to the bars of the rusted gate, trying not to cry. It was some solace that he wasn't letting her go because of her meddling. But every glimpse he'd offered her of what he really wanted to share with her was like a taste of heaven. How could all that glory be wrong? How could something so lovely be sinful?

At last she understood what May Belle had told her about a woman teasing a man until he lost all control. Gren had made sure to end things before that ever happened, curse him! The local libertine had suddenly—and unaccountably—turned honorable. She'd called up some innate decency in him, but instead of being gratified, she felt only a stinging pinion of regret.

Once she'd mastered her emotions, Sara slipped through the gate. It would soon be dusk, and she needed to find her way along the unfamiliar path before it grew dark.

The woods in this remote part of the estate were majestic but sparse—full of towering old-growth trees whose wide canopies had blocked out the sunlight and killed off bush and sapling below. She walked along, keeping religiously to the carters' lane, even though the mossy glades alongside her appeared tempting. She'd like to have laid her head on that velvety green carpet and had a proper cry. Except she suspected tears were beyond her. She'd drawn in on herself, turned parched and withered again, destroying all hope of normal release.

She stopped walking when she heard voices in the distance—the low baritone hum of men in quiet conversation, as though they feared being overheard. Sara crept closer, keeping behind the wider tree trunks, until she spied a large, disused woodshed in a small clearing.

There were two men near the open face of the shed—Sir Kenneth, mounted on one of his gleaming hunters, and a black-haired man on foot, holding the reins of a piebald cob.

Sara peered around the trunk of an oak, thankful her dark
pelisse provided some camouflage.

"'E's not 'appy," the black-haired man was saying. "The
goods 'aven't been the usual quality. Lank-haired, dull-eyed
skellingtons, that's what 'e calls 'em."

"These are harsh times in Cornwall," Sir Kenneth said.
"When the mines close, there is little food for man or beast."

"You're a mine owner, you know ovver mine owners. Get
'em to reopen the pits. Or lower your rents. Do somefing to put
the flesh back on these pitiful creatures. Or 'is nibs will go
elsewhere for . . . product."

Sara spun back out of sight, holding one fisted hand against
her mouth to keep from crying out. The two might have been
brangling over horses or cattle. Yet she was certain, beyond
any doubt, that the "product" they were discussing was young
women.

She risked another look, needing to commit the stranger's
features to memory. He was from London, she knew that much
from his speech. A very unsavory part of London. While she
watched, he turned in her direction to push away his horse's
questing nose. His face was slightly dished, as though in in-
fancy someone had flattened it with a board, and his short
black hair formed a fringe across his brow. Compared to the
strapping Sir Kenneth, he appeared almost willowy.

"I will speak to my people," Sir Kenneth now told him.
"See that they weed out the undesirables. There will be fewer
shipments, but I promise they will be of a higher quality."

"The quality always demands quality," the man jibed cryptically. "As you know."

"You can assure your master I will put things to rights at
once."

When the stranger mounted his horse, Sara quickly
crouched. She closed her eyes tight as he rode past her on the
track, barely a dozen feet away. She waited until she was sure
Sir Kenneth had ridden off before she resumed walking. Her
first instinct was to get Sadie and ride to Penwreath, to tell
Gren what she'd overheard. But even though this new wrinkle
would more than legitimize seeking him out, she couldn't face
him, not just yet.

Instead, she would write down everything she'd heard and seen, and send the note to Addie's care. Her friend would make sure it reached Gren's hands.

Sara was dazed and nearly spent by the time she staggered into the schoolroom. Far too much had happened in one short day. She'd discovered she was in love with Grenville Martyn only minutes before he severed all ties between them, *and* she'd learned that her employer was in league with the procurers who were stripping Cornwall of its young womanhood.

She didn't dare tell May Belle about Sir Kenneth, on the slim chance that she'd misjudged him. She couldn't tell a single soul about her feelings for Gren Martyn. Once again, she was reduced to expressing her deepest, most troubling thoughts in her journal.

But first, she had a letter to write.

Gren rode like a felon with a troop of militia on his tail. Cap lengthened his strides until man and beast were flinging over the ground, great clods of turf churning up in their wake. Damn the woman and her great mournful eyes. Damn her lissome arms that had been like a vise on his heart the whole way down from his farm. Damn her young, untried mouth and her rose-blushed cheeks. Double damn her wry bantering words that made sparring with her almost as pleasurable as kissing her. She wasn't a beauty, she wasn't alluring, and blast him if he'd ever met a woman who'd got such a firm hold on him. It was maddening.

He rode past Penwreath, out along the coast road, needing to wrestle with his demons before he was again in company with decent people. He'd wanted women before this and not burned himself to a hard cinder over it. There had been a girl in New York and another on shipboard coming home. Working young women with strong hands and a knowing look in their eyes. Proper young women who'd expected marriage after a few heated kisses. He'd read them like an atlas and kept away. So what if he'd tossed and turned in bed and bunk, wondering what he was missing? He'd never woken in a cold sweat, aching for an embrace, longing for a kiss, dying for a comforting word. Not like now.

Once he realized there were no solutions to his problem, save the obvious one he refused to even acknowledge, he walked his lathered horse back to Penwreath. He left Cap with an ostler and went striding into the Constant Star, pushing past his startled cousin. He needed a drink. Hell, he needed a whole bottle.

He never should have kissed her. It was his own fault for taking that one final taste before he set her aside for good. Only a nodcock would have indulged himself that way, as though he could have stopped with one kiss after he'd taken her in his arms. With Sara, need begat more need, hunger begat an insatiable appetite for the whole banquet. He knew he'd never have that completion with a respectable woman like Sara Cobb. So why in blazes had he let her stray so far into his life?

He pulled the cork from the whisky bottle with his teeth and filled a glass to the top. Blessed oblivion wouldn't be far behind. He was just about to down the entire glass when Lather sidled up beside him. "Brashear's carriage just went past," he said. "What odds he's on his way to Plymouth?"

Gren set down his drink, untouched. The best way to forget Sara Cobb was to get as far away from Penwreath as was possible. But before he could do that, he needed to finish up his work in Plymouth. This might be the chance he'd been waiting for, catching his enemy in the act.

"Get me a horse," he barked. "Cap's done-in."

Lather disappeared out the door. Gren raised the glass again, studying the dark amber liquid. In bright sunlight, Sara's eyes were the exact same shade.

God help me, he moaned silently, *I've turned into a blasted moonling.*

He took one long restorative swallow of the whisky, then set the glass down with a sharp clack.

Chapter Eleven

*T*hat same night, Sara sent Seth off to Needs Barrow with her note. It seemed fitting that the man who'd suffered the loss of a niece should play some part in bringing down the men who'd likely taken her.

She'd chosen her words carefully, not wanting Gren to think she was being fanciful or overwrought. It was imperative she set down only the things she had seen and overheard, and leave out any of her own conclusions. In a postscript she'd warned him, finally, about the mantraps. On her way back to the house, she'd seen a gamekeeper dragging a number of them into the woods on a sledge—great beastly things with their heavy chains dangling over the side.

Sir Kenneth's patience had clearly run out.

When she returned from the stable, she was agitated and could not relax. Some voice urged her to flee from this place. She knew the Spindles would take her in without hesitation. Yet she couldn't bear to leave Ileana. Amelie had deserted her, and Sara refused to do the same. After all, she wasn't in any real danger. And if it turned out that Sir Kenneth *was* involved with the vice peddlers, Ileana would need a friend close by. Sara couldn't picture Lady Brashear, stripped of her precious status, offering much consolation to her daughter.

If Sara's suspicions were correct, a nightmare would quickly ensue for the Brashears. Ileana would never have a season in London, the house would likely be closed up, and, although she was a little vague on the law in this case, Sara imagined Sir Kenneth would land in prison along with his confederates. Rank only protected a man so far.

She again wondered how Sir Kenneth profited from this wretched business. It seemed to her a great many girls would need to be sent to London to balance out the risk. Gren would know the answer, she was sure, but she no longer had the right to ask him. He'd been gone from her life for less than four hours, yet it felt like years.

At least she now knew why he had remained in Penwreath—he must have somehow connected Sir Kenneth, the man who'd condemned his brother, with the missing girls. Once again, she regretted not going after him and telling him about the dish-faced man. Gren might have been able to catch up with him before he left the district. Together, he and Sara wouldn't have had much trouble getting the fellow to implicate Sir Kenneth, especially if they brought Lord Denby into things.

Now Sara could do nothing but wait and fret. And ache.

The next morning when Ileana remarked that her father had gone to Plymouth for a few days, Sara was not surprised. It only served to corroborate her suspicions. She only hoped Gren had gotten her note in time to follow him. Hard upon this thought came her fears for his safety, one lone man going up against God knew how many hardened scoundrels.

No, Sara reminded herself, she no longer had the right to worry—she meant nothing to him beyond a passing conquest. She would make doubly sure he meant nothing to her.

"You are very distracted this morning," Ileana complained, looking up from a book of dress patterns.

"Is your father a fair man, do you think?"

Sara had spoken without gauging the prudence of her question, and the girl's face clouded in bewilderment.

"I've heard some talk in Penwreath," Sara explained quickly. "The villagers were angry when he closed the mines. I was wondering what you thought about that and about your father in general. You rarely speak of him."

"He wants little to do with me," she said with a tiny shrug. "He would certainly never discuss his business interests with me. I'm told I chatter mindlessly . . . like a magpie."

"Did he discuss these things with Amelie?"

Ileana got up from the window seat and moved to the edge of Sara's desk. "Amelie had few kind feelings toward our father," she said. "I never knew why. I was rarely home in those days, though she did tell me once she would kill to get out of his house."

Sara's eyes widened. Was it possible the girl had stumbled onto her father's nasty secret?

"I take it she was schooled at home."

"Mmm. She attended school in Truro for a time, but when she went on report once too often, Father brought her back to Tregallion. She had two different governesses then, Miss Durbin and Miss Castlereigh. I was terribly envious . . . both of them so pretty and gay. Not like the sour old spinsters at Miss Bonnet's school." She shot Sara a mischievous grin. "The odd thing is, both of them disappeared."

Sara had seen this coming. "Disappeared how?"

"They just vanished overnight. Miss Durbin took a few of her personal effects, but left most of her gowns behind. Miss C. took almost everything, but neither of them left a note or a message. I heard that Amelie cried for days when Miss Durbin disappeared. It was odd, though—she seemed rather grim after Miss C. left, but not at all grieved."

"You were home from school then?"

"Yes, it happened over Christmas. Mama declared that Amelie would have no more vagabond governesses and took on schooling her herself. My sister was months away from her comeout, so it didn't really matter."

Sara stabbed at a possibility. "And her coolness toward your father, did it begin before or after Miss Durbin disappeared?"

"After," Ileana said; then her expression darkened. "You don't believe she thought Father had anything to do with it?" She looked down at her twisted hands. "Oh, I know what they whisper about him and Mrs. Holcroft. But even if he's keeping a mistress, that doesn't mean he's likely to chase after every available female in the house. If anything, that would discourage him."

Ileana's logic was sound. Except that it hadn't discouraged

her father, as Sara knew from personal experience. The man still gave her chills.

"I am just trying to account for the missing governesses. You might say I have a legitimate interest."

"Well, if you must know, Amelie's feelings for Father changed around the time he had Gren Martyn's brother arrested. She apparently pleaded with him to withdraw his charges."

"But he refused."

She nodded. "Amelie was distraught . . . and so angry at him."

Sara could imagine. Her friend's brother taken away in chains and her own father the sole witness against him. No wonder Amelie had turned to Gren for solace when he came back to Penwreath. They'd each lost someone close to them.

"There are rumors that the charges were trumped up," Sara said.

Ileana's eyes flashed. "Those Martyns always had the villagers on their side. But I know what Gren Martyn did to Amelie. Hard to credit after they'd been friends as children. But Mama said that's what comes from consorting with the lower classes."

"And so the second governess disappeared after Jacob Martyn was hanged?"

"Yes," she said. "Four months later, as I recall. Though what the one event has to do with the other, I cannot imagine."

Sara suspected that link might explain volumes, and later that night she tried to piece together the things Ileana had told her.

Amelie was grieved when her first governess vanished, but merely grim when Miss C. left. The first one took no gowns, the second packed up everything. It sounded to Sara as though Miss Durbin had been lured away and Miss Castlereigh spirited away.

And who could have lured a pretty, lively governess from a comfortable position? Most likely a man who could offer her her pick of wealthy gentleman protectors. A man like Sir Kenneth Brashear. He'd made practically the same offer to Sara, though he'd couched it in such nebulous terms she'd thought he was referring to finding her a prosperous husband.

She didn't think that any longer.

So, she continued her mental tally, Miss Durbin ran off, Jacob Martyn was hanged, and Gren Martyn returned to Penwreath, determined to clear his brother *and* find out why the local farm girls were vanishing.

Sara wondered if Gren had suspected Sir Kenneth's involvement with the vice peddlers and mentioned it to Amelie. Amelie might have then concluded her father was responsible for the first governess's disappearance. And if the new governess also appeared to be at risk, the two friends could have arranged for her to leave the house in secret.

It was all starting to make sense now, Sara thought smugly. From one conversation overheard in the woods and a bit of prodding at Ileana, she was finally drawing all the lose threads together. It was a pity she no longer had the option of discussing it with Gren; he might be unwilling to volunteer any answers, but he'd surely have corroborated the ones she'd figured out herself.

She was just dozing off, when the gaping flaw in her logic rose up like a specter and jolted her awake. If Amelie had indeed conspired with Gren to thwart her father and rescue Miss Castlereigh, it didn't make any sense that six months later she was accusing him of attacking her—effectively giving her father the ammunition to destroy Gren just as he'd destroyed Jacob.

Sara's imaginary house of cards came tumbling down. And soon after, all her certainty about Sir Kenneth's involvement with the missing girls began to evaporate. The dish-faced man's mention of lank-haired, dull-eyed skeletons referred to nothing more sinister than horses or sheep. After all, at no time had either man spoken of young girls, even though there had been little need to guard their tongues in that secluded corner of the estate.

Feeling utterly miserable, and a fool to boot, Sara rolled over and thrust her face into the pillow. What she needed to do, rather than waste time sorting out a problem that did not affect her, was to begin advertising for a new position. March would

be here before she knew it, and she'd be gone from Penwreath—and Gren Martyn—forever.

Sara had no way of knowing whether Gren had acted on her
note and the anxiety was driving her to fits. Clearly, she
needed a major diversion. She decided to take Ileana on a
morning call to Needs Barrow, which would give her a chance
to assess her charge in company. She absolutely swore that she
had no ulterior motive; she would not ask the Spindles a single word about the errant poacher. Furthermore, if they happened to bring up his name, she would demonstrate only the
barest minimum of polite interest.

Of course, Ileana balked at first. Sara expected it after the
debacle of the dance lesson. She patiently explained to the girl
that it was unnatural for her to have no friends or confidantes
in the neighborhood.

"I have you," Ileana pointed out.

"A warden, whipper-in and general dogsbody does not
qualify as a friend."

Ileana sniffed, but her eyes were merry. "I fear you are not
getting paid sufficient if you are required to be all those things
to me."

"There's not enough gold in the kingdom to compensate
me," Sara drawled, and then laughed. Ileana was turning into
an adept sparring partner, a skill that would greatly improve
her chances of impressing the London wags.

Sara finally prevailed, as she had assumed she would.
She'd begun to suspect that Ileana was envious of her outings
to Needs Barrow and wanted badly to be part of them.

Ileana ordered up her mother's barouche and they set out
under a bright blue sky in the elegant, well-sprung carriage.
Sara purposely turned her head away as they passed the lane to
the Martyn farm and distracted herself by pointing out some
commonplace feature of the landscape to her companion.

Addie received them in her small comfortable parlor, settled them both on a sofa and then rang for tea and cake.

"It's such a pleasure to have you here again," Addie said to
Ileana. "Time was, you used to poke into every corner of the

house, your eyes wide and full of wonder. Aladdin's cave you called it."

"I was quite young," Ileana said, frowning down at the tatty throw cushion beneath her arm. "And I believe children have very little discrimination of taste."

Sara turned to goggle at her. What happened to her wry, charming pupil? Ileana had transformed into a miniature version of her mother, icy disdain and all.

"It *is* a rather unorthodox house," Addie said, clearly trying to make the best of her guest's stinging comment.

"Mama says it used to be the bailiff's cottage . . . on a much larger estate."

"The dower house," Addie amended. "For Regal Bluffs, which burned down in the last century. But Needs Barrow suits us."

"I suppose some people don't require much."

Sara quickly leaned forward. "Shall we see your brother today?" she asked, hoping to turn the conversation to a less perilous subject.

"He should be along any time now. He went to the Martyn farm to look after the chickens."

"Why?" Ileana asked archly. "Is Mr. Martyn too busy poaching my father's birds to take care of his own?"

"Ileana!" Sara cried. She was inches away from boxing the girl's ears.

Ileana turned to her with a pout of injured innocence. "Well, it's true, isn't it? Everyone says that truth is paramount, but whenever you attempt to speak it, people just glare at you."

"Mr. Martyn is away for a few days," Addie explained smoothly. Sara gave her points for diplomacy—and monumental restraint.

The conversation drifted to a halt after that; the three sat and fidgeted with the folds of their gowns. Sara was going to suggest it was time they left when Tristan came into the hall.

"We're in here," Addie called out. Sara imagined she was rolling her eyes in relief.

Tris was dressed in his usual simple country garb, but the ride across the moor had disordered his dark locks in a most appealing fashion. He appeared windblown and flushed and quite possibly the answer to every schoolgirl's dream of romance.

"Miss Cobb," he said, bowing—which he'd never done during any of Sara's previous visits. "And Miss Brashear, the queen of the ballroom. Broken anyone's toes lately?"

Ileana showed her teeth. "Ah, Mr. Spindle, king of sea and sand. A pity the tide still hasn't carried you off with all the other flotsam."

"I think I'd prefer to be jetsam," he said as he approached her.

"It doesn't matter what you call it—it's all debris to me."

He raised one brow. "I didn't know you had poetical inclinations, Miss Brashear."

"No, my inclinations are rather more departural."

"Oh don't leave us, pray. I consider it a service to the whole neighborhood to keep you here—and out of the homes of the faint-hearted and unsuspecting."

Addie motioned to Sara and they both crept out of the parlor. Sara doubted either Ileana or Tristan even noticed.

"That's what it was always like between them," Addie whispered as she led Sara to the library. "They would tease each other viciously and then be laughing the next minute."

"Still, Ileana was unforgivably rude to you at first. And I can't imagine why."

"Sara, she was nervous. Trust me—I was seated across from her and saw her face go all pinched and ghostly the instant she sat down. Plus, I think I've always made her a trifle uneasy. I am two years older than Tris, so I must have seemed ancient to her."

"I know the feeling," Sara muttered.

They settled on opposite sides of a cushioned window seat, both gazing out at the cove.

"So, do you think he's safe?" Sara asked after a time.

"Why wouldn't he be? Plymouth is not exactly the Barbary Coast."

"Plymouth?" she echoed blankly. "I was talking about Tristan, alone with my baby asp."

Addie laughed. "Forgive me. I was woolgathering and my first thought was that you were referring to Gren."

Sara forced herself to stick to her promise. "I would hardly be asking you about someone I've known such a short time."

Her friend gave her a cagey look. "No, but you'd be sending messages to him through me."

Sara shrugged with what she hoped was casual disregard. "Oh that? It was just a warning. I wanted him to spread the word that Sir Kenneth was putting out mantraps. For obvious reasons, I couldn't send any of the Brashears' servants to his farm. You know the politics hereabouts."

"Mmm, I do. I also know when a friend is telling me a galloping farradiddle." When Sara blushed, Addie quickly said, "No, no. I never pry. You'll tell me or you won't. But I *would* like to relate a curious sequence of events to you. How is it that the same day you went walking down the lane to Gren's farm—yes, Tris did mention that to me—you also sent us a note to pass on to him? And isn't it odd that we received a message from the Constant Star that night, saying that Gren was heading off to Plymouth and would we please grain the chickens?"

"Coincidence?"

"Poppycock."

Sara grinned. "And you never pry. . . ."

"Only when forced to."

"Well, there's nothing to tell. *I* think we should return to Beatrice and Benedick. In case there's blood to mop up."

"Or nice simmering pools of vitriol," Addie said as they went out into the hall.

The two women were still laughing as they came through the parlor door. Their timing couldn't have been worse.

Tristan, now standing before the fire, had just handed Ileana the large crystal that had pride of place on the mantel. As she shifted around at the unexpected sound, she bobbled it. Her eyes widened in disbelieving horror as it crashed to the fieldstone hearth and broke into a dozen glittering fragments.

All four of them stood staring at the scattered bits; then Ileana cried, "Sorry . . . I'm so sorry. I must be going. I *really* must be going."

She fled across the room, right past Sara, and out into the hall. Two seconds later, the front door slammed.

"Oh, Tris," Addie said hollowly as she came forward and knelt to collect the pieces. "I know this was one of your favorites. But I promise you she didn't mean it this time."

"I know," he said, casting a stricken look at the door. "I believe she was actually trying to show some interest in all my odd bits. What dashed bad luck."

Then he too went striding from the room, and a moment later they heard his boot tread on the stairs. Sara wondered if he'd been referring to the loss of the stone, or to Ileana running off in distress.

"I suppose I'd better take her home," she said to Addie, then added ruefully, "Maybe the next time we visit, you can serve us hemlock instead of tea. It couldn't make things any worse."

Addie walked her to the front door. "Sara, what's Gren really involved in? I'm truly not asking for personal details about the two of you. I just need to know if he's in any danger."

"It's funny—I keep thinking I should ask you or Tristan the same thing. All I know is that he's been looking into the girls who've gone missing."

Addie's face clouded. "Never say he's suspected in any of that."

She shook her head. How could she tell her friend that the only woman who'd gone missing from Gren Martyn's life was Sara Cobb?

Ileana was already waiting in the carriage, sitting stiffly upright, her perfect face marred by two blotches of crimson. Sara climbed in and sat down beside her.

"No one blames you," she said as the carriage moved off. "Everyone knows it was an accident."

"So you've heard about the first time? That silly shell?"

"Tristan told me. Hard to believe a rift in a friendship could happen over something so small."

"They were Amelie's friends, never mine."

"I'm not surprised, not if you spoke to them then the way you did today. Lucky for you Addie is a gracious hostess who can overlook certain lapses. I'm not sure you'll be as fortunate in London."

"London!" Ileana cried bitterly, half rising out of her seat. "How can I go to London? I am clumsy and gauche . . . and rude. I open my mouth and the most horrid things come out. And when I try to control it, it just get worse and worse. Tristan seems the only one who doesn't mind, but that's because he's as awkward as I am around people."

"Tris isn't awkward, exactly. He's more eccentric."

"And we were just starting to be civil to one another when I dropped that wretched crystal. He hates me again, you'll see. And who can blame him? I am exactly like that crystal, quite fine to look at, but cold and sharp-edged and . . . and—"

"Easily damaged?" Sara said gently.

Ileana started to weep into her handkerchief. "Yes . . . and I want to be brave and strong and sure of myself, the way Amelie was. The way you are, Miss Cobb."

Sara started back. "I'm hardly any of those things."

"You are . . . to me you are. You stood up to my tantrums and my sulks. You smuggle books to me you know Mama would never approve. I hear you've even got that skulking Holcroft in a pet. No, you are the only person I trust, dear Miss Cobb, and I don't ever want to lose you." She looked up over the crumpled square of linen. "I am going to ask Father if you can come to London as my companion. Then we shall never have to be apart."

Sara's throat constricted at the thought of endless months spent under the leering eyes of Sir Kenneth and under the harsh critical tongue of his wife.

What on earth had she reaped?

Chapter Twelve

Sir Kenneth returned home the day after Ileana's visit to Needs Barrow, to the general relief of the household. Lady Brashear had scheduled a lavish dinner at the end of the week, with a shooting party for the gentlemen to follow the next morning. Lord Denby would be there, as well as several notables from Bodmin and Plymouth.

Sara first learned of this from May Belle, who was busy preparing her kitchen for the siege. To Sara's surprise, Ileana told her she would be expected to attend, since there looked to be a surplus of gentlemen.

"And," the girl announced breathlessly, "I've prevailed upon Mama to invite the Spindles. I pointed out that I would be forced to spend the entire evening listening to Father's hunting cronies natter on about foxhounds and six-bar fences—pure punishment, as you can imagine—unless she could furnish me with a few guests closer to my own age."

"So you decided to offer Tristan the olive branch—again?"

Ileana hitched one shoulder. "This might be my only chance to apologize for my clumsiness. I seriously doubt I'll ever be in company with him or his sister once I am wed."

Sara was enlisted to gather flowers from the conservatory and oversee the rearranging of the drawing room furniture, where dancing was to take place after supper. These simple tasks took her mind off her own worries, and she found herself actually looking forward to a bit of festivity in a house that had begun to feel like the tomb of buried dreams.

The night of the party, she returned to her room after a lingering bath in May Belle's parlor and donned the amber velvet gown. She recalled what the dressmaker had said about her hair and finally settled on a loose topknot, with a few tendrils softening the line of her jaw. Finally, she drew her one adornment, a gold locket, from her trinket box, touching Gren's neckerchief wistfully before she closed the lid. There was no chance she would see him tonight, but she had dressed for him alone.

In the tiny mirror, she smudged a thin line of charcoal beneath her eyes, a trick she had learned from Miss Bonnet of all people, who'd vowed it turned Sara's eyes the color of gold. She dapped on a bit of plum-colored salve, a gift from Ileana, rationalizing that a woman past the first blush of youth was allowed to augment nature just a little.

These small embellishments must have made a remarkable difference; every footman she passed on her way to the salon turned to goggle at her. She discovered the reason when she came to a large mirror on the landing and happened to glance at herself.

Miss Prake had recut the bodice of the gown to meet with the current fashion. Sara goggled a bit herself at the sight of her breasts rising above the bead-worked bodice. She was about to race back to her room to fetch a tucker, when Sir Kenneth came along the hallway.

"Stunning, Miss Cobb," he pronounced. "You'll cast every woman here into the shade."

"Hardly, sir," she said, her jaw tensing.

He stood there examining her, his head tipped back. "You must come with us to Plymouth when we take Ileana to the winter assemblies. As I mentioned, there are gentleman there who would be delighted to make your acquaintance."

"That is very kind," she said. "But I fear I do not do well in company."

Just then her ladyship came sweeping out of the west wing, attired in a confection of cerulean satin and Belgian lace, and complaining of something to her husband. She bypassed Sara as though she were invisible.

Sara tried to keep out of Sir Kenneth's way in the salon, falling into conversation with Mr. Ivey and his plump wren of a wife. Ileana found two young people to talk to, the son and daughter of a baronet from Bodmin. The young man, spotty-faced and raspy-voiced, didn't look to give Tristan much competition, even though he could barely take his eyes off Ileana. When the Spindles arrived, they too were drawn into this group. Ileana became noticeably animated and focused all her attention on the spotty youth.

Interesting, Sara thought. And very transparent.

Lord Denby entered the room to a hum of acknowledgement and Sara turned from the vicar to observe him. Tall and hook-nosed, his gray-black hair thinning at the temples, he was attired in an elegant suit of brocaded silk that could have easily graced the courts of Whitehall. More interesting to Sara was the man at his side, a gentleman of perhaps sixty years, with the brawny shoulders of a pugilist and a thick mane of snowy white hair. His eyes gleamed with shrewd intelligence.

"That's Sir Robert Poole, the reformer," Mr. Ivey whispered to Sara. "Down from London. Denby's been showing him around the district. They stopped at my church earlier today. Wanted to talk about serving girls or some such thing."

Sara swung around to him. "Missing serving girls?"

Mr. Ivey shook his head. "No, teaching serving girls to read. Poole's got it into his head that we need to send both sexes to school."

"You forget I am a teacher, Mr. Ivey. I have to agree with Sir Robert."

The vicar smiled wanly. "I know, can't stand in the way of progress. If one can call it that."

Sara saw Sir Kenneth coming toward them. She quickly excused herself and began strolling about the room, staying one jump ahead of her employer and catching only snippets of conversations.

"Ileana's in fine looks. She'll outshine her mother, mark my words."

"I believe I recognize that fellow with Denby, some politician or other. Can't fathom why he'd bother himself with Cornwall."

And from two stylish young matrons: "I see the Spindles are out in company for a change."

"But did you see the coach they drove up in? Quite horridly decrepit, wasn't it?"

"Quite. Though I wouldn't mind being . . . um, driven . . . by that tall coachman. Utterly delicious." Both women tittered behind their fans.

Sara turned to stare at them as she reached a sickening conclusion. She went at once to Tristan and separated him from the others, drawing him to a secluded corner.

"Are you mad? Is *he* mad? A *coachman*?"

Tris shook his head. "Gren's just got back from Plymouth, and he apparently needs to talk to you. I may not be awake to every pursuit, Miss Cobb, but it occurs to me that you and Gren have formed some sort of . . . alliance. Something to do with this havey-cavey business he's always so secretive about."

"I am not involved with him in any manner," she assured him. "And how does he propose to deliver his message—sneak into the dining parlor dressed as a footman?"

Tristan grinned. "Wouldn't put it past him. Still, he'll find a way."

He led Sara back to where the others were animatedly discussing Walter Scott's latest book, but she was too distracted to participate—or to notice the series of dark looks Ileana kept casting at her, right until supper was announced.

Addie maneuvered beside Sara as the guests starting moving toward the door. "You've put your pupil's nose out of joint," she said under her breath. "Though I don't wonder you haven't noticed—you look a million miles away."

Sara scowled. "I'm worried, Addie. How could you have let Gren risk his neck like this? You are supposed to be the *sane* one."

"How dreadfully dull," Addie said. "And as for Gren Martyn, it would take a better woman than I to curb him. I am hardly my brother's keeper."

"He's not your brother," Sara said irritably. "And now I suppose I will have to slip outside at some point and meet with that vexing man. Is he waiting in the stable, do you think?"

Addie grinned. "Probably a lot closer than that. If I know Gren, he'll find *you*."

Sara gave a tiny grunt of displeasure. "It's not what you're thinking. I promise you there is nothing between Gren Martyn and myself."

Addie made no response, but her eyes continued to dance mischievously.

After an interminable meal where Sara fretted through each course—and kept staring fiercely at every footman who entered the room—the guests moved to the drawing room, where the carpet had been removed for dancing. A five-piece orchestra had set up at one end, and couples quickly formed on the polished parquet floor. Sara withdrew to a shadowed corner, watching as Ileana took her place for a country reel with the baronet's spotty-faced son. He was an awkward partner, and since Ileana was not well-versed in the steps, they frequently collided with the other dancers.

Tristan was hovering at the edge of the room, but when the next set began forming, he approached Ileana and virtually dragged her onto the floor. Sara saw him mouthing instructions to the girl, guiding her through the complicated steps.

Good for Tris, she thought. He hadn't given up on his chosen partner—not like some men she could name.

Lady Brashear, seated beside another elegant matron, caught sight of Sara and abruptly motioned her over. With a sinking feeling, Sara hurried toward her.

"A pity that gown does so little for your coloring," her ladyship remarked after studying Sara for a long, uncomfortable moment. "Then again, I mustn't forget it was fashioned to complement a young girl with fair hair." She leaned to her companion and said, not quite sotto voce, "I vow, Delia, one despairs of ever finding a governess who might actually be a credit to one's family."

"Can I get you anything, ma'am?" Sara asked between her teeth, aware that the color suffusing her cheeks was no blush, but the red heat of anger.

Lady Brashear sent her off to the punch bowl, the very last place she wanted to be since Sir Kenneth and Lord Denby stood conversing directly behind the refreshment table. Sara was forced to linger there, while the vicar's wife fussed with the punch ladle.

"You're to be commended," his lordship was saying. "In these lean times it's not every man who can offer such a charming entertainment. Not sure I could manage it m'self."

Sir Kenneth made an expansive motion. "A man's got to keep up appearances. And I wanted to give my girl a bit of a local send-off. She's to have her comeout this spring, as you know."

Denby leaned closer. "Your mines are prospering, then?"

He shrugged. "We haul out more rock than ore these days. I'm sure it's the same with your own mines." He paused, his eyes sweeping over Sara. She was about to move away, punch-less, until she heard his next words.

"I did have a notion that supplying mounts to the cavalry might bring in some extra blunt. I bought up a farm between here and Plymouth. But the only beasts I've been able to purchase are weedy things, undersized and without spirit. Now my buyer in London is threatening to cancel his orders."

Sara snatched up a half-filled glass of punch and spun away from the table in shock. The words "lank-haired, dull-eyed skellingtons" echoed ominously in her head. She must find Gren, tell him she was completely mistaken about Sir Kenneth and the dish-faced man. She returned to Lady Brashear in a daze and thrust the glass into her hands.

Tristan was nearby chatting with the vicar, but when he saw Sara's stricken face, he quickly disengaged himself. "What's wrong?"

"You must find Gren," she said urgently. "Tell him to meet me on the terrace in ten minutes."

Tris nodded once and went off.

Ten minutes later, Sara was standing near one of the French windows, every so often peering over her shoulder out into the darkness. The baronet's son came by and asked her to dance; she declined with a smile. Finally she cracked the door open and slipped outside. The night air was cool but not unwelcome, especially after the closeness of the drawing room.

Sara moved silently across the flagstones to the waist-high balustrade that overlooked the back garden. The lights from the house spilled a dozen feet beyond the terrace, to the point where rosebushes gave way to a small grove of apple trees. Beyond the edge of the trees, all was in darkness.

"Grenville!" Sara called softly. "Are you out there?"

She listened intently and thought she heard something moving through the trees. Probably not Gren, not if she could hear him. She was about to give up and go back inside, when the door behind her opened. A man came across the flags, tall and broad—and Sara had to bite back a cry of alarm.

"Dashed stuffy in there," Sir Kenneth said, fanning himself with one hand. "I don't blame you for sneaking out. It appears we are of a like mind."

"I must go back," Sara said. "Your wife will need me to re-fill her punch glass."

"My wife has lackeys to fetch for her."

Yes, and I am one of them, Sara nearly retorted.

"It's delightful that we can steal this moment away from the others," he murmured, attempting to take up her hand.

Sara placed both hands behind her on the balustrade—not a prudent move, since he closed in and slipped one arm about her waist. She smelled brandy on his breath. A great vaporous cloud of it.

"Sir Kenneth," she said stiffly, "this is hardly a fitting place."

"You've somewhere better in mind, my dove?" he purred, angling his body into hers.

Sara was about to thrust him away when an apple came plummeting out of the sky and bounced off his forehead with a hollow *bonk*.

He drew back with a startled cry. "What the devil!"

Sara had to smother her laughter. "Birds," she said, trying her utmost to stay serious. "Jackdaws carrying fruit from the garden."

"Jackanapes, more likely." He leaned far out over the balustrade. "You there—show yourself! I order you to come out."

During his momentary inattention, Sara quickly retreated back to the drawing room, thinking she owed Gren Martyn yet another debt of thanks—even if he were quite mad.

As she came through the French window, she nearly collided with Sir Robert Poole, who hastily begged pardon. Sara was a little awed—not by his rank, so much, but by his robust energy which seemed to enliven the very air around him.

"They say you are a reformer, sir," she remarked, once they'd introduced themselves.

He shot her a wry smile. "Yes, they do say that. Though there is most usually a very strong expletive placed before the word 'reformer.' "

Sara grinned back. "Since I have myself on occasion been called an *infernal* governess, you have all my sympathy."

They fell into easy conversation after that and Sara soon grew bold enough to bring up the trouble in Penwreath. "I wonder, sir, if you have heard anything of the young women who have gone missing from this district?"

He cocked his head. "Not a word. Though I will tell you, it's not uncommon in an area that has lost its industry for the younger people to go off to work in the cities."

"They don't just go off," she said in a low voice. "They are never heard from again. I've only just come to Penwreath, but I believe this has been happening for years."

He squeezed her hand briefly. "I must go—Lord Denby is beckoning to me. Some tedious political business, no doubt. But we are to overnight here for several days. Perhaps you and I can discuss this further in the morning. It's a troubling notion . . . most troubling."

Sara watched him stride off, still a little breathless at her own temerity. If Sir Kenneth was not behind the disappearances, that meant someone else in the district was. And there was nothing like a London muckraker to get to the bottom of things. She only wished she could find Gren and tell him what she'd set in motion.

Since she dared not risk the terrace again, she decided to go back to her room and write another note for Tristan to pass along. Much safer, in any number of ways, than seeking Gren out in person.

She was nearly at the door of the drawing room, when Ileana caught up with her.

"Where are you running off to?"

"My room," Sara said. "I—I've torn my hem."

"I must speak with you!" The girls eyes were shooting angry sparks, but Sara was too distracted pay her much mind. "You see, I've discov—"

"Tell me later," Sara said, setting her aside firmly. "I promise I won't be long."

With a swift smile of apology, she brushed past the girl.

As Sara approached the schoolroom, she was alarmed to see a band of light showing under the door. She opened it slowly and peered around the edge.

Gren Martyn was angled back in her chair, his long legs crossed on the desktop. He was dressed all in black: a long coachman's coat over a suit of broadcloth with an ebony kerchief knotted at his throat. His topboots gleamed in the light of a single candle.

Her open journal lay facedown on the blotter where she'd left it that afternoon. She fervently hoped he hadn't read any of her recent entries.

"Has Sir Kenneth recovered?" he asked with a wicked smirk as she came into the room. "Lord, I've been wanting to do that for ages. Pity I wasn't standing in a melon patch."

Sara refused to be charmed. "I cannot believe you snuck into this house. Are you purposely courting the gallows?"

He shrugged. "Man's got to be courting something." He pushed back from the desk and stood up. His eyes narrowed as he studied her, lingering somewhere in the vicinity of her bodice. "And on that note, let me express my admiration for your . . . gown. It never looked half so good on Amelie."

Sara set her chin. "I won't be cozened, Gren. Not now, not any longer. I thought you'd decided to stop wandering in—and then out—of my life."

"Maybe I can't help it," he said, half under his breath. "Maybe that fatal charm you once spoke of is your own." He raised his brows expectantly.

When her frosty manner didn't thaw, he frowned. "Ah, I see I've fallen from your favor, Miss Crab. And yet you smuggle notes to my farm and ask me to meet you on the terrace. You can't blame a man for getting his thoughts in a tangle after that."

"Nothing's changed," she assured him. "And even though I was not the one who insisted we keep apart, I'm more than willing to adhere to that arrangement. Something's come up, however, something you ought to know."

"What?"

"I gather you came to Tregallion to ask me about the note I sent you. But I was mistaken about Sir Kenneth, so you can just disregard it. He and the dish-faced man were discussing horses—"

"The devil they were."

"It's true. Tonight I heard him tell Lord Denby of a recent scheme to sell mounts to the cavalry. He claimed all the beasts around here were weedy and without spirit, and that his London buyer was complaining."

Gren mulled this over. "And you never once heard him refer to 'girls' while he was talking to the man by the wood-shed?"

She shook her head. "And yet the tone of their conversation was quite . . . clandestine. Almost as though they were speaking in code." She sighed. "It appears I have finally developed an imagination after all."

He grinned. "It's something in the air here."

"I know you went to Plymouth, and I'm sorry if it was me that sent you there on a wild goose chase."

"I went before I got your note. I was at the Constant Star when Sir Kenneth's coach drove past. I rode after him and followed him into town—and again discovered nothing."

"Again? You mean you've followed him there before?"

Gren looked a trifle put out. "You weren't supposed to know that. I really don't want to involved you in any of this, Sara. So no more eavesdropping, if you please. Sooner or later, it's bound to land you in trouble."

He gathered up the long coachman's whip, which was lying on the desk. "I'd best get back to the stable . . . where I belong."

A sudden panic swept over Sara. She ran to him as he

reached the door. "Be careful, Gren. Sir Kenneth has men posted all over the house tonight."

He shrugged off her concern. "Not in this wing he doesn't. I came up an old stairwell. . . . It rises from an ivy-covered outer door no one ever uses. Amelie showed it to me years ago."

Sara didn't care to think about him creeping into this schoolroom for assignations.

He took a step closer. "When we were children," he said.

He was inches away from her now, his strength and vital masculinity almost perceptible. She saw the expression of restraint tugging at his eyes, tightening his jaw, and she realized, perhaps for the first time, how difficult it was for him to leave her.

It was all she could do not to drag him back into the room, wrap her arms around him and keep him there forever. But since he'd made no actual overtures toward her, save a few sly verbal taunts, she grew flustered—and a little disgruntled.

"You'd better go," she whispered raggedly.

"Aren't you going to thank me first?"

"For what?"

"For not reading your journal." He nodded toward her desk. "I admit I was sorely tempted."

Her chin thrust up. "Trust me, there's nothing in there that could interest you."

"No? Perhaps you're right. Perhaps there was no point in reading it. . . ." His hand stroked over her cheek for an instant as he leaned in close and whispered, "Not when I see all the answers in your eyes."

Sara stood immobile for several seconds after he'd gone, leaning her head against the door, trembling all over from what she'd seen in *his* eyes. Tenderness, longing . . . aching regret.

She was just pulling herself together, when she heard a loud outcry in the hall—and then the muffled sound of men scuffling. She wrenched open the door and ran down the corridor. At the first turning, two men grappled in the shadows. A lit candle had fallen to the runner; Sara rushed forward and plucked it up.

"I've got you now, by God!" Sir Kenneth roared as he

thrust Gren hard against the paneling. "Housebreaking . . . thievery. Denby's here. . . . He'll see you sent to Bodmin in chains before the sun even rises."

"You won't find it so easy to hang me, Brashear," Gren snarled. "Not like with my brother."

"You're *all* vermin. Fit for nothing but the noose."

"I'll show you what I'm fit for," Gren cried as he launched himself at the larger man.

He got him by the throat, but Sir Kenneth shook him off and retaliated with a round-house swing. Gren ducked and came in close, landing a series of thudding punches below his ribs.

Sara was overcome by a number of simultaneous emotions: fear for Gren, a natural female distaste for men bloodying each other under her nose—and an overwhelming sense of repulsion once she deduced that Sir Kenneth had been coming to her bedroom.

The two men locked together again, pummeling each other and staggering in half circles, with neither of them prevailing. When Sir Kenneth caught sight of the heavy coaching whip lying a few feet away, he dove for it and came up flailing. Once, twice, he struck out at Gren, catching him hard across the shoulders.

Sara winced at the sound, and when Sir Kenneth drew back for a third blow, she ran forward and tugged the whip out of his hands. He reeled around with a cry of surprise, and the next instant Gren caught him with a powerful uppercut to the jaw. Sir Kenneth staggered a few feet before collapsing, face first, onto the runner.

"Sweet Jesus," Gren muttered, nursing his knuckles. "The man is an ox." His gaze darted to her face. "I knew you'd make a decent ally, Sara Cobb."

"You must go away," she said breathlessly. "This isn't going to blow over. He's not going to forget he saw you here— no matter how muzzy-headed he may be when he wakes up."

"I know," Gren said, poking at the inert form with his boot. "He might also happen to recall that you came to my aid."

"Oh bother. I'll—I'll think of some explanation. Now

please, you must go. Is there somewhere in Penwreath you can hide?"

He nodded. "Don't fret over me, sweetheart. Old Gren Martyn's still got a few tricks left." He went a dozen feet down the corridor, opened a small door that blended with the paneling and disappeared through it.

Then his head popped out again. "He was coming for you, Sara," he said almost matter-of-factly. "In case you hadn't noticed. Makes me wish I'd broken his blasted neck."

Sara didn't know what to do. If she woke Sir Kenneth, he would be after Gren in a flash. If she let him lie there in the hall, she'd have to answer for why she hadn't run for help. The only solution she could think of was to pretend a swoon. It would effectively give Gren a chance to escape and also explain why she hadn't roused her employer.

She retreated to the door of the schoolroom and settled herself in the right angle of the frame. As soon as she heard Sir Kenneth stirring, she shut her eyes and let her head dangle to one side.

He rose with an audible groan, and then began casting about in the dark hall like a spaniel at a field trial. "Where'd you go, dammit?"

He came blundering toward her. "Get up, Miss Cobb," he growled, shaking her by the shoulder. "There's trouble afoot."

"Sir Kenneth?" she said in a faint, faraway voice. "There were two men fighting beyond my door. . . . I was so frightened. I must have fainted."

"I caught an intruder sneaking through the corridor. The knave's run off, but we'll get him. By God, we will."

She insisted on following him back to the drawing room, where he announced to his guests that he'd caught a housebreaker. "It was that demmed Gren Martyn. The fellow beat me off with a whip and got away. He's likely somewhere on the grounds."

There was a general outcry, especially from Lady Brashear. Sir Kenneth mustered the gentlemen and led them out to the stableyard.

As soon as they were gone—and the female house guests

fled to their rooms to check on their valuables—Addie drew Sara into a corner. "What on earth happened?"

"What do you think? Gren tempted fate once too often."

"But he got away—"

"Barely," Sara whispered. "And of course Sir Kenneth recognized him. The cat's among the pigeons now, Addie. Although I doubt Sir Kenneth will connect him with your coachman."

"Tristan's gone off with the other men," she said. "He'll do what he can to set them on the wrong trail."

"Then he knows where Gren's gone?"

Addie nodded. "I expect Lather Pitt will keep him safe for a few days, at least until we can think of some way to get him out of Penwreath." For once her usual composure had deserted her. She plucked at the fabric of her gown and sighed. "I was fool to play along with him, Sara. Nearly as big a fool as you were to encourage him."

"Me?"

"You might as well admit it. You're quite green about the face—a remarkable display of shock and distress for a man you claim means nothing to you." She smiled wanly. "I actually thought you might be good for him, but not if it means he's so besotted he's turned careless. You know what Sir Kenneth will do if he catches him?"

"He won't catch him," Sara vowed. "Not while I'm here to prevent it."

Chapter Thirteen

*L*ady Brashear had retired to her room, Ileana had disappeared, and the remaining household staff had all gone belowstairs for a monumental bout of gossiping. So Sara had no difficulty sneaking into Sir Kenneth's study. If he was involved in anything illicit, she reasoned, there were bound to be papers here, some proof that it was he who was the vermin and not Gren Martyn.

None of his desk drawers was locked, not a good sign if one was hoping for the presence of incriminating evidence. Still, she searched through every paper, every invoice, until her eyes teared. After several fruitless hours, she thrust the final sheaf back into its drawer with a muttered oath. Nothing but mining business and the usual correspondence involved in running a large estate.

When she heard voices in the hall, she quickly doused her candle and crouched down behind the desk.

"The cur's got clean away," she heard Sir Kenneth say. "He unharnessed one of the coach horses in the drive and rode off. We checked his farm and forced the Spindle whelp to take us through Needs Barrow, but he's vanished."

"Do you think he knows?" This was a female voice—Holcroft, Sara was certain.

"Jacob Martyn was nearly illiterate, and he died before his brother came back to Penwreath. What could Gren possibly know?"

"They say he spends a deal of time in Plymouth . . . visiting brothels."

Sir Kenneth gave a guttural laugh. "Can't fault a man for

that. Those Martyns always were a lusty lot. And not just the men either, from what I hear."

"I don't like it," Mrs. Holcroft muttered. "I've an itching in my palms that bodes no good. So what's to be done now?"

"I'm taking the grooms and gamekeepers to search in Penwreath. Can't expect my illustrious guests to be riding 'cross country half the night. But first, I need a large brandy—and my pistols. If I have my way, Gren Martyn won't ever come before a judge, at least not a mortal one."

He moved into the study and lit a candle on the desk. Sara's teeth scored her lower lip as she shifted farther into the knee-hole opening. Fortunately for her, Sir Kenneth kept his pistols in the sideboard across the room.

"I'll pour you a brandy in the library," Mrs. Holcroft said from the doorway, "and tell the others to meet you there."

After she was sure they'd both gone, Sara raced through the house to the schoolroom. She needed to fetch her cloak.

She found Seth alone in the stable, all the able-bodied grooms having been recruited for the search. She asked him to saddle one of Sir Kenneth's hunters and when he balked, complaining that it wasn't fitting for her to go out alone at night, she explained quickly, "I think I know who's been abducting the girls in Plymouth. But I must get away before Sir Kenneth and his men ride out again."

She was trotting around the back of the house, intending to head for the wood carters' gate, when Ileana appeared from out of the shadows. She ran forward and grabbed the bridle, tugging the horse to a stop.

"You're going to him!" she cried. "Don't try to deny it. I went to your room before dinner to bring you one of my evening shawls and I—I saw your journal lying there. I read it, Sara, every word about you and Gren Martyn."

Sara swallowed her righteous anger. "Then you know why I cannot turn my back on him now."

"I'll tell my father. . . . I'll tell Lord Denby!" Ileana railed. "Please, you mustn't be taken in by him. Not the way Amelie was."

"Amelie was his friend. I don't think that's ever altered between them."

"Hasn't it?" the girl cried, nearly sobbing now. "You think yourself so clever, but you don't know anything. Gren Martyn didn't just force himself on my sister—he got her with child."

Sara nearly cried out in surprise.

"He did that to her and then denied everything. Is that a man worth risking your reputation over?"

Sara sat there blankly. There was no time to process this new revelation—she'd simply have to move forward on blind faith alone, taking Gren at his word that he had never touched Amelie.

Ileana pressed onward. "My sister gave birth a scant seven months after she was wed. Even though the baby was small, he was well-formed. Everyone who saw the child said the same thing. Everyone knew she had gone to her marriage already increasing. You must believe me—Gren Martyn is the worst sort of blackguard."

"Then why did Adeline Spindle defend him?"

"Maybe she's in love with him," Ileana sneered. "I seem to be the only female in Penwreath who is not."

"Your father intends to shoot him out of hand," Sara said intently.

"No!" Ileana cried. "That's a lie."

"Then at the very least he will testify against him for crimes he did not commit. Just as he did with Jacob. And I swear to you, Gren's only crime is poaching a few birds—which he's been sharing with the families on the moor. Is that something he should hang for?"

"I am not a judge," Ileana said.

"Then don't judge *me*. One day you might find yourself caring for someone unsuitable, someone with a questionable past. Then you will understand how little anything else matters, not rank or wealth, only the safety of the man you love."

Sara didn't realize Tristan had come out onto the terrace, drawn by their voices. He hurried down the steps now and took hold of Ileana's shoulders. "Go on, Sara," he said. "I'll see that she keeps quiet." He looked up at her. "Do you even know where you're going?"

•

Sara nodded, then choked out, "I'm so sorry, Ileana."

With a determined frown, she set her horse at a gallop toward the woods.

Ileana tried to struggle out of Tristan's hold. "And how will you keep me quiet, you great, meddling—"

Tris picked her up bodily, muffling her outburst with one hand, and carried her away from the house into the surrounding trees. "Sara needs to do this," he said in a low, even voice. "She needs to warn Gren to keep his head down."

"I don't care about Gren Martyn," she cried. "He can go to the devil."

"You ought to care. He saved your sister's bacon. And at great cost to himself."

She began to weep, with small, stuttering sobs.

"What is it, sweeting?"

She grasped his lapels with both hands. "Sara is my only friend," she uttered hoarsely. "And if they catch her with that man, they'll take her to prison. Then I won't have anyone, Tris. Not Amelie, not Miss Cobb . . . not even you."

"You don't want me," he reminded her, then added in a strained voice, "You told me I was of no consequence."

She hung her head, recalling exactly when those words had been spoken, and realizing now how much they must have stung him—even coming from a twelve-year-old child. "I was jealous . . . because you were paying so much attention to that ridiculous shell."

"So you destroyed your rival, along with any fond feelings I might have had for you."

"Y-yes. . . . But I was just a little girl, and I only wanted you to notice me. I didn't think about how angry it would make you."

"If it helps at all, I never stopped noticing you, LeeLee."

At his use of her childhood name, she started crying even harder.

"I am a terrible person," she sobbed. "Selfish and willful. And I've driven away everyone I ever cared about."

"Not so far away," he said gently. "And you're young yet. You could change."

The light of hope flickered in her eyes. "And you would . . . wait for me? To grow up a bit?"

His eyes narrowed. "*Mmm.* Not sure I could wait—"

Misery again clouded her face. It was too late for her, and Ileana feared her heart would cleave in two.

"In fact," he said as he drew her into his arms, "I don't intend to wait one minute more."

He kissed her then, a masterful, impetuous, breath-stealing kiss that nearly had Ileana swooning with relief and joy.

Ileana had never been kissed, but she'd heard a deal on the subject from her maid. Tristan Spindle's kiss was surprisingly satisfactory, especially coming from a scientific-minded young man who like to grub about with disgusting sea creatures. From his proficiency, to say nothing of his intensity, she deduced he'd also been grubbing about with a number of fallen women.

This pleased her beyond all logic. He'd tasted the heady wine of sinful passion out in the wide world, but had come back to her, experienced and ardent, and chosen instead the sweet May wine of Tregallion.

Ileana decided there was nothing for it but to kiss him back. After all, she finally admitted to herself, she'd been secretly dreaming of this moment for nearly six years.

Sara was canny enough not to bring a Tregallion horse to the Constant Star. Instead, she left the gelding in the woods at the edge of town, making her way on foot toward the back of the inn. It was very late and she prayed someone was still up and about inside. She scratched at the back door, relieved when Lather Pitt himself opened it.

"What the devil do you want in the middle of the night?"

"Gren Martyn," she whispered sharply. "I need to get a message to him."

"Go look for him at his farm."

"He's not there. Sir Kenneth caught him inside Tregallion. He and his men are not far behind me. You've got to warn your cousin. *Please.*"

A hand snaked out the door and dragged her into the

kitchen. He motioned her forward with his candlestick. "Come with me."

She followed him down a steep narrow staircase into the cellar of the inn, where sacks of grain and crates of produce were piled high. He went down another half flight of stairs to a smaller room lined with wine bottles and casks of ale. "It be on your head," he muttered ominously, "if aught happens to him."

She heard a low grinding noise and watched as a portion of the wall slid to one side, wine bottles and all. He thrust her into the opening and quickly closed the partition.

Sara shivered. The darkness was thick about her. What had Gren said about a darkness blacker than any imagining? She stretched out her arms and was able to touch the walls on both sides. A priest's hole, she thought, or a cache for hiding smuggled spirits. But why had the landlord put her in here? What possible reason—

She gasped softly when she sensed someone behind her. He took a step forward, his body close against hers now. Two arms reached around her, one hand coming to rest on her waist, the other just below her breasts. He pressed her back into the curve of his body, and Sara shivered again as his warm mouth drifted along the nape of her neck. "Daft," he whispered like a sigh. "Lovely and brave . . . and daft."

He was kissing her throat now, lingering on the throbbing pulse at its base. Sara arched her head back, vowing that if this was the only time given to them, she would take full measure.

With a groan he spun her around, never easing his hold, and caught her mouth, kissing her roughly, hungrily. Sara stretched up, arms twining around him, spine curving inward to meet him, every sense awakened by his touch.

He'd never kissed her standing before. It was almost too much to absorb—the melding of bodies, the fitting together of parts and planes she'd have thought awkward or uncomfortable. Noses shifted by nature to just the right degree. Hips and shoulders angled by instinct to interlock like puzzle pieces. Hands found purchase, limbs nested into hollows . . . and the glorious sum was a rare multiplication of their separate energies.

Sara's skin was aflame, yet not nearly so hot as the fire that licked inside her.

Gren undid the clasp of her cloak, thrusting the fabric off her shoulders to pool at her feet. The cool air assaulted her, but as he lowered his head to nuzzle her throat, flames danced over her again, the blood coursing like molten metal through her veins.

His mouth caressed her collarbone, then slid lower.

"Sara . . . ah, Sara," he murmured into the hollow of her breasts.

She clutched at the thick silk of his hair, overcome by sharp, aching need. Her trembling limbs were holding her upright, yet she swore she was no longer touching ground.

She sighed raggedly when he stroked one hand over her breast, groaned deep in her throat when he pressed a kiss there. Her arms tightened around him, her hands savoring the contours of his back—ribs and spine and shoulders all cased in rippling muscle. The image of his naked torso swept over her, and she wanted to rip away the layers of broadcloth, to stroke the heated skin beneath.

Gren tugged the pins from her topknot, hissing his pleasure as her hair cascaded over them both, rippling and satiny and alive with an energy all its own. Catching a handful of it, he tugged her head back. He didn't need to see in the dark to know how she responded; he could feel her straining against him. She was everything he'd imagined she'd be—fierce, passionate, full of reciprocal hunger.

He'd warned her that things had gotten too complicated between them, but they weren't complicated any longer. He knew the price he would have to pay, and it didn't matter, not now. He swung her back against the wall, kissing her deeply, pressing into her so that she would understand the fullness of his body's response. She did not shy away, but locked her fingers in his hair, tugging his head down and kissing him all the harder.

When they broke apart at last, to breathe if nothing else, he could barely stand. He clung to the wall, panting, nearly sobbing, until she crept forward and found him.

"You'll save Brashear the trouble of hanging me," he

rasped as he hooked his arm about her waist. "Now leave off kissing me, Miss Cobb . . . or I'll surely swoon."

Sara tucked his head against her shoulder. "Faint heart," she murmured.

He laughed low, under his breath, a warm exhalation against her collarbone. "Not faint," he rebutted. "Frustrated."

"Very well . . . I know better than to tease you." She dropped her arms and stepped back from him. It was easy this time, mainly because she suspected he would never again be completely out of reach.

"Just tell me one thing," she said as she shifted her shoulders to the wall beside him. "What did you mean in the schoolroom when you said all the answers were in my eyes?"

He was silent a long while. Sara knew kissing came easily to a man like Gren Martyn. Expressing his feelings was perhaps a bit harder to muster.

When he did answer, his voice was halting. "I—I meant the answers to the questions I'd never dare ask you, Sara. To be with me . . . stay with me. I'm still not certain what it is that draws me to you . . . maybe the laughter in your eyes or your rare sense of justice . . . even your sometimes brutal honesty. But it's strong, sweeting, stronger than anything I've ever felt before." He traced her cheek in the darkness. "And now this. . . . Coming to me, risking everything. When I have nothing to give you in return."

She wrapped her arms around him, laid her face against the hollow of his throat. "Then we'll be renegades together, you and I." She felt him smile. "Anyway I had to come, Gren. Sir Kenneth intends to shoot you on sight. There will be no trumped-up trial this time."

Before he could respond, they heard voices in the room beyond them, muffled but audible through the wooden partition. Gren set his hand lightly over her mouth and drew her into the deepest recess of the chamber.

Sir Kenneth's barking voice penetrated the wall. "I know he's here, Pitt. You've abetted him before."

"I bin in my bed these three hours past," Lather protested. "It was a slow night, what with so many of the villagers up to Tregallion to help out with th' party."

Sara heard the sound of bottles being knocked about and glass breaking.

"I know you've a secret cellar for storing smuggled brandy," Sir Kenneth said. "It's common knowledge in Penwreath."

"'Tisn't here, sir," Lather said. "'Tis beneath my barn."

"Take me," Sir Kenneth ordered.

"But, sir—"

"Take me now . . . or I'll put a torch to the whole festering pile. That would be fitting, eh Pitt? After you burned down my carriage house last year."

Lather's voice deflated. "As you like, sir. Follow me."

Once they'd gone, Gren tugged off his long coat and set it on the stone floor for Sara to sit on. He settled next to her, leaning back against the rough-hewn wall.

"Gad, I forgot how much I hate the dark," he said, taking up her hand and stroking his thumb over it. "You've no idea what having you here means to me."

"Does it mean enough that you'll finally tell me what's going on? Ileana accused you of something quite terrible just before I rode off. I need to know how you and the Brashears have woven this tangled web of hate and revenge."

He didn't speak at first. She could almost hear his mind humming.

"It began with Amelie's first governess," he said at last.

"Miss Durbin."

"Mmm. When she disappeared, I'd not yet returned from America. Then they hanged Jacob, and I came home. Not long after, Amelie told me her father was pressuring the new governess, offering to set her up with one of his wealthy cronies in Plymouth. He'd let slip that her predecessor had given way to his blandishments and was currently living in London as the *cher amie* of a titled gentleman."

"That is not precisely a crime," she pointed out.

"It's called procuring, Sara, and it's against the law. Because the peer undoubtedly paid Sir Kenneth handsomely for Miss Durbin's favors. Anyway, Amelie was understandably distressed."

"So you *did* help Miss Castlereigh escape from Tregallion."

"We—Amelie and I—found her another posting, off in Shropshire. Meantime, she hid at Needs Barrow."

"So much for the mystery of the disappearing governesses. Though I had begun to figure it out for myself. Sir Kenneth's been dropping hints that he knows a few well-heeled gentlemen who'd be pleased to take me under their wing." She coughed once. "I thought he was referring to marriage."

"Green girl," he chided.

"Not any longer. And now what about you and Amelie, all that wicked gossip?"

She felt his withdrawal, even in the dark.

"Grenville, if I am to throw in my lot with you, I think I deserve to hear the truth."

He gave a weary sigh. "It's a common enough tale. Amelie came back from London with a babe in her belly—begot by a young officer she had fallen in love with. A decent fellow, in spite of how it might appear . . . a wounded naval hero, but quite poor. Her parents whisked her home when they saw where things were heading. And, of course, they knew nothing about the baby."

Sara couldn't begin to imagine Amelie's state of mind—torn from the man she loved, banished to the wilds of Cornwall. And facing the worst sort of scandal on top of it.

"Amelie came to me," he continued, "pleading that I help her run away to him before her condition started to show. But I thought of a better plan, one that would make the Brashears welcome any suitor with open arms. Amelie would blame me for deflowering her—knowing that Addie would counter any accusations she made. It worked like a charm. The Brashears didn't know whom to believe—they just wanted their soiled daughter off their hands. Roger Woode came down from London right afterward, and they practically threw her at him."

"Is she happy now?"

"I believe so. Marriage and motherhood have tamed her . . . or so she writes."

"That's the best testament to friendship I've ever heard. That you'd let yourself become the neighborhood byword to save her from being shunted off to some distant place to bear her child—and then give it up to strangers. Besides that, you kept the man she married from being tarred by scandal. It was nobly done, Gren, giving her a fresh start like that."

"It wasn't just our friendship made me do it. I had other reasons."

"Yes. . . ." she prodded him. "What about those reasons? I know only the barest details. The one thing I *am* sure of is that Sir Kenneth is involved in something questionable. Tonight I overheard him speaking to Mrs. Holcroft—"

"More eavesdropping?"

"Shush! When he went riding after you, I sneaked into his study and looked through the papers in his desk." She sensed his incredulity. "See, you've got yourself a fine accomplice. I shrink from nothing. Unfortunately, I found only legitimate business correspondence. Then he and the housekeeper started talking outside the door. She asked him how much you knew. She sounded nervous, but he reassured her that your brother had no opportunity to speak with you before he died. He sounded . . . smug." She set her hand on his sleeve. "So what did Jacob know, Gren?"

"Very little, I'm afraid. He did stumble onto something but had only the sketchiest details."

"And how did you learn of this? Sir Kenneth said he was barely literate."

"Jacob left me a deathbed testimony the night before he was hanged, transcribed by one of the inmates. It took months for the paper to reach me. I'd been lingering in Penwreath to make sure Amelie was settled and to spend time with the Spindles. I was just about to pack up and leave when a stranger showed up at my door with this soiled, wrinkled document." His voice grew strained. "I couldn't leave after that. Not until I discovered why my brother had been murdered."

"And you're sure it *was* murder? I imagine men are sometimes hanged for poaching alone."

"Not in Cornwall, not during these lean times. No, Brashear needed him out of the way because Jacob had actually seen him conducting his foul business in one of the brothels in Plymouth. A pity he couldn't recall which one."

"*What?*"

He chuffed. "Jacob was drunk as a parson. He'd gotten

woozy in a hallway and managed to crawl into a dark room. When he came to, he was lying behind a sofa. He heard two men speaking, negotiating the terms of a shipment . . . a shipment of girls who were being sent to London to be auctioned off."

"Wait," Sara said. "I've been wondering about this for days. How does selling a few country girls to run-down brothels in London put money in Sir Kenneth's pocket? The man appears to be swimming in gold—even Lord Denby remarked on his extravagance. Yet his mines are no longer profitable, and after reading his papers, I know he doesn't invest in commerce or shipping."

"You're forcing me to tread in delicate waters, my girl. Do you really want to know?"

"Of course I do."

"In London, among the well-padded nobility, a pretty, fresh-faced virgin can fetch hundreds of pounds at auction. Sometimes thousands."

Sara hissed an indrawn breath. "That's completely depraved."

"Welcome to the Age of Excess," he drawled. "I'm something of a libertine myself, and it shocks me."

"At least that first governess had a choice, but these girls . . . carried off and sold on the block like animals." She set her hands over her face, pressing her temples to make them stop throbbing. "You could have told me all this right from the start," she said. "I might have paid more attention to Sir Kenneth's comings and goings, for one thing."

"It was too risky," he said. "These people are not the sort you want to cross. When Sir Kenneth discovered Jacob and realized he'd been listening, he trussed him up and tossed him into a canal. But we Penwreath lads swim like fish. Even jugbit, Jacob was able to get free and drag himself from the water. But the fool went back home. Two days later, the militia from Bodmin took him away in chains."

"I'm so sorry, Gren."

"It's been more than two years now, and I'm still trying to find some link between Brashear and this mysterious bawdy house. But whenever I follow him to Plymouth, he never sets foot in a brothel. There's a grain warehouse near the waterfront where he stops off most times. I've been inside after dark and searched the place. Beyond a small office, it's just a normal warehouse."

"Perhaps his confederates meet with him there?"

"No. I've kept watch and he was the only one to enter or leave"

"A back entrance?"

"The back bay opens directly onto the barge canal."

She gave a tiny moan of vexation. "How could your brother not recall which brothel he was in?"

Gren chuckled. "They do all start to look alike after a time."

Sara poked him in the ribs, then tucked up her knees and tried desperately to think of a solution to their problem. Gren's life might depend on it.

He must have heard her growling under her breath. "Are you angry that I waited so long to tell you?"

"Not angry over that," she muttered. "I'm furious at the Brashears. Gross hypocrites, both of them. Lady Brashear, the petty autocrat with her nose in the air. And Sir Kenneth, forcing the servants to endure his pompous Bible reading each night, as though a few passages from the Scriptures would keep his soul from Perdition." She *humph*ed abruptly. "And to think how I've been awed and cowed by them, it just makes my blood boil. I'm—I'm only surprised that . . ."

"What?"

"That Amelie could have left her sister at Tregallion, with a father she suspected was a monster."

"She had no choice. Lady Brashear would hardly have let Ileana go off with Amelie, a daughter she considered sullied. Besides, Ileana wasn't at Tregallion most of the year. She was at Miss Bonnet's Improving School."

"True. . . ."

"And I assured Amelie, once I got to know you, that you would be the best bulwark between her sister and any danger in that house."

"Bulwark?" she echoed. "That's flattering. And not very accurate. In case you didn't notice, I wasn't behaving with much propriety around you for the past month."

"Two different things entirely. It hardly meant you wouldn't look after Ileana."

"Mmm . . . I left her in tears tonight. Though Tris manfully came to her rescue."

"It's been quite a night for such things, one way or another. Though I never thought I'd be thanking *you* for rescuing me."

She sniffed. "I don't recall you thanking me, as a matter of fact."

"Easily remedied." He had her half across his lap and was kissing her lustily before she knew what he was about.

"Stop trying to distract me," she grumbled, trying not to grin. "One of us has to keep a clear head."

"My head is quite clear. My body, on the other hand . . ." His fingers sidled up from her waist.

She slapped them away. And then chuckled. "I never realized how incorrigible you are. But would you try to be serious? You're a wanted man now. Officially, I shouldn't doubt, since Lord Denby is at Tregallion. Although I did mention the missing girls to his friend, Sir Robert Poole—"

"Poole? He's something of an agitator in the Commons. 'The lone voice' is what they call him. He might be just the person to aid us."

"Shall I go fetch him?" she inquired slyly. "I daresay there's room for another body in this cubby hole."

"Well, we can't do it alone," he said.

A plan had begun stirring in Sara's brain. "You know, I could put this all to rights fairly easily. What if I were to convince Sir Kenneth that you were not housebreaking, but rather on your way to my bedroom—at my invitation? They can't hang a man for being . . . amorous."

She felt his body tense. "Do you think I'd let you sacrifice your good name for me?"

"I suppose it hasn't occurred to you that after staying here with you all night, my reputation will be in tatters. Anyway, my good name is worth a lot less than your life."

"Brashear will still maintain that I was in the house illegally."

"Then what are we to do?"

"I could take a ship to America."

Sara's heart twisted. "But we are still at war."

"That's never stopped a man from getting in—or out—of a country. Ask any smuggler. I can't stay here in this hole, Sara. You know how I feel about being trapped in the dark."

"You can't run, Gren, not when you're so close to finding the proof you need."

"You think I want to run? But there's no other way out, not if my only option is seeing you disgraced for helping me."

"I rather think that's my decision to make."

"Ah, Sara." He wrapped his arms around her and Sara clung to him, distraught and so afraid of losing him. She could feel his heart beating beneath her cheek, steady and strong. How had the world gone so topsy-turvy that a decent man like Gren Martyn was reduced to hiding in a cellar, while those who plotted and carried out a poisonous evil had the law on their side?

He murmured, "I can't imagine why you'd want to throw in with a shiftless layabout like me."

She read the doubt behind his teasing tone. Her hand drifted over his face, caressing features she didn't need to see, they were so ingrained in her memory.

"That's easy. I never felt truly alive until I met you. I was hiding in the shadows and you drew me out. Your kindness to me that first night, for one thing. And your concern that day in the woods. You made me feel . . . validated. Which I badly needed just then, since everything was falling apart around me. And there's another thing, Gren—you kept coming back. We'd tiff and spar and throw hasty words at each other, but you never really left."

"I told you tonight. . . . I couldn't keep away."

She pushed back from him a little. "I hate to admit it, but you also gave the teacher a lesson in humility."

"Me?"

"Yes, you. I didn't quite know what to make of you at first, brimming with confidence and easy charm, which was odd really, considering you were usually on the wrong side of the law. Besides that, you were benevolent, in spite of owning very little. You made me realize that a person's measure has little to do with wealth or titles. You thought yourself as good as any man—something I suspect you brought back from America—and I so admired you for that. I still do."

She heard his gravelly sigh.

"I am a better man than I was," he admitted. "Overlooking a few dozen flaws, I believe I can finally say that. And a lot of it's due to you, Sara. I spent more than two years stoked with anger, with no thought except avenging my brother. But after I met you, my focus shifted from clearing Jacob's name to bringing down the men who'd been luring those unlucky girls away from Cornwall." His hand tightened on hers. "Because, you see, if the Brashears *had* dismissed you, you might so easily have become one of them."

Sara's throat constricted. She recalled, even if he did not, that from their first meeting he'd been determined to look after her, to keep her safe.

And then the full portent of his words filtered into her brain, and she rose abruptly to her knees. *"That's it!"*

"What? What odd start's taken hold of you now?"

"Listen," she said, pulling him close. "I think I have a solution. All it requires is that we enlist Sir Robert Poole."

She sensed him frowning in the dark as she related the plan that had formed, full-blown, inside her head. By the time she was done, she knew he was scowling deeply.

"No, absolutely not. Out of the question. It's beyond daft."

"Grenville . . ." she muttered mutinously. "I'll do it with you or without you."

"You'll not do it at all, not while I have breath in my body to stop you."

She gripped him by the shoulders and kissed him long and hard—until, in truth, he had no breath left to deny her anything.

Chapter Fourteen

*G*ren Martyn sat waiting in a back booth of the Constant Star's empty taproom, fighting off an occasional stab of apprehension. He wiped his damp palms along his breeches and stared out the window across the room. It was the first daylight he'd seen in two days, and he was simultaneously experiencing the normal relief of a prisoner freed from a dark cell and the clammy fear of a captive set down in a sun-bleached Roman arena, where danger lurked on every side.

He prayed Sara was right, that the man he awaited was honorable and just. It occurred to him that his imminent visitor lived in London, the very place his unknown adversary dwelled. But what were the odds that a lauded reformer was also the power behind the dealers in human flesh? Well, stranger things had happened. He'd keep his guard up and keep an eye on his cousin, Lather, who stood behind the bar with a fowling piece close at hand.

There was a small commotion in the hall, heralding the arrival of Sir Robert Poole, who entered the taproom a few seconds later. Gren had barely glimpsed him the night of the party. He was now impressed by the man's sheer physical presence, the brawny shoulders and ham-sized hands, the thick mane of white hair and blunt features that reminded Gren of an aging, but still formidable, lion. Yet in spite of Sir Robert's robust aura, he was almost dwarfed by the man at his side, a towering, muscle-bound brute in the livery of a groom.

The giant at once made his way to the bar, leaned over it and leered knowingly at Lather.

"I see you've brought a bit of insurance," Gren said as he rose to greet his guest.

Sir Robert smiled coolly. "You told me to come alone. I am as alone as you are."

"My cousin owns this place. I could hardly ask him to leave."

"My groom owes me his life. I could hardly ask him to risk mine."

"Fair enough." Gren nodded as he sat down.

Sir Robert settled opposite him, tugging off his gloves as he gazed about the room.

"I enjoy these old hostelries," he pronounced with relish. "The very beams and bricks steeped in history. Though not always the sort of history we read in books, eh, Mr. Martyn? In Cornwall, the bricks are more like to render up the ghosts of smugglers and wreckers—and poachers."

"I'm not a ghost yet, Sir Robert. And have no itch to be one before my time."

"Then you'd better do a proper job of convincing me why I shouldn't hand you over to Lord Denby."

"I don't deny I've been a poacher—and a smuggler briefly, though that can be blamed on the folly of youth. I did have a respectable trade once, but was called away from it by the death of my brother here in Cornwall."

Lather came by with two glasses of stout. Sir Robert thanked him, then returned to gazing expectantly at Gren. "Go on. . . ."

"Since I had no trade, I helped myself to the bounty of the land."

"Not your own land, alas."

Gren shrugged. "A hundred years ago there were few boundary fences in Cornwall. The moors and the meadows and the beech woods belonged to everyone."

"So you fancy yourself a victim of progress—"

"This is not about me. Only in that Sir Kenneth wants me out of the way because I know my brother was a victim . . . a victim of Brashear's lying, murderous slanders."

Sir Robert's jaw tensed, "I'd advise you to choose your words carefully, Mr. Martyn."

Gren quickly controlled his temper. "Sorry, sir. There's a lot at stake here."

With a rumbling sigh, Sir Robert said, "I looked into your brother's case after I got your note yesterday, and I see nothing irregular. He was, as I understand, taken as a poacher and a horse thief. The first crime I imagine might have been overlooked if the second were not so serious. Stealing a man's horse is still punishable by hanging in most of England."

Gren leaned forward. "The only person to testify against Jacob was Sir Kenneth Brashear. He claimed he saw my brother steal two of his hunters from their paddock. The day Jacob was taken, Brashear's men found the beasts grazing near my brother's farm. Now I'm no expert on the law, but I do understand what the word 'circumstantial' means." His voice lowered a notch. "I'm also familiar with the expression 'being set up.'"

An expression of increasing interest had narrowed Sir Robert's broad face. "And why would Sir Kenneth—a most respected gentleman I am told—perjure himself to harm a local farmer?"

Gren drew a soiled wrinkled piece of paper from his vest and slid it across the table. Lather had fetched it from his farm only that morning. "This might furnish you with a few answers."

Sir Robert began to scan the document carelessly. Gren noted the exact moment the man's eyes widened, and then shifted back to the top for a more thorough read.

When he was done, however, the great snowy brows meshed and Sir Robert shook his head. "It's too preposterous," he said. "I'm sorry, but there's nothing here that would hold up in court."

"Not even as a deathbed testimony? My brother was hanged the next day at dawn."

Sir Robert thought for a moment, then splayed the blunt fingertips of both hands over the paper. "Let us suppose this is all true. How could you begin to prove any of it?"

"Miss Cobb, the Brashear's governess, overheard Sir Kenneth several times in clandestine conversations. Once with a man from the East End. They spoke of 'his nibs' in London complaining of unsuitable product coming from Penwreath, that shipments were lank haired and dull-eyed. Miss Cobb points out they might have been discussing livestock, but there's not a farmer or stockman born who ever refers to a beast's covering as hair. It's always coat or hide or fleece."

"Quite true," he agreed. "I have myself dabbled in sheep breeding. I believe you are correct on that score. And what else did this most acute governess overhear?"

"Two days ago, the night I fled, she heard Sir Kenneth and his housekeeper in private conversation. The woman was nervy. She asked him outright what I knew. He vowed I could know nothing, that Jacob had died before he could tell anyone what he'd learned. So whether or not I'm right about his involvement with the missing girls, he's up to something shady. Something my brother knew about—something he died for." Gren touched the edge of the paper. "And if he suspected something other than this, why did he dictate *these* words for me to read?"

"Why, indeed?" Sir Robert murmured. He took a long swallow from his mug and then set it down with a thump. "But even if you have the right of things, what can be done to incriminate Brashear? He's apparently covered his tracks all this time."

"Miss Cobb has a plan," Gren said. "We thought that if I could convince you to give me the benefit of the doubt, you might be willing to help us carry it out."

"Why should I believe the word of a poacher? What surety can you offer me of your character? That is, besides the apparent trust and affection of an impressionable young governess."

Gren looked him in the eye and said with some heat, "She is a deal more than that. But I won't deserve a woman like Sara Cobb until I can clear my brother's name and get my own life underway again."

Sir Robert gave way to a bemused smile, then quickly obscured it. "I take it Miss Cobb is still in the neighborhood. According to the Brashears' servants, she disappeared the night you fled from Tregallion."

"She's in a safe place," Gren said. He'd had Lather take her off to the Curry's farm the morning after the house party. "She

could tell you a few things, though. About Sir Kenneth prey-
ing on the young women who serve him. You might also want
to inquire of his elder daughter in Somerset, a Mrs. Woode.
Brashear lured her first governess into vice."

"But you don't know this first-hand?"

Gren's fist slammed onto the table. "First-hand, second-
hand? What the devil difference does it make? Half the carrying out of the law is rumor and speculation—and the other
half is damned lies."

Sir Robert laughed outright at this. "And they tell me
you've never been to London. Quite amazing. And sadly, quite
true."

"And as for people to vouch for me, there's Lather Pitt over
by yon tap—"

"An accomplice to smugglers, so I'm told."

"And Mrs. Woode."

"She's too biased . . . a disgruntled daughter according to
the tattle."

"There's Miss Adeline Spindle and her brother, Tristan. I
dare you to find fault with them."

Sir Robert tapped his forefinger against his upper lip. "Except for one small thing. They'd be happy to lie for you because they are your close relations."

Gren goggled at him, almost fearful that a mortal man could
be so omniscient.

"Well, are they not?"

"No one knows that," Gren hissed. "None save the Spindles
and myself."

"*And* the Spindles' retired groom, who was apparently
privy to his master's benevolence toward your mother. You
see, I have a fairly thorough spy network when I need to get to
the bottom of something."

Gren shook his head slowly. "There's no proof. Just an old
letter we discovered in a trunk, which my mother had written
to Arthur Spindle. No more than hints. . . ."

Yet Gren believed it implicitly. Shortly after his return to
Penwreath, the three of them had tripped over the truth and
embraced it in the musty attic of Needs Barrow. It explained so
much—why the widowed gentleman had always welcomed

Gren into his house, why he had given Jacob the money to send his brother to America. Gren only wished he'd known while Arthur was still alive.

"There is another who would speak for me," Gren said gruffly. "But he's across an ocean, in a country we make war with on a regular basis."

"Who?"

"Mr. Duncan Phyfe of New York."

Poole appeared astonished. "Duncan Phyfe, the cabinet-maker?"

"The same. I worked for him nearly six years, apprentice and journeyman both."

Sir Robert's piercing eyes grew dreamy. "I'm fortunate enough to own one of Mr. Phyfe's inlaid satinwood sideboards. Exquisite." His manner changed perceptibly, from wry caution to smiling acceptance. "Well, why the deuce didn't you say that at the start? There's no chance a man with such inspired attention to detail would have allowed a rascal in his shop for half a decade." He held out his hand to Gren. "Peace then, Mr. Martyn. I will do everything in my power to help you uncover the truth."

Gren shook his hand a bit hesitantly, then launched into the details of Sara's plan, all the while marveling that his quest for justice might possibly be nearing an end—and all due to the elegant lines of a satinwood sideboard.

It was fate, sure as anything.

Sir Kenneth was lunching with Lord Denby and a few other guests, having taken a break from scouring the countryside for Gren Martyn, to restore himself with a hearty meal. After three days of searching, he was beginning to lose hope of ever finding the knave, which, naturally, had heightened his desire to squash him like an insect.

He was also uneasy over the continued absence of Miss Cobb. The servants were starting to remark on it, and it wouldn't be long before Denby's valet learned that this was the third governess in three years to have gone missing, Sir Kenneth prayed his lordship had himself experienced the ingratitude and waywardness of the serving classes and would not think to tax him on the matter.

He already had enough to worry about inside the house. His wife had turned an icy shoulder to him after she'd sussed his ultimate destination in the east wing the night he caught Gren Martyn trespassing. His protestations of being foxed and getting lost on the way to the privy fell on deaf ears.

Holcroft's continued mutterings and dire predictions were also starting to unnerve him.

As a result, he found himself in a state of agitated wariness.

Denby was just making his apologies for Sir Robert Poole, who had been called away unexpectedly that morning, when a footman appeared with a note for Sir Kenneth. "This was left for you at the gatehouse, sir."

He snatched it up and scanned it quickly. Though the message was familiar—"Come to the usual place"—the handwriting was not.

Troubling . . . very troubling.

In spite of his sense of foreboding, he rose smoothly from the table and excused himself to his guests. "There's been a development in the matter of the housebreaker," he said. "I believe I must see to it."

He rode off down the drive, but once out of sight of the house, he veered to the left, heading for the abandoned woodshed. His horse was fresh and mettlesome, so he set the beast at a gallop through the trees and within minutes was approaching the clearing.

A gangling young man on a bay cob waited there. Sir Kenneth peered through the foliage, unable to place him. A shiver of apprehension traced its way up his back.

The youth called out before Sir Kenneth even cleared the wood. "'Ee best hie it to th' house in Plymouth. His nibs is come from London. Wants a word with 'ee . . . *instanter*." Then he reined the bay around and pelted away toward the carters' gate.

Sir Kenneth had a mind to give chase; his hunter could have easily outdistanced the stocky cob. But no, the fellow had been waiting in the proper spot—and the message had been clear.

He rode slowly back to Tregallion, wondering if he dared to

ignore the summons. He needed to be *here*, needed to run that pernicious Martyn to earth. But he knew the character of the man who awaited him in Plymouth. Not someone you could easily say no to. Not if you valued your neck.

Chapter Fifteen

*I*t was coming on to dusk when the farm girl descended from the mail coach in the cobbled yard of the West Wind. There was little to distinguish her from the numerous young women who came to Plymouth seeking work—a faded, homespun gown hanging limply beneath a pilled woven shawl, thick woolen stockings tucked into heavy brogues. Yet her ancient straw bonnet was perched above a gleaming braid of coffee-colored hair, and her amber-hued eyes were exotically tipped at each corner.

She fiddled with her shabby valise, walked up and down a few times, seeming uncertain about approaching the back door of the inn. A prosperous-looking couple on the pavement watched her for several minutes before they came forward.

"Are you lost, dearie?" the apple-cheeked woman asked her.

"No, jest a mite scairt. My ma sent me to find work at the West Wind. I be from Penwreath way.... My da's lost his place in the mine, an' we've seven to feed back home."

The couple shared a look of commiseration.

"This is most timely," the man said. "The Mrs. and I are in the market for a maid. We'd come to Plymouth for the hiring fair, but found no one to suit."

The girl weighed her options. "P'raps I might do for 'ee.... I be stronger than I look an' can cook a bit. Ah, tedn't possible, though. Ma wants me to work at this here inn, it bein' respectable an' all."

"I promise you, my husband and I are quite respectable," said the woman with a warm chuckle.

The couple then spoke a few words in an undertone. "We'd be willing to give you a try," said the woman at last. "And I think we can offer a better wage than the landlord of the inn. He's a notorious nipfarthing . . . and hasty with a slap."

The girl thought for a moment, then bobbed a curtsy. "Anne Canard is my name, ma'am."

"I am Mrs. Ritchie. Of Salfash Parish, west of Plymouth. And this is my husband, Mr. Charles Ritchie."

"We were on our way to dine at the Red Lion," Mr. Ritchie said as Anne fell into step behind them. "We'd be happy to buy you supper . . . to seal the deal, so to speak."

"Ma sent me away with only a half a pasty," the girl complained. "I do have a gnawin' pain in my innerts."

They settled her in a booth in the back of the Red Lion's bustling dining parlor. When a steaming kettle of stew appeared at the table, Mr. Ritchie himself ladled it into a bowl for her. She knew she should have been impressed by his kindness and generosity, but the soup tasted more than a little bitter. Both Mr. and Mrs. Ritchie fell to eating and kept urging Anne to empty her bowl. But before long she began to feel unwell. This troubled her greatly; she was a sturdy girl and rarely ever sick.

When they set out for the livery, where the Ritchie's carriage awaited, the girl found she was having trouble walking. She stumbled on the pavement and quickly apologized. "Forgive me, ma'am . . . sir. I be feelin' a bit muzzy."

"No matter," the woman said. "You're doubtless just weary from your journey."

They hadn't gone another ten feet before she collapsed to her knees.

Mr. Ritchie promptly scooped her up and between them the husband and wife got her back on her feet and moving forward. A passerby would have had to get very close to note that the girl was not actually walking.

"Took the chit long enough," Mrs. Ritchie huffed under her breath. "Considering you emptied half the bottle into her bowl."

The girl was groaning now, but neither of them paid her any heed.

*   *   *

Sara felt them lower her onto a soft, flat surface. When she risked opening her eyes, she saw she was lying in a gaudily decorated bedroom. Gaudy, but not very clean. There were greasy streaks on the purple velvet draperies, and the satin comforter below her was mottled with tea stains. At least she prayed they were tea stains. On a scuffed night table of French inlay a lone candle burned.

She heard footsteps in the hall; they halted outside the open door of her room. She craned her head up imperceptibly. Mrs. Ritchie stood there, and facing her was a tall, well-set-up gentleman with tawny hair.

Sir Kenneth Brashear in all his glory.

Sara knew this was the part where she was to leap up and escape from the room or climb through the window. She'd had strict orders not to linger once Sir Kenneth had been compromised. Still, she reasoned, where was the harm in listening in for another minute? They thought she was drugged, after all, and she had a pistol in her skirt pocket if things got really sticky.

"What do you mean you sent no message?" Sir Kenneth hissed. "I saw the boy large as life. He told me his nibs was waiting for me—I was forced to leave a rather important houseguest in order to race down here."

"Monk Abelard's not been in Plymouth for nigh on six months," Mrs. Ritchie said, then added in a hushed fearful voice, "God be praised."

"Look . . . I still have the note in my pocket." He drew it out and handed it to her.

"Not one of my bully boys," she said. "I'd know their scrawl if I saw it. 'Pears you were duped." Before the further implications of this could dawn on her, she continued, "Still, I'm glad you've come. Now you can see for yourself that we're only bothering with quality goods, as instructed." She sketched a wave toward the bed.

Sara quickly closed her eyes.

"This one will fetch a fine price in London. She's fairly clean, for one thing, and well-fed. Hard to believe she hails from one of your seedy tenant farms. She's got the makings of a little beauty. . . . Just requires the right setting and she'll shine like a jewel."

Sir Kenneth made a noise of annoyance. "Well, maybe the trip wasn't a total waste. Let me have a look at her before she wakes up and starts in to screeching."

Sara knew it was absolutely time to make her escape. What she hadn't counted on was how lethargic the small portion of the drugged soup had left her. Heart pounding, she surreptitiously groped for the pistol.

Sir Kenneth approached the bed and leaned down—Sara nearly grimaced when she felt his breath on her face—then with a stuttering cry reeled back.

"T-take her out of here!" he whispered urgently. "Before she is awake. Cosh her on the head and throw her into the canal. *Take her I say!*"

The woman wavered in the doorway. "But, sir, I thought you'd—"

"It's a trap," he seethed. "She knows me, she works for me, for God's sake. I must leave at once."

Sara mustered all her courage. He mustn't be allowed to flee.

"It's too late," she said coolly as she sat up and leveled the pistol at him. "You're right, Sir Kenneth, it is a trap. For once the fox stepped into his own snare."

He glowered at her. "You think I am going to quail before a lone female?"

"Not quite alone."

Keeping the pistol trained on him, she slipped carefully off the opposite side of the bed and shifted backward to the window. The room was one flight up, and below her in the narrow street ranged a number of armed men, among them Tristan Spindle and one devilishly handsome poacher. She motioned several times against the glass with her free hand without taking her eyes, or the pistol, off Sir Kenneth.

"Robert Poole's men are outside," she said. "You haven't a prayer of getting away."

"Oh, don't I?" he growled as he swept the lit candle onto the floor, plunging the far end of the room into darkness.

Sara fumbled, one-handed, to get the window open as Sir

Kenneth scrambled across the mattress toward her. As frightened as she was, she couldn't bring herself to shoot him. Instead she turned and put a bullet through the window. It shattered outward, but Sir Kenneth was upon her before she could lean out and cry out for help. They grappled in the dark, while the woman in the hallway screamed for assistance from below.

The useless pistol was wrenched from Sara's hand, and an instant later the blunt stock smashed down on her temple. She forced herself not to go under—Sir Robert's men would be pounding up the stairs any second. Sir Kenneth struck her again, this time with his fist, and the last thing she saw was a hazy expanse of faded carpet rushing up to meet her.

She came to as they were carrying her through a narrow, dimly lit passage. Sir Kenneth had her under the arms and the man who called himself Mr. Ritchie was holding her legs. She scrunched her eyes closed and prayed they hadn't noticed her return to consciousness.

They carried her awkwardly up a set of stone steps and Sara nearly groaned when they dropped her onto a hard wooden floor. When she heard them moving away, she opened one eye. She was lying in a cavernous building, stacked high on one side with sacks of grain. Wheat chaff floated in the air like dandelion floss. This had to be the warehouse Gren had told her about, a warehouse with an underground connection to the brothel. Even in her dazed state, she was beginning to make sense of things.

"Fetch my carriage," Sir Kenneth said to his confederate. "And bring it around to the end of the wharf. I need to get her away from here."

"What about the canal? It's right out back."

"No, I can't risk anyone finding her near this place. If you recall, the last time we threw someone into the canal, he managed to escape."

Mr. Ritchie slipped out the door to the street, while Sir Kenneth went into a small office and busied himself collecting things in a large canvas satchel. Metal clanged, chains rattled, and Sara wondered sickly if he'd changed his mind about the canal.

He carried the satchel to the back of the building and slid open a large door. Immediately, the dank fetid scent of canal water assaulted her. After he threw the heavy satchel into a boat—Sara heard the water slosh as the craft bobbed from the impact—he returned and scooped her off the floor. She forced herself to remain limp as he half dragged her to the edge of the loading dock, but she cried out involuntarily when he flung her over the edge.

She blacked out again when she slammed into the bottom of a small rowboat.

She was so cold—shivering and aching, her stomach roiling inside her.

When the nausea finally overcame her, Sara rolled onto her side and vomited up the tiny amount of stew she had swallowed.

Right onto Sir Kenneth's pristine boots.

She was lying on the floor of an open carriage. Sir Kenneth loomed above her, driving at a dangerous pace, face rigid, jaw set. He'd trussed her arms to her sides, but since he hadn't blindfolded her, she could see they'd left Plymouth far behind. Rugged countryside spread out all around them beneath a starless night sky.

"Where are you taking me?" she cried.

"Where no one will ever find you."

His response confirmed Sara's worst fears. And since it was unlikely her protectors were anywhere close by, she had only her own wits to rely on to get away from him. She felt around with her right hand, relieved to discover the knife Gren had given her was still in her skirt pocket. Thank God Sir Kenneth hadn't searched her. Unfortunately she'd refused a second pistol, pressed on her by Tristan. At the time it seemed her accomplices wanted to arm her like a pirate queen. Now she wished she'd heeded them.

Sir Kenneth turned his carriage from the road somewhere near the sea—Sara could hear the distant crashing of the surf—and set his horses across a stretch of flat heath. Not far

ahead a group of buildings rose up like shadowy specters from
the featureless landscape. When Sara recognized them as
abandoned mine workings, a dread unlike any she'd ever experienced surged up in waves from her belly.

He drove into the midst of the buildings and pulled up.
After detaching one of the carriage lamps, he threw her over
his shoulder and moved off at a rapid, jouncing walk. Sara's
stomach began to protest—it would serve him right if she
vomited all down his back.

After he tossed her to the ground near a foot-high, round
wooden hatch, he stood glaring down at her. "You forced me
into this. You're the only person who can link me to the
Ritchies."

"And to the dish-faced man," she pointed out, since it
couldn't worsen her situation any to admit how much she knew.

He didn't respond at first and then gave a snort of recognition. "Ah, you must mean Cockney Joe Fowler. How in blazes
do you know about him?"

"I was out walking near the woodshed last week. And
you're wrong. . . . I'm not the only one who knows. I also told
Gren Martyn."

"He's no threat to me. He'll be dangling from a gibbet before the year is out."

He pivoted around and returned to the carriage, where he
retrieved the canvas satchel and carried it back to where she
lay. She watched, wide-eyed, as he drew out a stout iron bar
and methodically began prying the rotting planks off the hatch.

"Are you going to throw me down an abandoned mine shaft?"

He stopped tearing at the wood and turned to sneer at her.
"What? And have some sheep herder's dog find you within a
week? No, I'm going to leave you where no one will find you
in a hundred years. I might not even kill you directly. I'm thinking I could chain you down there and enjoy a bit of sport first."

Sara's throat went dry. She desperately tried angling the
knife in her pocket to saw through the rope on her right
wrist . . . with little success. Once Sir Kenneth had removed
the last of the planks, however, he tugged her to her feet and
undid the knots himself. "You'll need your hands," he said as
he pushed her roughly toward the opening.

Sara toyed with the notion of making a run for it. But she'd seen the stock of a pistol jutting from his waistcoat; it was better to take her chances in the mine than being shot at like a fear-crazed doe.

"Down you go," he said. "There's an iron ladder just below you."

Sara saw the two curved metal handles that jutted above the opening. She groped for them with trembling hands and began what felt like an endless descent into the black hole.

Sir Kenneth had affixed the lantern to a length of rope; it dangled near his boots as he followed her down, but did nothing to illuminate the shaft below her. The deeper she went, the more Sara understood what Gren meant about the overwhelming darkness of the pit. It hunkered there waiting for her—airless, dense, nearly obscene.

When they finally reached bottom, Sir Kenneth's lantern illuminated a low-roofed stone chamber with three tunnels running off it. He looked about, and then with a shrug drew out his pistol and began prodding Sara along the center one. She had slipped her knife from her pocket, but feared to use it so long as he kept the barrel lodged between her shoulder blades.

It was amazing how clear-headed she felt now that her panic had receded—and a very good thing. She knew she'd get only one chance to strike at him and she had to make it count.

The walls around them were scarred with pick marks and the silty floor was dark with wet patches. Every half dozen feet a brace of wooden beams had been erected to reinforce the roof, but they appeared as rotted as Gren Martyn's fences.

No, she told herself as she marched along, better not to think about Gren. It would do no good to imagine his distress when he entered the brothel and found her gone. If only she'd fled as she'd promised to do. What did it matter that by remaining she'd gained the answer to another large part of the puzzle? She was likely to die before she could tell anyone.

Gren had warned her that eavesdropping would get her in trouble. God, why hadn't she listened?

Finally Sir Kenneth caught her by the upper arm. "This place should do as well as any," he muttered as he set down the lantern.

He thrust her face-first against the pock-marked wall. "Put your hands behind you," he said with a nudge from the pistol. "You'd like to get your claws into me, eh, Miss Cobb? But I don't fancy returning to Tregallion with your scratch marks all down my face."

Sara heard him fumbling in his coat pocket for the chain he'd brought. This was it, she thought. Do or die. She whirled around and drove her knife deep into his right shoulder, then, quickly skittered away. He gave a ragged cry—and a heartbeat later the lantern went out.

The tunnel was now blacker than Hades.

"You're dead, you little bitch!" Sir Kenneth growled.

An arm slid around Sara's waist, a hand clamped over her mouth. "*Shssh*," a voice breathed into her ear. She was drawn swiftly away from Sir Kenneth, fifteen or twenty feet along the tunnel. Then there was a soft sigh on her neck, and a slow, sliding kiss along her throat.

Dear God, he'd found her! He had come for her after all, down into the darkness he hated.

"Who's out there!" Sir Kenneth shouted, the loud cry echoing along the tunnel. The timbers above Sara's head creaked and groaned.

Suddenly the comforting arm was gone from her waist. She felt him brush past her, moving silently toward the spot where Sir Kenneth stomped and fumed in the dark. Her cat-footed poacher.

"Who d'ye think I be?" he called softly in broad Cornish. "'Tis a dead man come to pay his respects, you filthy, lying cur. You put me in the ground and now I'm thinkin' it's time I returned the favor."

"Gren Martyn, is that you? Stop playing these damned games."

The voice that responded was ghostlike, disembodied, seeming to come from no set direction. "Tedn't a game, Sir Craven. 'Tis serious as the grave."

"You think you can scare me? I'll have your hide before this is done. . . . You'll rot in irons until they hang you. Unless I manage to put a bullet in you first."

"Hard t' kill a man who's already dead. But ' ee be welcome

to try. Except that 'tis never prudent to fire a pistol in an old mine shaft."

Sir Kenneth's voice turned conciliating. "Listen . . . if you let me go, I'll make a bargain with you, promise to see that you're transported instead of hanged."

The specter scoffed. "Bin hanged once already. . . . Even a great inflated bogey like you can't do it twice to a man."

"*I* didn't hang you. Was the judge in Bodmin ordered it."

"Ah, but you had no trouble lyin' to him. And all because I caught you in the wrong place. Now I've caught you again in the wrong place. . . . But it won't be me suffers for it. Not this time."

"*He* made me lie!" Sir Kenneth snarled. "You don't know how powerful he is."

"Then tell me his name. What other devil makes this devil dance?"

"I dare not," Sir Kenneth choked out hoarsely. "It would mean my life."

His loud panicked breathing reached Sara, and then the sound of his booted feet running deeper into the tunnel.

"Ah, that tedn't the way out," the spectral voice called. The bootsteps slowed, then halted. "*Or is it?* A pity mine owners never set foot underground. You might've got used to the dark. Now tell me the name of the man you call master, and I'll gladly show you the way out."

"I can't, damn you!" Sir Kenneth bellowed. "Damn you to hell!"

"I be there already. I'm only waitin' on you to join me."

The support timbers all along the passage were creaking ominously as Gren slipped back beside Sara. "We need to get out of here," he whispered urgently, and then began guiding her swiftly along the dark tunnel, keeping one outstretched hand on the wall.

Soon Sara spied a faint beacon in the distance—light flowing down the entrance shaft to the chamber below.

Sir Kenneth was still ranting behind them. "Don't leave me! Don't you dare leave me here!"

"It's this way!" Gren called out over his shoulder. "Follow my voice."

There was no immediate response. When Sir Kenneth did

answer, his tone was subdued. "No . . . no point in going back now. . . . I know I'm done for."

Sara swung around to Gren in alarm just as a pistol shot sounded, the report echoing painfully through the close confines of the tunnel. Seconds later, the walls and floor began to vibrate, accompanied by a deep rumbling that seemed to emanate from the very rock itself.

Gren snatched up her hand and together they flew along the tunnel, careering off the walls, but never letting go of each other as they raced toward the light.

Behind them the noise of timbers collapsing and rock faces shattering was deafening—and it was coming closer by the second. When they reached the base chamber, Gren cried, "Up!" and thrust her high onto the ladder an instant before a dense cloud of dust engulfed them.

Sara sped upward, blinded by the dust and barely able to breathe, missing every third rung, but climbing, climbing, knowing that if she faltered or fell, Gren would suffer for it. Finally a pair of arms reached for her, drew her away from the black pit and its spewing maelstrom of dust.

She collapsed onto the ground, lay there choking and wheezing, focusing with her remaining strength on the mine entrance, waiting, praying, for a dark head to appear at the lip. But all she could see was the thick cloud of pulverized debris that swirled above the open shaft. Then Tristan was beside her, drawing her into his arms.

"Where's G-gren?" she stammered against his shoulder. "Oh Tris, I thought he was right behind me."

"Hush now," he said. "He's likely waiting for the dust to clear."

She was only vaguely aware of the armed men encircling them in the hazy lantern light, of Sir Robert standing near the pit.

Finally Sara broke away from Tristan and staggered back toward the opening.

"Gren!" she called, falling to her knees. "*Grenville!*"

But there was only silence below her. Silence and a black well of oblivion.

Chapter Sixteen

Sara keened softly, her face pressed to the withered grass. Endless minutes had gone by, and there was still no sign of Gren.

Tris raised her in his arms again, soothing her with gentle words. She looked up at last, wondering why his nose and mouth were now obscured by a handkerchief, why his dark hair and clothing were powdered with a layer of dust. It took several seconds before she understood who was holding her so tightly to his chest.

"Gren!" she sobbed, thrusting her head into his shoulder. "Oh, Gren! Thank God."

"Sara," he sighed, increasing the pressure of his arms. "Easy, sweetheart. It's over now."

"I thought . . . when you didn't come up . . . I couldn't bear it."

"I'm sorry I frightened you," he said, nuzzling her head with his chin. "I started up after you, but by then the dust was too thick. So I dropped down and ran into one of the other tunnels. For a minute there I thought the whole works was caving in on my head."

She drew the handkerchief down and gently touched his cheek, where a long gash ran below his eye. "You're bleeding."

"I'm alive, Sara. . . . And so are you. That's all that matters." His jaw tightened. "I'm afraid I can't say the same for Sir Kenneth. The center tunnel's completely blocked." He stroked his hand over her hair. "But how are you faring? Anything broken?"

"I've got a hellish headache. He—he clouted me with my pistol. And then struck me on the chin."

He tipped her head up, examining her face. "You'll have a few nasty bruises come morning. Anything else?"

"No."

"Good," he said, shaking her gently by the shoulders, "because I believe I am going to strangle you for not keeping to our plan. You promised me you'd end the ruse the instant Sir Kenneth appeared."

She smiled weakly. "I meant to get away. But the drug they gave me was more potent than I thought, even though I swallowed very little of it. The hardest part was tipping the stew over the edge of the table without them catching me. Ah, but Gren, they seemed like such a friendly, harmless couple."

"Vipers," he spat. "Sir Robert's men are holding them in Plymouth."

Sir Robert himself came over then; he set a hand on her shoulder.

"Bravely done, Miss Cobb. It appears Mr. Martyn was right—you are much, much more than a governess. My compliments, ma'am."

"I'm taking her home now," Gren said as he drew Sara to her feet. "If you've any questions tomorrow, she'll be at Needs Barrow."

He nodded. "I should go back to Tregallion to break the news to Lady Brashear."

"How will you tell her he died?"

Sir Robert's cheeks narrowed. "As an old political hand, I think I can come up with something plausible. The charges can be brought after the shock of his death has worn off."

"No charges against Brashear," Gren said unexpectedly. "Not on my account. I got what I wanted, an admission that he lied about Jacob."

"Then I'll see what I can do about avoiding an inquest. It was an accidental death, wasn't it?"

Gren nodded. He was looking at Tristan, who had just driven the carriage up beside the open shaft. "Let those living at Tregallion go on as they were. I don't want any more innocent lives ruined."

Gren knows, Sara thought. He knows how Tris feels about Ileana.

"I'll go with you, if you like," Tris said to Sir Robert. "The women will need someone familiar to lean on." He paused, gazing into the gaping hole. "I can't believe Sir Kenneth's final resting place ended up being Wheal Adeline."

Sara looked up sharply and immediately regretted it when her head throbbed.

"This was my father's mine," Tris explained. "But the tin ran out years ago. I suppose it's my responsibility now. I'll round up some Penwreath men to dig out the body."

"Might take weeks," Gren said. "It sounded as though the whole roof collapsed in that center tunnel."

Gren was driving the carriage one-handed, his left arm wrapped around Sara. They'd crossed the heath and were tooling along the graded road toward Penwreath.

"I was never aiming to kill Brashear," he told her. "I only wanted him to confess. When it came to the sticking point, I was more concerned with getting you to safety than destroying him."

"You didn't have to destroy him. Once it all came out, he'd have been ruined . . . disgraced." She added in a hollow voice, "I have a feeling he didn't fire that pistol into the roof supports."

"No, maybe he actually did the honorable thing in the end."

Sara couldn't believe the whole sordid business was finally over. All the solutions to all the mysteries were finally out in the open. Except one.

She shifted around. "How did you find me, Gren? After they carried me to the grain warehouse I feared you'd never be able to follow my trail."

"It wasn't so difficult. Once I saw where they'd taken you, not a brothel, by the way, but a gaming hell—and curse my brother for being so foxed he couldn't remember that little detail. Anyway, I realized the place was less than fifty feet from Brashear's warehouse."

"There was a tunnel—"

"I figured that out as well. I got inside the place just as he was rowing off with you. He didn't go far, just to a wharf where a carriage was waiting. I ran to get Sir Robert's men and we followed you here."

"Why didn't you try to stop him along the way?"

"He had quite a head start. We didn't want to risk charging him and have him end up shooting you. It seemed safer to wait until he stopped. When he drew up at the mine, we left our horses and crept in from the road. I slipped into the shaft about two minutes after he went down the ladder." He turned to glare at her. "I still think I should wring your neck, Sara Cobb. I never took an easy breath the entire time."

"I stabbed him in the shoulder with your knife," she said gamely. "He wasn't expecting that. I discovered I couldn't shoot him outright in the gaming hell. But by the time he'd dragged me into the mine, I think I could have cut his heart out."

"He saved us both the trouble. Though it's a pity. . . . I doubt we'll ever find the man in London now."

Sara looked at him through her lashes and said primly, "You mean Monk Abelard?"

Gren tugged the horses to a halt, then sat there staring at her.

"Sir Kenneth and Mrs. Ritchie thought I was drugged," she explained. "So they didn't bother to guard their tongues. Now, aren't you glad I didn't run off as soon as Sir Kenneth appeared?"

He smiled at her, slow and mirthless. "I've spent a hundred sleepless nights trying to conjure that name. *He* was in the room with Brashear the night Jacob overheard them talking. Except Jacob thought he was called *Abe* Ballard. 'Abe Ballard's the link' is what he said in his testimony. I hired a solicitor in London to trace him—and wasted my money.

"Now at least you've got a name. I imagine a man who spreads such a dark shadow, even to faraway Cornwall, should be easy to find. If not to catch."

"That's up to Sir Robert now," he said, setting his hand on her knee and rubbing it soothingly. It sent ripples of pleasure dancing up her spine. "I've other things to occupy me now."

He clucked to the horses and Sara again curled up against

him. "You were splendid down there in the dark," she said sleepily. "Just in case I forget to tell you in the morning."

He sighed. "It's funny . . . how some of the things we learn have a value we can't begin to understand at the time. I hated working in the pit, but if I'd never been down there, never grown accustomed to the dark, I couldn't have got you away from him."

Sara tweaked him in the ribs. "You're starting to sound like one of those fanciful Cornishmen again."

"And I suppose the unimaginative Miss Cobb doesn't believe in fate."

"I believe in you, Gren Martyn. Miss Bonnet always said fate was nothing more than a chance taken and a deed done. She claimed we create our destiny by our own hands."

"Go to sleep, little schoolteacher," he grumbled fondly as he tightened his arm around her drooping shoulders. "It's been a long night."

Gren carried her, still half asleep, through the front door of Needs Barrow and up the stairs to one of the guest bedrooms. An anxious Addie had met them in the hall and insisted Sara needed a bath and some doctoring. Gren had brushed her aside, declaring that rest was what she required most.

Sara clung to him after he'd set her down in a wide tester bed. "Stay with me," she murmured.

He tapped his knuckles against her chin. "You wouldn't have a clue what to do with a wicked fellow like me."

"Shows all you know. I could use my newly discovered imagination."

He laughed softly. "It's a tempting offer, but hardly fair to the man you're going to wed."

She gave him a pouty frown. "And what man would want to wed me?"

He studied her thoughtfully, his little governess all covered with gray dust. She was languid and kittenish and utterly desirable. "You've got a point. There are those serious eyebrows to get past. And that fatal tendency to manage people."

"Don't forget my thick waist and indiscernible bosom," she added with a wide yawn.

"Oh, I doubt I could ever forget your bosom," he drawled as he leaned close and stroked his mouth over hers.

Sara closed her eyes and smiled. "Mmm . . . I don't wonder all the women in Penwreath sigh after your kisses, Gren Martyn."

"Not any longer," he whispered as she drifted off to sleep.

He removed her heavy brogues and then drew a coverlet over her. Afterward, he stood watching her, a little tic playing along his jaw.

He hadn't been completely honest with her, and it was starting to gnaw at him.

There was something he had to do, now that his life was his own again. He toyed with the notion of waking Sara and telling her. It was foregone that she wasn't going to like it, females being habitually unreasonable. Still, he couldn't let her wake up tomorrow and find him gone. That would be unimaginably cruel after what she'd just been through.

He sat on the edge of the bed, and gently roused her. "Sara. . . ."

"Mmm?"

"I've got to go away."

Her eyes opened, still hazed with weariness. "I know. . . . You just told me you couldn't stay."

"I mean for a while . . . I'm not sure how long."

"Christmas is coming. You can't be gone for Christmas."

"I'll try to be back by then."

"Where are you going? Can't I come too? And who will feed your chickens?"

He nearly smiled. "I know you're not making much sense of this. Addie can answer all your questions in the morning."

"I am making sense," she protested. "You're going away, but you'll be home before the New Year." She rolled onto her side and clutched at her pillow as her eyes closed again. "It will be lovely," she murmured. "Christmas in Cornwall. . . .

He bent and gently kissed the small bump on her temple and the ruddy bruise on her chin.

"Forgive me, Sara," he said gruffly. "It's for the best."

Chapter Seventeen

*W*hen Sara awoke, just after noon, Addie was sitting beside the bed neatly darning the lace trim on a lawn petticoat.

"They've all been and gone," Addie said. "Tristan, Sir Robert . . . Gren. I've been sitting here like a bulldog to keep anyone from disturbing you until you woke up on your own." She leaned forward in her chair. "Gren told me what happened last night. It must have been dreadful for you, Sara. How are you faring?"

"I'm feeling rather fine, actually," she said, rubbing the side of her face as she sat up. "Delayed reaction maybe. What did Sir Robert want?"

"He went back to Tregallion early this morning and found Mrs. Holcroft packed up and ready to run. Turns out she'd been one of the procuresses for the man in London. When she decided she wanted an easier life, she blackmailed Sir Kenneth into hiring her and apparently ended up abetting him. The handbills were her idea. Sir Robert's men found dozens of them in a trunk in her parlor."

"I searched the wrong room," Sara muttered under her breath.

"Lady Brashear is planning to go to her sister in Truro after the funeral . . . well, providing there is a funeral. And Ileana is going to Somerset to stay with Amelie." She paused. "Tris is to take her."

"Ah . . . I knew the two of them patched things up the night of the party."

Addie's eyes danced. "Better than that. Tristan apparently

swept her right off her feet in the garden. He now has every intention of marrying her."

Sara grinned widely. "Nothing like a scientific young man to induce the proper chemical reaction. But how will Lady Brashear take it, do you think?"

"She has other more pressing concerns than her daughter's future. Her own, for one thing. And she must realize that Ileana will never have a season. Not now."

"I imagine Ileana and Tristan will have to wait a while . . . mourning period and all that."

"It won't hurt them any to wait. They're both still so young. Though once Tris leaves for Somerset, Sara, it will be just the two of us at Needs Barrow. Do you mind staying on?"

Sara was about to remind her that she had nowhere else to go. She certainly couldn't return to Tregallion. Then she recalled that she *did* have someplace to go . . . maybe not tomorrow or the next day, but soon. A very shabby, very muddy shambles of a farm. She could barely wait.

"Of course I'll stay and keep you company," she said. "And it won't be just the two of us, after all. Gren will be about."

Addie frowned slightly. "Not for some time though."

"What? What do you mean?"

"He said he told you last night . . . that he was going away." When it was clear her words still hadn't registered, Addie said, "Gren's gone, Sara."

She scrambled out from under the coverlet and crouched there, her heart racing. "Gone?"

"I told him it was wrong to rush off and leave you to face the aftermath alone. Gren assured me Sir Robert would see to everything. He wouldn't tell me where he was going or for how long, just that he had something he needed to set in motion as soon as may be."

Sara reeled back. "I don't believe it."

She taxed her brain, trying to recall what they'd talked about last night, but she'd been like a woman in a fog, befuddled by relief and joy. It was something about Christmas . . . and chickens.

"I can't remember what he said," she uttered mournfully.

"Oh, Addie, what if he was saying good-bye, what if he never comes back?"

Addie patted her hand. "Nonsense. You can't possibly doubt that Gren cares for you. Tristan said he was like a wild man last night when they broke into the gaming hell and you weren't there."

"I thought I knew how he felt, but he's never told me. Not outright. Oh, I'm such a fool for leaping ahead, for assuming things . . . just because he kissed me a few times. May Belle True warned me he was free with his kisses."

"He's not free with his friendship or his loyalty, Sara. And he gave you those in full measure."

Sara clutched her pillow to her chest and laid her cheek on it. "I woke up feeling so wonderful and now . . . it's all gone bleak and gray again."

"I think I'm going to brain that man the next time he sets foot in this house."

"No," Sara said with a tiny sigh. "Maybe it's better that he's gone off. Maybe Ileana and Tris aren't the only ones who need to wait a bit before they take such an important step."

"Never tell me *you're* uncertain of your feelings."

Sara grinned wistfully. "I think I knew Gren Martyn was the man for me an hour after I met him. And nothing since then has shaken that certainty. Not all the accusations or gossip. Not even that hellhole of a farm. It's Gren, I'm thinking, who needs to come to terms with this. After all, I'm hardly the sort of woman to tame a libertine."

Addie shook her head. "You are exactly the sort of woman for him. Amelie always said Gren was looking for something fixed in its orbit, something . . . enduring . . . to guide him. Like Lather Pitt's inn—a constant star. And until he found it, she predicted, he'd never keep a steady course." Addie chuckled. "Amelie was very taken with all things nautical. Which is why it wasn't surprising when she fell in love with a former naval lieutenant."

"And you think that is what I am to Gren, a fixed point?"

"You just told me yourself that you never wavered in your affection."

"So what am I to do now, Addie? Wait and see if he is as unwavering?"

"Yes, you must wait. And trust."

"Gren's free now," Sara mused, half to herself. "He accomplished all that he set out to do. But I imagine it's left a hole in his life, not having that goad any longer. I suppose he just needs time to find something to replace it."

The words made a deal of sense, but she still didn't feel very comforted.

"And he did try to explain last night," Addie pointed out. "There is that in his favor."

"I just wish he'd made sure I was fully awake before he told me," she grumbled.

"You'd have clouted him on the head."

Sara gave her a wan smile. "Precisely."

Sir Kenneth's body was exhumed after nearly a week of digging. No one ever told Sara whether he'd died from a bullet wound or from the falling rocks. She hoped it was the former.

As promised, Sir Robert Poole managed to avoid an inquest. The general tale was that the unlucky Brashear, while searching for Gren Martyn, had gone into an abandoned mine shaft and set off the cave-in. Gren was exonerated when Sir Robert "revealed" that the poacher had secretly been investigating a local smuggling operation for the Home Office. He had been inside Tregallion waiting to rendezvous with Sir Robert when Brashear caught him.

Sara thought the story sounded rather cobbled together, but the coroner accepted it, which was the main thing. The villagers, on the other hand, seemed to know exactly what had transpired in Plymouth and all that followed. Sara found herself the recipient of genial nods and grateful smiles whenever she ventured into Penwreath.

Sir Kenneth's funeral service was limited to the immediate family—Amelie came from Somerset to stand beside her mother and sister, but she departed again the same day and did not visit Needs Barrow. Ileana and Tristan were to follow her within the week.

On the day before Tris was to leave, one of the workmen who'd been clearing Wheal Adeline rode up to the house with a sack slung over his horse's withers.

"Copper," he said, emptying it onto Addie's pristine carpet. Jagged clumps of dull metal spilled across the floor. "The seam was runnin' above the tin workin's. Biggest one I ever come across . . . and I bin minin' copper these twenty years."

Sara and Addie just stood staring at the bounty spread before them. Tris crouched down and hefted one nugget, weighing it in his hand. "It looks fairly pure," he said wonderingly.

"A' course 'ee ought to have a minin' engineer take a gander at the place, but it 'pears to be a major strike."

Things heated up at Needs Barrow after that. Tristan sent Ileana off to Somerset in the care of Miss Prake; he needed to stay behind and determine whether the seam ran deep enough into the rock to make it worth digging out. The engineer's report was encouraging, and Tristan returned from his bank in Bodmin with enough funds to set up a proper operation. It appeared he would now have something more than his jars of sea creatures to offer Ileana.

Sara was elated over the Spindles' sudden turn of fortune and kept her dubious opinions about mining to herself, especially since she was partaking of their hospitality.

She never returned to Tregallion House, which was to be closed up. Lord Denby offered to find posts for the house servants, save Mrs. Holcroft, who had been taken off to Bodmin under the watchful eye of Sir Robert. May Belle refused the magistrate's offer to rule over his kitchen and opted, instead, to cook for the Spindles. Seth also came to work in the stable at Needs Barrow, where Sadie appeared one day, as if by magic.

Sara began taking long rides out onto the moor, always keeping far away from Beebe's Brook and the small run-down farm in the hollow. She made sure that the Gramblers and the Currys had all the surplus food from May Belle's kitchen. There were other families up on Bodmin whom she met eventually, people who expressed a new surge of hope now that Wheal Adeline had reopened.

And still there was no word from Gren.

Tris complained bitterly over his absence. "He needn't go

down in the pit," he said one night over supper. "I'd just like him to advise me on how to get the most ore with the least danger to the men. I've ordered every book on mining I could find, but I could still use some first-hand advice."

"Well, don't look at me," Sara huffed. "I haven't a clue where's he's gone."

One afternoon, less than two weeks from Christmas, Addie found Sara in the back parlor writing out advertisements for a new post.

"So, you're giving up then?"

"Just being practical."

"He will come back, Sara."

"He gave all his chickens to the Gramblers," she said darkly.

Addie restrained a chuckle. "That doesn't mean he's left Penwreath for good."

"He also knows how to write. A letter . . . a note . . . something to hold onto would have been nice."

Addie's mouth tightened. Sara picked up on it at once. "What is it?"

"Nothing."

"Adeline Spindle, if you know something—"

"He's back," she said baldly. "Tris ran into him in Penwreath yesterday. They shared an ale in the Star, and Tris told him all about Wheal Adeline. Gren, apparently, told my brother next to nothing."

"Men are so inept at shaking information out of each other," Sara muttered. "Well, at least Gren didn't go off after Monk Abelard and get himself killed, which is what I've been fearing."

"You never said anything to me," Addie cried softly, clutching at Sara's hand. "I'm sorry this mine business has made me so distracted. You've been fretting and I barely noticed."

"I've been taking it out on May Belle," Sara said with a grin. "Her theory is that Gren went back to America . . . to make his fortune so he could come home rich as a nabob and sweep me off my feet." She gave a wistful sigh. "As though that was ever a problem."

"So now that he's home, I expect you'll want to ride over and visit him."

Sara thought for a moment. "I don't believe I will. Remember, I am the constant star, and I think I should remain fixed right here."

"Are you sure?"

When Sara nodded, Addie said, "Just remember, you always have the option of going there. Though I don't blame you for wanting him to come to you for a change."

He always came after me, Sara refuted silently. *Always.*

Sara still felt confused. It was clear Addie expected her to visit Gren, yet Sara was not sure it was the right course to take. If he had lost interest in her, she certainly didn't want to confront him on the matter. Nothing could be more humiliating. Then again, not knowing where she stood was driving her into a bad case of the dismals. She decided to seek the counsel of May Belle, her first—and least complicated—confidante in Penwreath.

The cook was making honey buns, thumping viciously at a large clod of dough as though she was fending off a back-alley footpad, but she looked up with a smile when Sara came into the kitchen. Sara sat down beside a bowl of raisins and started to arrange them into neat rows on the flour-dusted table.

"You're looking peaky," May Belle observed between thumps. "That young rogue still playing least in sight?"

"Mmm . . . although he is back at his farm."

And not lying dead in some East End rookery, she added to herself, forcing herself to look on the bright side.

May Belle glowered. "Fine lot of good that does you."

"The thing is," Sara said, popping a few raisins into her mouth, "I'm not sure what it means. Now, you've had some experience with men—"

"Buried two husbands, so far."

"That's not exactly what I was getting at. I was just wondering whether you thought it was a bad sign that he hasn't come to see me."

May Belle stared off into space for a moment. "There's

signs and then there's *signs*," she said cryptically. "Mayhap you should ride over there and put the question to him."

Sara frowned. "That might be a bit risky. Suppose he is not disposed to see me?"

"No risk, no gain," May Belle pronounced.

"I'm not sure I'm up to the task," Sara confessed in a low voice.

May Belle stopped kneading and looked across at Sara with an expression of sympathy. "Here's the one thing I do know, pet. Men've got different ways of showing how they feel. Some come courting with flowers and fancy words. Others, well, they go off and do something to impress their lady."

"He went off. . . . But I am *not* impressed."

"Not yet," said May Belle with a wink.

"He'd better do it soon," Sara grumbled, "before I fall into a permanent funk."

"A funk, is it? Then perhaps you *should* ride over."

Sara shook her head. "No, he already thinks I meddle too much in his life. I'll just bide my time here."

On a chilly windswept day a week before Christmas, a shabby coach pulled up at the door of Needs Barrow. A handsome young woman emerged, followed by a thin gypsy-eyed gentleman and a nursemaid carrying a young child. Ileana came out last, fussing with the hem of her pelisse.

Sara was at the edge of the garden collecting evergreen boughs for decorating the parlor. She watched as Addie flew from the house, exclaiming her surprise as she embraced her friend. Sara studied Amelie Woode, the young woman whose wild nature had at last been tamed by love. She was much like her sister, tall and tawny-haired, though a bit less willowy. Her husband was neither elegant nor imposing, but he could barely take his eyes off Amelie or their child. Sara now understood why the girl had given up everything to be with him.

Tristan appeared and herded them all into the house, his hand at Ileana's elbow. A short time later Sara gathered up her basket of greenery and followed them. She hovered just inside the parlor door, not wanting to intrude on the reunion. Tris was down on the carpet, literally at Ileana's feet, dangling his watch fob for the gypsy-eyed baby, while Addie and the Woodes watched from the sofa—all of them chattering like magpies.

"But where is our Gren?" Amelie cried at one point. "I was sure he'd be here. Time was, you couldn't keep him from Needs Barrow at Christmas."

Addie and her brother shared an awkward look. "We've not seen much of him lately."

"Why, you must send a groom to fetch him. Mr. Woode has never met him, for one thing, and for another, it's only fitting that he finally get to see his namesake, Roger Grenville."

At the sound of his name, the baby looked up from sucking on Tris's fingers.

Ileana turned in her chair and gazed questioningly at Sara. This was the first contact they'd had since the wrenching scene in the garden of Tregallion.

"Sara?" she asked softly. "Why isn't he here with you?"

There was only perplexity in her expression, no smug gloating that Gren had deserted her, no harsh recrimination for Sara's part in the death of her father.

Sara eyes filled with tears. She stepped forward and gave Ileana's hand a brief squeeze. "It doesn't matter. I'm . . . I'm so happy to see you again."

Ileana leaped up and hugged her. "They wouldn't let me visit you," she whispered intently. "Mama and my aunt from Truro . . . they said you were no better than you should be. But I stuck up for you and told them you were more of a true lady than anyone I had ever met." She grinned. "Mama was so incensed, she choked on a piece of scone. We had to pound her on the back for fully two minutes."

Sara quickly hid her smile. She knew she would always cherish that image. "I'm sorry about your father, Ileana."

The girl sighed and an expression of sadness momentarily clouded her face. "It was a terrible shock at first. But we're all bearing up, as you can see. Spending time with baby Roger has been very . . . healing." She drew Sara further into the room. "Now come, you must let me introduce you to my sister and her husband."

When Mr. Woode stood and bowed, Sara was struck by his

calm, intelligent eyes. Amelie also rose, holding out one hand.
"Miss Cobb, at last. I've heard so much about you." Her eyes
held a meaning far deeper than her polite words. "I've nothing
but admiration for the woman who managed to turn my vexing
little sister into someone I could actually stand to be around."

Ileana made a rude face at her, and then both of them
laughed.

Sara suddenly felt like a complete outsider.

Spindles, Brashears, Woodes . . . everyone around her was
related in some way to another person in the room. Amelie was
further connected to the Spindles through the childhood pact
they had sworn. The only one missing from that little coterie
was Gren.

She caught Addie's eye. "I think I'll take a walk and let all
of you catch up on old times."

Her friend shot her a look of concern, but Sara smiled back
and shook her head. *I'll be all right.*

Sara went out through the French door, lingering on the terrace that overlooked the cove, still close enough to hear them
laughing and teasing each other. She heard it when the baby
grew fractious and Amelie begged to be excused. When her
feelings of isolation became too much to bear, she made her
way down the shallow steps to the drive and somehow found
herself at the stable door.

Seth looked up from cleaning a bridle, his eyes beaming.
"Did you hear the news, Miss Cobb? They found our Bessie in
London. She'd run off to a charity home before some dirty fellow could get his paws on her. But she was afeared to come
back to Penwreath, thinkin' she was sullied just the same."

"I had heard. And I'm so very glad."

"It was 'cause a'you, miss . . . you and Gren Martyn.
There's people about in Penwreath say we should raise up a
statue."

Sara laughed. "Great heavens. Just buy Mr. Martyn a drink
the next time he's at the Star."

"And what about you, miss? What would you like most?"

"If you would saddle Sadie for me, that would do nicely."

She set out along the cliff road in the opposite direction
from Beebe's Brook, ruminating over the question Seth had

just asked her. What *would* she like most? Something to soothe the pain inside her, she thought, to ease the longing for a man who had gone away without any explanation. That was what she really wanted—an explanation.

And by God, she thought as she hauled Sadie around, that was what exactly what she was going to get. Regardless that she'd made up her mind to wait, she couldn't bear the gnawing anxiety one minute more. She was finally going to shake some answers out of Gren Martyn.

Sometimes it seemed that was all she'd ever done with him—followed him about saying, "Tell me . . . tell me." As it turned out, he *had* told her everything she needed to know—except maybe the most important thing of all.

Once again she heard the sound of hammering as she approached the hollow. Sara wasn't prepared, however, for the sight that met her eyes when she crested the hill above the farm.

A large wooden framework had been joined to the cottage, a full two stories high it was and set above a stone-and-mortar foundation. Gren was straddling one of the raised crossbeams, wearing only a homespun shirt above his corded breeches, in spite of the weather having come on so chilly. Sweat had soaked through the shirt so that it clung in patches to his back and chest.

Sara urged Sadie down the hill and leaped off almost before the mare had come to a stop.

"Go away!" Gren called from his perch without looking up from his hammering. "You're not supposed to be here." He punctuated his irritation with a loud *bang, bang, bang!*

"I will not go away. I will sit here in your front yard until you talk to me."

"I'm working," he said.

"I'm waiting," she shot back as she settled on a large rock and crossed her arms.

He swung down from the beam and came stomping over to her. She didn't like the look on his face one bit, but refused to cower. Barely slowing his momentum, he swooped low, scooped her up and carried her back to Sadie. He tried to throw her onto the saddle, but Sara got her hands around his neck and would not let go.

"You've ruined everything, you know," he growled, trying to peel her off him. "Now if you would just go back to Needs Barrow and forget what you saw."

He finally got free of her and set her on the ground. She pushed away from him, stood there panting and fuming.

"What have I ruined?" she cried. "Your life, your future . . . any chance of happiness? Because that's what you've done to me, Gren Martyn. It's as though you fell off the planet."

"I've been busy . . . as you can see."

"So this farm, which you neglected for years, is suddenly more important than the people you care about? And why are you finally fixing it up? Are you planning to sell it and slip away to America one night, like the sneaking cat-footed poacher you are?"

He rocked back on his heels. "What ever happened to the demure Sara Cobb who blushed at every other word?"

"She's gone," she said, suddenly deflated. She stumbled away from him and sat again on the rock. "I don't know who I am any longer."

He sighed deeply and eased down beside her, nearly unseating her. But Sara clung doggedly to her spot. She'd learned how to do that, hold on to what was hers.

"What am I supposed to say to you? You come here full of steam over some imaginary slight—"

"Imaginary?" she huffed.

"Do you see any signs that I am about to sneak off anywhere?"

"I see you fixing up your house. Has Tristan's new mine overseer made you an offer?"

Gren put both hands over his face. "Lord help me. . . ."

"Well?"

"I had some idiotic notion you might enjoy a surprise."

"My only surprise was waking up the morning after the cave-in and finding you gone." She flicked her fingers toward the partially completed addition. "And now this."

He shifted around and took up her hands. "Has it possibly occurred to you that I'm building it for someone other than

Tristan's blasted overseer? Someone educated and well-bred, who isn't used to living in a one-room cottage?"

The truth dawned on Sara with a wild acceleration of her heart. "You mean it's for me?"

"Of course it's for you, ye daft woman." His eyes glittered. "I intended to bring you here on Christmas morning."

One hand raised weakly to her mouth. "Oh, Gren." Her whole body was trembling as relief flooded through her. She wasn't even aware that tears had pooled in her eyes.

"Ah, Sara, don't cry," he crooned as he cupped her face, gently tracing a thumb beneath each eye. "Please don't. I was a wicked thoughtless fool not to tell you sooner. You've got such a prickly exterior, I sometimes forget how easily you bruise. I promise I won't forget again."

"I thought you'd changed your mind," she choked out. "I thought you didn't want me."

"Never," he whispered as he enfolded her in his arms. "You're the only thing in my life that makes any sense. Even when everything I'd been working toward started slipping away, you were right there, steadfast and abiding."

When Sara gave a watery chuckle, he raised her chin. "What?"

"Nothing. I'll tell you another time. Just a wise thing Addie said."

"Women and their secrets," he muttered.

"You're a fine one to talk," she said, nodding to the house beyond them.

"Come on," he said as he drew her to her feet. "Let me show you."

Gren laid a relaxed arm over her shoulders as they stood and observed the unfinished facade together. Sara felt the muscular weight like a benediction—a piercing reminder that some burdens were welcome beyond words.

"There will be three rooms up and three down," he said, pointing. "And I was thinking you might want to use the old cottage as a schoolroom . . . in case the odd miner's brat wanders by."

Sara's eyes gleamed. What had he said to her that day in the woods, that she would find the students she required? She'd never have dared to imagine, back then, that her life would turn out like this.

"It's beyond wonderful, Gren." She shot him a sly glance. "Hmm . . . it will have walls, won't it?"

He *tsk*ed. "Females are so demanding."

"But where did you get the money for supplies?" She gripped his arm. "You didn't steal it?"

"You'd like that . . . more grist for your Robin Hood myth. But no, it happens I got the money from Sir Robert. He thought I ought to have something to compensate me for giving up two years of my life doing what should have been the government's work."

She nodded, again impressed by the statesman's sense of justice. Then something occurred to her and her eyes narrowed. "And the others at Needs Barrow, they knew about this . . . surprise . . . and agreed to keep it a secret?"

He nodded. "I told Tris last week after I returned from London, but asked him and Addie to keep it a secret. I've been buying supplies in Penwreath, so I assume May Belle knows, since village gossip sticks to her like gooseberry jam." He pulled her closer. "And just so you don't think me a completely heartless cad, when I met up with Tristan I did ask how you were faring. He said you seemed quite jolly."

"Jolly?" she echoed in disbelief. Her eyes blazed for an instant. "You asked a *man*?"

He looked away, cheeks narrowed in sheepish amusement.

Sara tugged on his sleeve. "But I still don't understand. Not a single one of them told me not to come here. Just the opposite, in fact. They kept saying, 'Go if you want to, it's your decision.'"

"That's because they know you, Sara Cobb. If they'd said 'you absolutely mustn't go,' you'd have been galloping off on Sadie the next instant. So they, *mmm*, finessed you a bit."

"I should be furious with them . . . and with you. I probably wouldn't even have come today, except that Amelie and her family arrived unexpectedly. I suddenly felt so alone in the midst of all that happiness and I needed the one person who could make that feeling go away."

"Oh, Sara," he whispered, stroking one work-roughened

hand over her cheek. "God, I've missed you so much. It's barely been three weeks but it feels like forever."

"I know. I still don't understand why you had to rush off."

"How could I have stayed? I wanted to carry you off that night, but to where exactly? I had nothing to offer you, Sara, nothing but a run-down joke of a farm."

"It wouldn't have mattered," she said staunchly. And then lapsed into broad Cornish. "I be stronger than I look, an' I can cook a bit."

He grinned. "So I'm told, Miss Canard. But even a layabout poacher's got his manly pride. So I racked my brain until I thought of something I could do that might just make a difference. It was a wild notion and I knew I had to act quickly, before the utter improbability of it hobbled me. I—I kept reminding myself of what your Miss Bonnet said, that fate was no more than a chance taken and a deed done."

"I wish you'd told me before you left. All I remembered was asking you about your chickens."

"I didn't know myself where I would end up. London seemed the biggest gamble, so being a contrary Cornishman, that's where I started."

"And have you any intention of telling me what you were doing there?"

"Better yet, I'll show you."

He took up her hand and led her across the barnyard to the work shed. "Go on," he said, prodding her inside.

The first thing Sara noticed were the shiny new woodworking tools scattered over the plank table. More compelling was a number of foot-high wooden miniatures sitting on the shelf beside it: a walnut writing desk, a satinwood sideboard, and a harp-backed dining chair.

She picked up the sideboard to examine it. "So this is what you learned in America," she murmured. "Are these for a doll house?" To her untrained eye, the detailing seemed far more intricate than a child would require. "They're . . . quite beautiful, but they seem a bit large."

"They're samples," he said from the doorway. He came forward and took the sideboard from her, his long fingers stroking lovingly over the inlaid surface. "Facsimiles of what the full-

size pieces will look like. I've been working on them for a
while now . . . well, actually since the day I first kissed you.
Something to keep my mind off my wayward inclinations
where you were concerned."

She gave him a droll look. "Yes, that worked."

He arched one brow. "Are you complaining? Anyway, I
took them to London, to see if any of the better-grade furniture
dealers were interested."

"And?"

He nodded, and then grinned. "It looks like I can give up
poaching."

Sara threw herself at him. "You must be so pleased! And
Jacob would be so proud. It's what he wanted for you."

"I know." He pressed her head to his shoulder. A moment
later she felt the muscles in his arms tense. "*Hmmm* . . . there
is one other thing I do need to tell you."

Her breathing hitched. *He is finally going to say it.*

Instead of sounding ardent, however, his voice was hesi-
tant. "I—I told you once that I was low-born, but there's more
to it than that. Addie and Tris . . . they aren't just my friends.
There's a fair chance they're my half siblings."

Sara's smile was serene. "That's the *one* thing I had figured
out, Gren. Somehow."

"You're not shocked?"

"Not a bit. I first noticed your resemblance to Tris that day
you were together in the cove. And there's the way Addie
treats you—bossy but fond. Just like a sister."

He tugged at her ear. "I *meant* shocked about my being
a . . . bastard. It turns out that before Arthur Spindle was wed,
he was apparently very taken with my mother. My father was
not the easiest of husbands. Addie, Tris and I only learned of
this after I returned to Penwreath. We came across a letter in
the attic at Needs Barrow."

"It must have felt like a blessing at the time, Gren, to discover they were family. You'd just lost your only brother."

"I'd never understood why I was always welcomed in that
house," he said, rubbing the back of his head. "The unschooled
raggedy farm boy. I finally knew why."

"It doesn't matter to me at all. Does it trouble you?"

He blew out a breath. "If you'd ever met Jonas Martyn, you wouldn't ask. Bad blood there, wild blood. No, I got the better part of that bargain. Plus here's a bit of irony for you. After rushing off to London, thinking I needed to secure our future, I come home to discover that Wheal Adeline is bursting with copper."

"And?"

"I have a part share in that mine, Sara. Turns out Arthur Spindle left it to me—the Spindles never mentioned it when I came back from America because the tin played out shortly after their father died." He sighed. "Looks like I'm not done with the pit after all."

"Yes, but I wager it will be the best-run pit in Cornwall."

"So what do you think? Are you primed to take a gamble? A poacher turned cabinetmaker . . . turned mine owner?"

Her eyes danced impishly. "Are you asking me to invest capital in your new venture?"

He tugged her off her feet and growled, "You? You haven't two shillings to rub together. No, Miss Prim, I am asking you to invest in *us*. Because it occurs to me every so often— mostly late at night or when you're vexing me beyond words—that I love you." His voice lowered to a gruff whisper. "I do, Sara. I stopped fighting it that night in the cellar of the Star."

She gazed up at him, needing to commit this moment to memory—the affection brimming in those bright blue eyes, the ardent smile that curled his beautiful mouth.

"I've waited a long time to hear you say that."

His arms tightened. "I don't suppose you'd care to say it back."

She leaned up on tiptoes and pressed her lips to his ear. "I love you, will always love you. And have loved you . . . since the moment you put me up behind you on Cap and dragged my arm around your waist."

His amazed smile slowly widened. "Is that true?"

"I could feel your heart beating, and your hair was tickling my nose. I felt safe and warm and . . . home."

His eyes melted. "Ah, sweetheart. I had no idea. It took me

a bit longer, I'm afraid. And once I did know how I felt, I feared I'd have to batter down all your maidenly defenses."

"You could have done it with a feather duster."

"Then kiss me, Sara Cobb. And make it last . . . because I have to get back to work."

She squirmed away from him, and said in mock dismay, "No, Gren, you're all sweaty."

"And will be again," he promised slyly as he stalked toward her.

She danced back from him, out the door and into the barn-yard. "I'm thinking you need to go under the pump."

"Not a chance."

"Go on, get under the pump." She leered at him shame-lessly. Bless the man, he had turned her into a complete hussy. "You know how much I like it."

"*No!*" He darted forward to grab her, but she scurried to-ward the house, then stood grinning wickedly with her back to the fence.

He crossed his arms and glared. "I'm not going near that pump."

"*Grenville . . .*" she muttered warningly.

"I'll freeze my backside off."

She was laughing as she flew toward him and wrapped her arms around his neck, holding on tight. "Don't 'ee be worryin' about gettin' warm. We'll put 'ee in th' barn with Nelly th' cow."

He lifted her off her feet with one arm and kissed her soundly. "The hell you will."

When there was still no sign of Sara by the time darkness fell, Addie went down to the kitchen. May Belle looked up from the melba toast she was tenderly preparing for Roger Grenville Woode.

"Sara apparently rode out hours ago," Addie said, "and I'm starting to get anxious. I don't suppose she mentioned where she might be going."

"She didn't say a word to me. But I'll give you three guesses where she went."

Addie sighed. "I suppose the waiting just got too much for

her. I honestly thought she'd be able to hold out until Christmas, even though I've wanted to tell her the truth a dozen times. I vow I could box Tristan's ears for promising Gren we wouldn't say anything. I'm almost relieved Sara's finally taken things into her own hands."

"It was only a matter of time," May Belle said sagely. "I know my Sara Cobb. You set a hurdle in front of her, she'll balk sure as anything. She'll fret and stomp and fuss. But you put something she wants on t'other side, good Lord, that girl will jump. And a nice proper little jumper she turned out to be."

Epilogue

New Year's Eve blew in cold, sharp-edged, and frosty. In Tregallion Wood, an icy, salt-stung wind rattled the bare branches of the trees and turned the dead grass into brittle, glittering lace. The caped stranger had left his horse beside the wall and come through a rusted iron gate. He now trod an overgrown path lit only by an indifferent moon, his boot steps crunching on the rimed bracken. He tugged his collar high against his throat, anticipating the moment when he would be inside—and warm. Soon now, very soon.

He'd been forced to flee, turned on by his own kind. Like jackals they were, eager to feast on their leader. But he'd evaded them. Gold had helped, and he had plenty of that. He'd come clear across England to pay back the ones who'd betrayed him. Brashear was dead, he did know that. The man had a wife, however . . . and daughters.

He lost his way after he passed a tumbledown woodshed, cursing as he found himself moving deeper into thickets of dense shrubs and entwined saplings. When he stepped into a small clearing, the moonlight shone for an instant on his fleshy face. It was deeply pitted with scars from an illness that had almost killed him as a child. But he'd survived and grown strong. That marred face had earned him a new name in the rookeries of London, where the pimps swore there was not a strumpet alive who would let him touch her.

Ah, but he'd taken plenty, willing or no.

Now he was moving downhill, into a small hollow, the ground cover thick with knee-high bushes. He drew back with a cry as a large bird, startled from sleep, flew up with a whir of wings, batting his face for an instant before it gained altitude and flew off.

He cursed again, feeling out of his element in this misbegotten wood, where the stripped winter branches rose high above him like the fingers of those long dead.

Better to concentrate on the work before him. Once he finished up at Tregallion House he had another call to pay. A small farm beyond a brook, that's what they'd told him in the village. He'd paid a great deal of his hard-won gold to learn the man's name. Martyn. The twice-damned poacher who'd poked his nose into things that didn't concern him.

He stroked his hand savoringly over the hilt of his knife, thinking he'd take a very long time finishing him off. And even longer with the poacher's doxy, in the house above the cove.

The constables would have a pretty bit of work before them when they found the trail of bodies he'd left behind. They'd see that it was never wise to cross—

S-n-a-a-c-k!

A cry of surprise burst from his lungs. His first thought was that he'd blundered into a patch of thorny brambles or that some fierce small animal had leaped up and bitten him high on the leg. Then the lancing pain assaulted him, and he reeled in shock.

He reached down instinctively, his gloved hand coming away wet and dark. Tearing off the glove and biting hard on his lip, he groped again, feeling cold metal beneath his fingers . . . and teeth, a dozen jagged teeth, most of them lodged in the flesh above his knee.

He screamed then, a long drawn-out cry, as fiery agony caught him mid-section. As if in reply, the deep baying of a large dog echoed in the distance.

His hackles rose.

He tugged urgently at his shackle, gritting his teeth against the increased pain. But the trap was staked to the ground, immovable, and he could only hobble around it in a crazed circle, like a lame jester.

"No!" he wailed, his head straining back. "*N-o-o-o!*"

The barking came closer, and with it, the urgent shouts of men. He began to tremble. It was unthinkable, to be trapped and held, like the weakest of creatures. He was strong, driven, powerful—and he'd been minutes away from taking his final revenge.

Again he wrapped his fingers around the sides of the trap, heaving with all his might. Muscles swelled, sinews stretched, his eyes bulged. Yet the frozen ground held fast to the iron stake—which might just as well have been hammered into his heart.

He sank to his knees, eyes blazing. Let them come for him, then. . . . Let them try to take him alive. He'd been a master of scoundrels—and the occasional gentleman—for nearly two decades. Maybe it was time he met his own master.

When he fell onto his side, the metal jaws moved with him, the dull clanking of the heavy chain sounding his fate.

"God help me," he groaned.

But there was no answer, no succor, only the keening of the wind from the sea . . . and the darkness of the vaulted sky above him. Only the wind and the darkness.

SIGNET

The Barkin Emeralds
by Nancy Bulter

"A writer not to be missed."
—Mary Balogh

On behalf of her mistress, Miss Maggie
Bonner is returning a rejected betrothal
gift to Lord Barkin in Scotland. But
when she is mistaken for his intended,
she is kidnapped by a dashing pirate.

0-451-21175-8

Available wherever books are sold or at
www.penguin.com